£2

THE
APPRENTICE

THE APPRENTICE

The Story of a Nonentity

by

Joseph Tomelty

The Blackstaff Press

First published in 1953 by Jonathan Cape Limited
This Blackstaff Press edition is a photolithographic facsimile
of the first edition printed at the Alden Press and is
unabridged with the exception of the preliminary pages.

This facsimile edition first published in 1983
by The Blackstaff Press
3 Galway Park, Dundonald, Belfast BT16 0AN

British Library Cataloguing in Publication Data

Tomelty, Joseph
The apprentice.
I. Title
823'.914[F]   PR6039.0/

ISBN 0–85640–286–9

*To
the memory of
my father*

PART ONE

1   'IS IT YOU WHO's wanting the reference?
Is that why you are hanging about?'

'Yes, sir.' The boy's voice echoed in the
empty schoolroom. He knew the master was not interested
in him; indeed, disliked him. He would force him to read
aloud and join in the laughter of the class at his stammer.

'Wasn't it a reference you wanted?' The boy knew the
master had a habit of asking him everything twice, pretending not to hear the first time.

'Ye . . . ye . . . ye . . . yes.'

'What age are you?'

And the boy quickly snapped out: 'Fourteen.' He was
glad the word came to him so quickly.

'What age did you say . . .?'

The word 'fourteen' was still in the boy's mouth. Somewhere about the roof of his mind; or was it the echo?

Words beginning with 'f' were always hard for him to say.
He seemed to have to draw them from the pit of his stomach.
The other boys would coax him to pronounce words beginning with that letter, so that they could laugh when he made
sounds suggesting a vulgar expression.

He rocked from one foot to the other, beating his left thigh
with his hand, trying to force the word from where it stuck
in his mind. Then he closed his eyes, shutting out the hairy
nose and the bulging eyes of the master, and spat the word to
the dirty, dusty ceiling.

'Fourteen years of age,' said the master, 'and two hands
higher than a duck. The Corporation had better watch out
or you might sue them for bumping your bottom on the
pavement.' He laughed, but closed his mouth suddenly as
his false teeth dropped.

7

Taking the roll from the press, he peeled its pages back with his forefinger.

'Here we are: Francis Price. Born May . . .' He tightened his lips and started writing.

'Yes, you are fourteen. What work are you going to?'

It dawned on the boy that he was leaving school for ever. There was no need for him to face the master. He could not use the cane on him now; so again he spoke to the ceiling.

'I'm gonna be a painter.'

'A painter like Augustus John or Sammy Duggan?'

'Like Sammy Duggan.' The boy had never heard of the other man.

'You mean you are going to be a house-painter, a white-washer, a bug blinder?'

The boy nodded.

'Why don't you say what you mean? Well, what are we going to say about you? If we tell the truth we can only say your writing is hopeless, your reading worse, your spelling appalling, and your drawing of the pot stick variety.'

The boy wanted to say that he could read; he could read quietly to himself, but not out loud the way the master wanted. He looked at the clock, and heard the scratching of the pen as the master wrote.

'I am telling all whom it may concern that you are honest, and I suppose I must add, obedient, and that you are punctual. Were you ever late for school?'

The boy shook his head.

'You must practise the deaf and dumb signs; they'll be a great help to you in later life. Take refuge in the thought that Napoleon was a crowl of a man.' He folded the paper and slid it into an envelope. The boy reached up for it, and the master shouted: 'Go and wash your dirty paws first.'

In the school yard he let the water from the tap flow over his hands. There was no towel and he had no handkerchief, so he shook his hands above his head, scattering the beads of water about the lavatory door. He stared for a moment at the disappearing flecks, for the door was warm with the sun. He saw the pencil mark on the door frame. He had made this mark on the frame about a year earlier. He had measured himself, thinking that he might join the English Navy and get away from the things he feared. But he was too small. Now, he moved to where the mark was, and stood close to the frame, but he had not grown at all since then.

'What's keeping you, boy?'

He hurried back to the schoolroom. The master was putting on his coat.

'Well now,' he said, 'we'll know where to go when we want our houses painted. Be sure you put the paint right side out.'

The boy took the envelope, and as he left the school the master called after him: 'Farewell, parental scenes, a sad farewell. . . .'

His schoolbag fell from his shoulders. He wanted to lift it and hurl it over the school wall. It had little in its tattered belly: a jotter whose blue lines were nearly rubbed away, a three-half-penny writing book that blotted every time a pen touched it, an arithmetic with pages missing, a catechism fingered and dirty, and a pencil, teeth-peppered at the end.

Release from school was, he felt, the beginning of his freedom. Going to work would mean he would be away from home now from early morning until six or seven in the evening. Yet he knew he could take no chances with his aunt. The thought of her stirred a fear inside him; he was not sure whether he had wet the bed last night or not. He was in no hurry to get home. He never was. And today was different; he could dally — if she complained, he could say that the master had kept him waiting for the reference. . . .

She would have the soup heated, and he would stand at the end of the table where she would watch him eating it. She would listen to him trying to keep from vomiting as he gulped down the carrots, the parsnips and turnips that she loaded into his bowl. She would never cut these roots fine; they were so big that it was like swallowing broken sticks. He

9

would wait, as always, until she turned her face to poke the fire, or went outside to talk to a neighbour; then he would spoon the mess into his hand and put it in his pocket. At the first opportunity he could rush to Kelly's stable yard and empty his pocket to the hen that Kelly won for playing cards.

He hated his aunt. She had made him hate her. When he heard her at her prayers he wondered whether God did not hate her too. But God loved everybody; that was what the priests said in the pulpits, and the Protestant preachers at the street corners.

He walked up the street slowly. He stopped to look at the inscriptions on the gable of Greer's wall. 'UP THE REPUBLIC DAMN YOUR CONCESSIONS ENGLAND WE WANT OUR COUNTRY.'

He did not know who wanted the country, or why. All he knew about the Republic was that it had a green, white and orange flag, and that if the police found one in your house they could put you in jail for having it. It was the letters which fascinated him. How badly shaped they were! He would be a signwriter when he had served his apprenticeship.

2   HIS AUNT WAS A TALL, thin woman with a violent temper. 'Don't tempt me, boy, or I'll be hung for you,' was a common remark of hers. He got quickly out of her way when she spoke like this; but often she was quicker than he was. It seemed to him that she must have the longest arms of any woman in the world. Her arms were snake-like in their reach and movement. She was cruel, very cruel. None of the other women in the street ever beat their children as she beat him.

Once she tried to pull the tongue out of his mouth, and he had bitten her fingers. She had shown her fingers to all the neighbours, and they agreed with her that he was vicious, a case for a reformatory. And once when she threw him to the ground, she tried to jump on his body, but he caught her ankles, and she fell back, her head hitting the kitchen sofa. She lay moaning and calling out that she was dying. When he brought in the neighbours, they lifted her to the sofa. Hearing her version of the incident, they again agreed that a reformatory was the place for him.

He did not remember his mother. She had died when he was three years of age, and his father had sold out the home in Liverpool and come to live with his sister. Now his father was dead.

He remembered his father, a thin man with a pale face and large eyes, and a wooden arm. He remembered him sitting by the fire, sharpening his penknife, which he would try on his wooden arm, shaving off little ribbons. When he put the knife away, he would take a little bottle of stain from the mantelpiece, and stain the new whiteness of the arm.

His aunt, his father's sister, disapproved of him because he had been a British soldier. She had a habit of saying: 'They were not good Irish that wore the khaki uniform of the British army.' She was a Republican and had spent a week in Belfast jail for having attempted to smuggle messages into Republican prisoners when she visited them. The neighbours respected her, not only on account of this, but because the boy she had been engaged to was shot during a pogrom in Belfast. She had his photograph in the kitchen in a coloured frame, with the words 'He died for Ireland' under it.

The boy never understood what Simon Clarke meant when he had said: 'Frankie, that's what happens in Ireland. The louder you sing "God save the King", the better. The louder you shout "Up the Rebels", the better. The louder you shout "I believe in God" the better. You can get away with bloody murder, provided you shout these things loud enough in the right places.'

When his father died, his aunt was afraid that he might be given a military funeral with the Union Jack wrapped around his coffin; so she buried him at her own expense, and the neighbours spoke well of her because of this.

He entered the house noisily. When he entered quietly she would accuse him of spying on her. She was standing beside the fire, her right elbow on the mantelpiece. He glanced at her, seeing her nostrils widen as she turned her head to the fire. What was she going to use on him this time? He saw the shiny bulb-shaped top of the poker; and in the hearth lay the long shafted brush. She turned her head, and fear fixed the boy's eyes on her white, cruel face.

'Don't look under your eyes at me,' she said. 'Go upstairs and have a look at that tick.'

It was a trick of hers to get him up the stairs so that she could beat him. If he remained below, he could run to the street or out into the yard: upstairs he had no chance of escape.

Pulling back the brown hairy blanket, he looked at the stain on the coarse mattress. It recalled the shape of Australia on the map in the schoolroom.

She tried to walk quietly, but the stairs creaked. She was coming to beat him. At school he had only to remember it, and he could plainly feel the sting of the hearth brush on his arm, her toe on his shin, or the poker on his head.

She was in the room now, closing the door behind her. The window was open; if he screamed loud enough perhaps she would not be so brutal.

'Do you see that bed? What in God's name am I going to do with you? A dirty, lazy loafer that won't rise at night! I'll beat the dirty habit out of you.'

Now she was at him with the hearth brush, hammering at his upraised elbow, until his arm fell lifelessly, exposing his forehead. He rushed towards the door, but she caught him with the brush on the head, and he cried out as the blood ran down his brow.

'That's right! Yell like blue hell and let the neighbours think I'm murdering you. But the neighbours know what you are — a dirty lazy loafer that has me washing after you day and night.'

He looked at her through the mist of blood and tears. The saliva was churning white on her angry lips. She made towards him and he dashed through the door and down the stairs.

'I'll give you something to yell for . . .' But he was in the yard before she finished, and was holding the latch of the yard door as tight as he could to prevent her following him. He listened. Her footsteps were heavy on the creaky stairs. She crossed the kitchen, throwing the hearth brush on the hob.

He bent over the water barrel, splashing the rain water about his face, looking down at the drops of blood as they spread themselves into queer shapes, like skeleton worms. He pulled up the sleeve of his coat and twisted his arm so that he could see his elbow. Near the point, which was wrinkled like the unsucked teat of a sow, the bruises were silky grey, turning as he looked to a dark blue.

Why could he not cure himself of this awful habit? Did she think he wet the bed just to get hammered with a brush or a poker, or whatever else was handy? If only she knew how often he had prayed to God about it. She must know that it was not his fault. She saw to it that hours before he went to bed he was not given anything to drink. He had sucked stones at night when his mouth was dry, and once had swallowed a stone by accident. Long afterwards he had the fear that, buried inside him, it kept him from growing.

'This soup is here for you if you want it . . .' he heard her shout. Grey lumps of bread floated on top of it. He pushed the sodden bread to the side of the bowl, trying to get at the clear liquid. It was hot, and the first spoonful he put in his mouth made him cough violently.

'I'll give you something to cry for,' she said, mistaking the sudden fit of coughing for weeping.

She was coming towards him and he moved into the hallway. He was sorry he had not taken the soup with him, for here was a chance to move into the yard to get rid of the bread, the carrots and the turnips.

'Did the master give you a reference?'

He felt in his pocket.

'Look at you, you'll have it filthy.' She snatched the envelope from him.

The outside door was knocked, and he heard a neighbour calling her. Walking quietly to the fire he spooned the bread, carrots and parsnips from the bowl into its red heart. As the fire burned them into black blotches there was a sizzling, and he was afraid she might hear it.

The neighbour was saying: 'It's just a pot of jam I tried as an experiment. But our ones wouldn't lip it. I made it from a vegetable marrow that I bought at the market.'

He liked the soup now. There was nothing in it but barley.

She came into the kitchen again, put a small pot of greenish jam on the table, and cut a slice of bread. Taking a little of the jam on the point of the knife, she tasted it. Her face puckered and she spat into the fire. She plastered the jam on the bread and pushed it towards him.

The jam was sweet, so sweet that it nearly made him feel sick. He toyed with the bread, playing for time until he could get away from the table to the yard and scrape the jam off.

She was reading the reference, with her eye screwed into a round magnifying glass chipped at the edges.

'It doesn't say much about your learning,' she muttered. She shook her head, and said loudly: 'He says you're honest. You're honest because I made you honest, for I'd have cut the thieving hands from your body.'

He knew what she meant; the incident was fresh in his mind. He was standing before the priest with the rimless glasses and the black teeth. He was guilty of stealing a shilling from the money he had collected with the pin-hole card for the Foreign Missions. The priest was telling him what a mean action it was; he was depriving some poor black baby of its due. He wanted to tell the priest that he stole the shilling because he was hungry. His aunt thanked the priest and then hurried into the church forcing him to his knees to ask God's forgiveness for committing this awful sin.

'That reference would hardly carry you to the top of the street,' she said. Then her eye caught the uneaten bread in his hand. 'What's the matter with it?'

'The jam is too sweet,' he stammered timidly.

'Get it into you. Go on . . . eat it. . . .'

The sweet jam stuck in his throat, forcing him to vomit.

'Take yourself to the yard, and not vomit here . . .' He ran quickly up the hall to the back door. Bending to the water barrel he scooped some water down his throat.

He scraped the jam from the bread with his finger, and rubbed his finger against the wall until it was clean. If he put his head into this barrel and the water ran up his nose, he would be dead . . . But that would be taking his own life, and God would send him to hell.

'Wash your hands and go and see Simon Clarke about your job,' she called.

He could have whooped with joy at her words, for he loved going to Simon Clarke's house.

3   SIMON CLARKE was getting him started as an apprentice. His aunt did not like Simon. He was an ex-soldier. She regarded his interest in the boy as reeking of the charity of the British Legion.

He was a big man; not tall, but everything about him was big; his hands, his eyes, his face. His feet looked enormous, and his boots were always thickly soled and heeled with layers of rubber. Since the boy's father had died, Simon's visits to the house were rare. Before that he would call every Saturday night, and his father and he would go out, as Simon said, 'For a glass of goat's milk.' Simon would bring him back sweets, or a water pistol, or a couple of lucky bags. The boy thought of him as the only kind person he had met except Sally Blair. Simon was an uncommon name. In the chapel when the priest, doing the Stations of the Cross, called out; 'The fifth Station; Simon helps Jesus with the Cross . . .' it seemed to the boy that it was what Simon Clarke would have done, had he been there.

His aunt would never agree that Simon was kind. She said that he was knee-deep in Freemasonry (the boy wondered what that meant — Simon was a painter and not a mason), and that he hated everything that was Catholic.

He lived on the Shankill road, where all the people were Protestants. The boy used to be frightened to go near his house; there was writing on a gable which made him run past it. 'To hell with the Pope' was printed in big letters. Simon laughed at his fears: 'Frankie, don't you worry about the Pope. The Pope, son, would give all the Irish tears for a smile from England. For God's sake, son, don't let these bloody sayings and slogans worry you.' He had a way of talking about things that made him seem important. He would never speak of the King, but always of 'Geordie the Fifth'. He would say terrible things about kings and cardinals. Reading a book about some famous man, he would put it down, laugh, and say; 'Bejazes, you're a boy and a half!' — as if the man he was reading about were beside him.

When the boy knocked on the door, Simon appeared wearing glasses that seemed to have bandages of thread everywhere on them.

'Ach, it's yourself, Frankie, come my son, come in.' As he brought Frankie within, he said: 'I'm in the middle of Napoleon's life. I say, Frankie, the bold Boneyparte was a bit of a lad . . . Chase that cat down and park yourself.'

The boy pushed the cat gently, but the animal crushed back further into the chair.

'Get down off that chair, McCusker. Where are your manners?' Simon shook the chair until the cat fell from it.

'Look at that, Frankie, he's as lazy as cut-the-bags. He's a buck and he's been out on the randan this past week; and when he does that he'd sleep for a fortnight.

'You have arrived just in time,' Simon said. 'I'm gonna make some tea, and I've a nice bit of lamb's liver here to fry.' He kept talking about Napoleon as he prepared the meal.

'Well, Frankie,' he said when he motioned the boy to the table, 'tomorrow morning you start work. You start on the road of life. A long road, boy. Puddles and puddles of trouble. You know, Frankie, there's times I ask myself what's it all about? It's about something, you know, if only we could find out . . .' Suddenly he stopped and got up from the table. 'Look, Frankie, come here and I'll show you something.' He led the way up the stairs. On the landing he stopped, and pulling the curtains aside from the window he looked out at the wall opposite. 'Look Frankie, look out through this window. See that window-sill opposite?' The boy nodded. 'Look at the corner. That's a pigeon crulged in there. She's been sitting there on two eggs this long while. If she could talk she could tell you what it's all about. Why does she sit on that draughty window-sill on her two eggs? What makes her do it? She has the answer, Frankie, but she can't talk . . .' He was going down the stairs. 'No, son, she can't talk. But I watch her sitting on the eggs, day after day, night after night, with the knowing nod of the Sphinx about her. It's a puzzle, son, it's a puzzle.' He poured out the tea, saying as if to himself, 'It's a puzzle.' Near the edge of the table lay a book of gold leaf. The boy stared at it.

'I'm doing a bit of gilding, Frankie — a church notice-board. Some minister or other has got a new degree conferred on him. He proved Luther was right in something he said, and wrote a book about it, so this is what he gets for it; more letters after his name. As I say, Johnny, it's all a bloody puzzle. When you think about it, it makes you laugh. Some Catholic will write a book proving Luther was wrong, and some school of learning will add letters to his name for it, just as some Protestant will say Luther was right, and get letters after his too. It's laughable ... Have you ever thought about this city you're living in, Frankie. Of the ghettoes in it? The Protestants are stuck in one district; the Catholics in another, the Jews somewhere else. I tell you, Frankie, if I was dictator here for about five years, I'd change the whole set-up. These creeds and classes have made the place a bloody purgatory for themselves. But you're only a child with no head for that kind of talk. As you get older, talk to me and I'll put you wise about a few things in life to avoid; only don't ask me the point of living life as we do in Belfast. Ask the pigeon.'

Simon stretched himself on the sofa, made a cigarette, and lit it. 'Now to business,' he said as he exhaled the first pull. 'Tomorrow morning, at eight-fifteen precisely, you'll present yourself at the office of Messrs. George St. Clair, at 84 West Cyprus Street. You'll ask for Mr. Pyper, and you'll tell him you are the boy Simon Clarke was speaking to him about. It is a dacent firm, Frankie, a firm that you need never be ashamed to say that you served your time with. But one word of warning: if your first foreman happens to be a man called Eustace Crawford, watch your step and be careful, for he's an embittered old bastard ... Now don't look alarmed. That's an innocent word meaning exactly just what it says.' His cigarette went out and Frankie rolled a bit of paper, lit it at the fire and brought it over.

'What makes your hand tremble so much, Frankie?'

The boy looked at his hand but made no answer.

'You know, son, it's unnatural for anyone like you to have such a shaky hand. Maybe it's just excitement. I mind when I was joining the army, I just could hardly see a thing in front of me, I was that excited. Twenty-one years in the army, son, and never fired a shot. There's a record for you. You see, son, I was handy with the pen, and the old maxim is still true; the pen, Frankie, the pen is mightier than the sword. Did you never write that in your copy book at school?'

18

Frankie stammered out that the only thing he ever wrote in his copy book was; 'Cleanliness is next to Godliness'.

Simon grunted a laugh and said, 'If that's the case there's a big lot of atheists about.' He raised his shoulders higher on the sofa.

'You must watch your breathing, Frankie. Try and control it more. Concentrate on it. Say to yourself: "Here is a breath and I am not going to waste it. I am going to use it to say so many words." A stammering man can be his own greatest handicap.' Simon's eyes were on him, wider than he had ever seen them before; they almost frightened him.

'What about your aunt?' The quietness of the voice reassured him. Frankie felt he could not talk about her. Although this house was far away from where he lived, she seemed to be here with him. He knew he must answer Simon's question, but he burst into tears.

'That's it, son. Cry your fill. It will ease you. Never think it unmanly to cry. Go on, weep as much as you like. Tears to the soul is as good as salts to the body.'

Simon cleared the table. 'You could have been reared in many a happier home,' he said, as he poured milk into a tin plate for the cat. Then, taking Frankie's hand he led him to the sofa. 'Many and many a time, I had thought of taking you over to live with me. But the obstacles were many, legal as well as religious. Yes, there was your immortal soul to be thought of and all the labels that civilization has invented to torture itself with. I was fond of your father, Frankie, and I knew your mother well. You don't remember her?'

He shook his head.

'She was a wee angel of a woman with just the smallest cast in her eye; and yet do you know, far from it having an unsightly effect, I must say it made her face more attractive.'

There was a long pause, then Simon said slowly: 'Always remember, Frankie, there's a bed here for you any time you feel you want it. But now that you have started to work, your aunt might soften a little towards you. I daresay she's bought you a pair of overalls. If she could buy you two pairs, when one pair would be in the wash, the other would be handy. Now, Frankie, I want you to do a little errand for me. As you are passing the library would you leave this book in for me?' Frankie reached for the book, turning over the pages when Simon gave it to him.

'The book wouldn't interest a youngster like you. It's a study of the diseases of the heart; I got it out because I felt a pain in my old ticker. But I think it was just a touch of nervous wind, that was all. Still, you know, it's best to check these things in time.'

Simon left him at the door, patting his head as he said: 'Report to me as soon as you can, I'd like to know how you fare on your first job.'

Frankie walked slowly. A bright bottle like a huge flash-light was shining in a chemist's window. Beside this bottle was a picture of a near naked man with golden hair. The man's body was perfectly made, and underneath were the words: 'You can have a body like this by taking Streno night and morning.' A small jar of it, cost five shillings; to the boy that seemed a fortune; but he made up his mind on the spot that once he started to work, he would save money to buy 'Streno'.

He stood there, his forehead touching the glass, his eyes filled with the golden brown of the man's body. It was not because the man had a perfectly shaped body that he admired the picture — it was because he looked so happy. He was always there; snug and warm in this window, with the colour from the bottle shining on him. Even at night when the blind was down, and the lights in the shop were out, he would still be snug and happy.

There was a queue at the library. One man wanted a book on family sickness; and when the girl attendant inquired what the sickness was, he said that his wife was 'expecting'. The attendant, a thin, small girl with a sharp nose and rimless glasses, kept beetling the books with a heavy stamp. Frankie made up his mind to ask for a book about nerves.

'Mr. Clarke wants a book on nerves,' he stammered.

'Nerves? What kind of a book on nerves?' she asked.

'Just a book about nerves.'

'Yes, but there are thousands of books about nerves; there's one published every week.'

He wanted to say that it was a book about not being able to climb, about how to keep his hands from trembling. He rocked from foot to foot.

'I'll give you Majonksy's book; it's fairly comprehensive. It's used as a text book.'

He knew she was using big words to show off; she was always like that. Once when his aunt sent him for a book, this girl puzzled him by asking was it fiction he had wanted, and when he said it was a just a story, she was quite angry with him.

He left the library, hurrying to the brightest lit shop window, and opened the book. It had many drawings in it, shaped like meat hanging in a butcher's shop. At the beginning it had big words which he could make nothing of; he tried to skip them but they would crop up again and he knew it was useless for him to try to read the book without knowing what they meant.

He hid the book down his trousers, lest his aunt should see it. Maybe somewhere in the middle there might be bits he could understand; maybe he could find out how to keep his hand steady, and how to rid his mind of the fear that came over him when he tried to climb.

4   'THERE'S A PAIR of overalls, try them on and see if they fit you.'

He held the overalls close to his body, the legs curled on the floor, and he tried to lift them by pulling them close to the fork of his trousers.

'Put them on the right way.'

He made to unbutton his trousers, but suddenly remembered the book.

'Take yourself upstairs, and not undress there, you shameless brat,' and her wet hand slid down his ear.

He cried, mounting the stairs, and her threat was after him; 'I'll give you something to cry for. . . .'

He pushed the book under the mattress, and stood drying his eyes. He looked at the overalls in his hand; not knowing how to wear them, whether they should be next his skin or over his trousers.

'Do they fit you?' she called.

He pulled them up as he came down the stairs, frightened that he might trip as he descended and that he might dirty the overalls as he walked in the kitchen to let her see them.

'They need sewing at the legs and arms. Take them off you and I'll fix them, and hurry — this is your confraternity night.' He took the overalls off. 'Damnation take you, look at you, trailing them on the floor. Is that all the respect you have for them. Now wash your face and comb your hair. Don't go into the house of God like a dirty tramp.'

He washed his face, using the water from the barrel. He forked his fingers through his damp hair. She would never let him use a mirror; she said the devil was there.

When he was ready she took his medal from the tin canister on the mantelpiece and left it on the table.

'There's your medal,' she said.

He picked up the medal and put it in his pocket, his fingers feeling the little raised figures of the Holy Family. He did not like going to the confraternity; but he could not stay away from it, for the prefect of the section to which he belonged lived just two doors above him. He knew if he ever 'mitched' a meeting, the prefect would ask his aunt the reason. It was the prefect who made him dislike the confraternity. He was a smallish man with a bald head; his eyes looked as though he was always crying, his nose was crooked, and his chin shot down like the tongue of a boot. When he laughed, his upper lip almost disappeared, and his long chin reached up to the point of his crooked nose. He had a peculiar way of walking, as if he used the sides of his feet. He attended all the Gaelic classes, and could speak Irish; he was never known to curse or drink; and was in all the sodalities and confraternities connected with the church. Every Saturday he collected for the black babies, and every Sunday for the white babies. Sally Blair's father had called him a 'religious informer'. It was said he was in everything connected with the church except the crib at Christmas.

Frankie often prayed to God to make him believe as the other boys did. The priest preached to them, taking for granted that everyone believed in God. The priest would say that Jesus wanted them to be happy, but Frankie knew it was hard to be happy when you were hungry. It was all very well for the priest to point at the picture of the Holy Family and say: 'There you have the example of perfect harmony and happiness, Jesus, Mary and Joseph.' Jesus could be happy for he had a smiling woman like Mary, with her gentle eyes and kind face. Jesus knew that Mary never wanted to pull the tongue out of his mouth, nor dance on his body, nor beat him with a poker, or a hearth brush.

He joined the crowd as they walked up the long street to the church. The crowd closed in as he climbed the steps of the church. He felt suffocated. It was the feeling of going where he did not belong. If he could believe! If God would only whisper a few words in his ear; 'Don't be afraid, son, I am God, I exist. I will reward the good and punish the wicked.'

He looked towards the prefect who was marking his roll book, and stood up to show that he was present. The prefect might mark him absent, and tell his aunt he had not attended; sometimes when you got behind one of the church pillars it was difficult for you to be seen.

The priest climbed into the pulpit, and there was a great

23

noise of kneeling when he tapped the ridge of the pulpit with the crucifix which hung from his neck. 'Let you all stand up now and sing one verse of Sweet Holy Child.' They rose almost lazily and sang:

> Jesus, teach me how to pray,
> Suffer not my thoughts to stray,
> Send distractions far away,
> Sweet, Holy Child.

When they sat down, the priest said they were not singers at all. 'All keep silent now, and think about God, and about your dead friends. Think, too, about those you love, and pray for them, that God may increase your love for them, as well as for Him.'

Frankie thought about love. There was no one he loved, except Sally Blair; but he knew that was not the love the priest was talking about.

He prayed for his father because he was the only thing, the only image he could escape to; even if his memory now recalled only a wooden arm, he knew it was something real, yet it frightened him to be thinking of a dead thing as being real.

He wondered about the place called hell, and the other called purgatory. He thought of his father in hell, of his wooden arm crackling in the fire . . . But would God burn people? He remembered a priest saying that no one knew whether God's hell was one of fire, for no one knew the mind of God. It was hard to believe that God, looking down at his father, would think, there's another one to burn in hell. His father had shouted before he died, and all the neighbours said he was raving. Once he looked into the room where death fluttered, and his father was crying out for a new suit. He remembered a woman standing at the door and she was laughing. She was the prefect's mother. But maybe it was funny to hear a dying man talking like a child.

But what had the priest been preaching about? He would

have to find out in case his aunt asked him, but he knew that to ask the boy beside him would make him stutter so badly that the prefect might hear him, and come down on him again. He decided if his aunt asked him, he would tell her the priest had been preaching about sin; he nearly always preached about that.

A soft drizzle of rain was falling. At the corner of his own street he stopped with Alec Devlin and some other boys. Devlin was waiting for Sally Blair; he kept looking up the street, saying, 'I wonder is that rain on for the night?'

Devlin did not attend the confraternity; his mother said she would not force anybody to do anything he did not want to do, or to go anywhere he did not want to go. She would let the children crowd into the kitchen of her house on a wet day, and she was the only woman who had bought her son a pair of real football boots.

The others knew that Devlin was waiting for Sally, but they never made fun of Devlin about her. They knew that when Devlin climbed up the street lamp to put the light out it was because he did not want anyone to see Sally and him standing in the doorway. Sally and Devlin were 'boy' and 'girl', but Devlin's mother was against his even speaking to her; she said Sally was going around like a bitch in heat. Frankie's aunt did not like Sally, nor did the neighbours at the bottom of the street. He had heard one woman telling his aunt that she might expect nothing else, for Sally Blair's mother had been a Protestant, and like the rest of the 'love' Catholics, the faith was far back in her. The woman was the prefect's mother and had his long chin and little pig's eyes.

Sally came down the street and they all greeted her. Frankie admired her; he liked the black and white dress she wore going to school, and her long black stockings that disappeared under her short skirt. Often she would buy sweets, and it did not matter how many were standing at the lamp-post, she would give the sweets out; sometimes she had only one left for herself. Once she had given him a bun;

25

she had only taken one bite from it, then handed it to him, behind her back so as no one would see her. The bun, he remembered, was sweet and when he touched the open part where she had bitten he imagined he was kissing her lips. He thought often about her; next to Simon she was the only one who was kind to him. He knew she could never be his girl. Devlin was nice-looking, and everyone admired his black curls and his brown eyes. His mother loved him so much that she would have given him everything in the house. He wanted for nothing. He could go to any picture house he liked, or any football match. He had a racing bicycle and roller skates. Once, when half a dozen of them were in Devlin's kitchen, she lifted his head and kissed him. Devlin pulled away from her, saying the others would laugh at her. Frankie noticed they did laugh, everyone except himself.

Sally came nearer the lamplight, and took a nail file from the pocket of her black blazer.

'I hear you're left school, Frankie.'

'Yes, Sally.' He looked at her large eyes, her red cheeks and at the white blouse with its striped tie.

'It's well for you. I've got to start in Green's Academy on Thursday next.'

'What are you going to learn there?' Devlin asked.

'Shorthand and typewriting. I'll type your name for you, Frankie . . .'

'Will you?'

She nodded, and he saw Devlin catch her hand, then drop it as someone approached.

It was the prefect. When he passed, Sally muttered: 'Chinny chin chin . . .'

'Don't, Sally, he'll hear you,' Devlin whispered loudly.

Frankie turned to go, but Sally stopped him. 'You are in a big hurry,' she said.

'I must go, Sally; he saw me talking at the confraternity and he might tell my aunt . . .'

'And would she beat you for it?' This was another thing

that made him like Sally more. She always seemed to know what he was going to say, and she could help him by cutting in.

'Don't you know well enough she would beat him. Sure he hasn't the life of a dog,' Devlin said, kicking playfully at the bottom of the lamp-post.

A band started to play somewhere, and the other boys rushed away to follow it.

Devlin climbed up the lamp-post and put the light out, then backed into the doorway pulling Sally slowly with him.

As Frankie left them Sally caught his hand and crushed a coin into his palm. 'It's a threepenny-bit,' she whispered. Then she walked into the dark doorway. 'Good night, Frankie,' came from Devlin, and 'Cheerio,' from Sally.

He was glad that his aunt did not ask him what the priest had been preaching about. She had his overalls ready, and ordered him to put them on so that she would see what they looked like. And when she satisfied herself that they fitted him, she said: 'Take yourself off to bed, and not have me shouting the lungs out of myself trying to waken you in the morning.'

He sat on the bed, feeling the bottoms of the overalls. This was his first time for long trousers, and he longed to see himself in a mirror.

'I don't hear you at your prayers,' she called up.

He fell to his knees, heavily, so that she might hear the thud. He rhymed out the Our Father and the Apostle's Creed.

'What way is that to be galloping through your prayers. It's God you are praying to.'

He recited loudly:

Jesus, Mary and Joseph, I place all my trust in thee.
Jesus, Mary and Joseph, assist me in my last agony.
Jesus, Mary and Joseph, make me a good boy.

The bed was hard, coarse and damp like a cement wall.

27

Of late he had taken the pillow and pushed it under him to get some warmth. But she had come on him one night, and tore the pillow away; even now he was afraid to chance it again. He curled his feet up against his hips; pressing his toes at the same time with his hand; it was so cold.

From outside came the sound of running feet, and then the music of a band. A torch for a moment shone through the bleary window. When the sounds of the band faded, he pulled the bedclothes over his head, breathing down his shirt almost in grunts to warm his body. He remembered that in the stable of Bethlehem the ox had blown its breath on the infant Jesus. The breath of the ox was longer and warmer; he had watched one once, and its breath came like that of a man exhaling a long pull of a cigarette.

5   WHEN HIS AUNT wakened him in the morning, instinctively, he felt the bed; it was wet. He looked out through the window, rubbing the breath of frost from the glass, but all he could see was the grey sky. On the other side of the street was a bread cart, the horse stamping one of its hind feet, sending up tiny sparks from the road.

He came downstairs and stood at the end of the table. He lingered over the two slices of bread she put before him, knowing the longer he chewed and kept the bread in his mouth, the more filling it could be.

'Are you going to fall asleep again over your breakfast?'

He gulped down the warm tea.

'Be attentive. Do what you're told, and keep you hands to yourself. And don't give cheek,' she told him.

The tea was down. Was it spreading the soft bread like porridge over the bottom of his stomach? When his stomach

28

was empty did it dry in until both sides met, like a pig's bladder he had seen drying in the sun? When food was put into it, it flattened again ...

'Do you hear what I've said to you? I'll put you from day-dreaming. . . .'

He answered her, moving from the table, but saw she was not following him. She sat at the fire toasting bread for herself. Her skirt was pulled up; her legs were naked, and he could see her knees discoloured and wrinkled.

The bread she was holding close to the fire fell from the fork; she turned and caught him looking at her.

'The hungry eye sees far; the covetous one farther. . . .'

The screech of a mill horn came up the hall.

'There goes the horn for eight o'clock. Be off to your job, if you want to start today.'

He hurried away. When he knocked on a door with a plate which said, 'GEORGE ST. CLAIR. House Renovators and Church Decorators', no one answered it. He waited, still tapping the door with his knuckles. A small man came up the street.

'Are you the new apprentice?' he asked.

Frankie nodded.

The man looked at his watch and said: 'Still five minutes to go. I think I'll have a smoke.' He crouched on his hunkers, lighting his pipe and looking up at Frankie.

'You're small enough anyway. You'll do for getting into the corners,' he said. His eyes were cruel and he kept them half closed so that they looked like slits. Could he be Eustace Crawford, the foreman that Simon had spoken about?

Two more men approached. 'Good morning, Eustace,' said one of them.

'You have your share of it.'

The second man looked down at Eustace, and Frankie could see an expression of dislike on his face.

'You're the new apprentice,' said the taller of the two men.

Frankie stammered out, 'Yes . . .'

'Are you a stutterer?' Eustace asked, without looking up.

The tall man winked at Frankie and shook his head, and the boy knew that he too disliked Eustace.

Eustace got to his feet and took a key from his pocket. He opened the door and pointing to another inside the yard, he said, 'There's the office, go in and report.'

The door Frankie knocked was marked 'Private'. Through the glass pane he could see a girl with a small mirror in her hand, powdering her face. When he entered, she closed the powder compact with a little click.

'Mr. Pyper will be down shortly. You're the boy Simon Clarke has recommended?' She eyed him, as she wet her finger and smoothed her eyebrows. 'What school did you go to?' From the way she smoothed her eyebrows as she spoke, Frankie felt that it did not matter whether he answered her or not. 'Did you hear what I asked you? What school did you go to?'

He stammered out the name of the school.

'Is that the Falls or the Shankill district?'

He knew that she asked him this to find out his religion. If he said the Falls she would know he was a Catholic.

He told her the school was on the Grosvenor Road. She would not know now, because both Catholics and Protestants lived in this locality.

He could see his answer did not please her, for she widened her eyes and gave a little cough.

Mr. Pyper came into the office. He was a small thin man, with large yellow veins in his neck. His face was sad. His head was nodding all the time, and he kept looking at the ground as though he had lost something. He ignored Frankie, and reached out for the bundle of letters on the counter. He read the envelope of each letter and his head shook more quickly as he threw them one by one back to the counter again.

The girl muttered something about the new apprentice.

30

He turned to Frankie. 'You are Simon Clarke's friend? Let me see your reference.' He read the reference as if it annoyed him.

'Well, that wouldn't pass you into Heaven. But we shall take a chance on Simon Clarke's account. Now a word or two before you start. We are a respected firm. We give all our apprentices a reasonable chance of becoming first-class tradesmen. We are decorators, not whitewashers. We are respected by all denominations, we won't tolerate any sectarian tittle-tattle, for as we do work for Protestant as well as Catholic, for Jew as well as Gentile, for English and Scotch as well as Irish, or Hindoo for that matter, we must keep balanced perspectives. If you are attentive and obedient as well as willing, you'll emerge at the end of five years a qualified tradesman, you understand?'

'Yes, yes, sir.'

'I notice you have a stammer, a handicap in a way. Still . . . We are prepared to do a lot for you. Now, in return we ask you to do something for us. We ask you to be honest, to be clean and to shave every day, when you reach that stage of course, you understand?'

'Ye — yes, sir.'

'Now a few general remarks. Never regard the property of the people you work for as your own; you must never be a thief. I think that the most awful word in the English language. Another thing, too, you must be very careful about . . . are you listening?'

'Ye — yes, sir . . .'

'This is important. You'll find in the various houses you work in a certain type of servant girl — a scatter-brained type, with nothing else in her head but tittle-tattle and with a weakness towards flirtation. The type usually keep you from your work; now remember any tig-toying with girls of this type is strictly forbidden. A report of this nature means instant dismissal, you understand?'

'Ye — yes, sir.'

'Your wages will be ten shillings a week with an increase every year until you finish your time. Now go outside and report to Mr. Crawford, one of our foremen.'

Frankie thanked him and left the office. Outside he looked about for Crawford. The tall man told him that he had gone to the wallpaper store but would be back directly. 'Did you get a lecture in the office?'

Frankie nodded.

'I suppose he told you to lay off servant girls?'

'Yes.'

'What a bloody hypocrite! You couldn't trust him with a corpse. Servant girls are an obsession with him.'

Crawford approached. 'Come on, my lad, look alive.' Frankie walked to meet him and Crawford gave him a bundle of wallpaper to carry.

When they arrived at the job, Frankie saw it was a house called the Sycamores; he wondered why for there were no trees about the place. He followed Crawford into a room which was bare and smelled strongly of paint. Crawford sat down and filled his pipe.

'Keep moving about, give the impression of noise; pretend you are working. . . .'

Frankie stamped his feet loudly through the room.

'Don't do a bloody cart horse act; move about as easily as you can, and at the same time make as much noise as you can, until I finish my smoke.'

When he stood up again, Crawford asked: 'What's your name?'

'Frankie Price.'

'What price, half price?' Crawford laughed; then he said: 'There's a bucket there, if you want to use it. Don't go near the toilet upstairs; and be careful here, for the owner is a friend of the boss.'

He put Frankie to work on the wall with a bit of pumice stone. He disliked handling the pumice stone; when his finger nails touched it, it set his teeth on edge; but he worked on until sweat came out on his forehead, for he knew every now and then the eyes of Crawford were on him.

When the chimes of a church bell came to the room Crawford made him stop work until he counted the strokes. It was twelve o'clock; time for lunch.

Crawford gave him a small packet of tea, telling him to take it to the kitchen where the mistress of the house would brew it for them.

'Take your own tea with it too.'

'I haven't got any.'

'How the hell do you expect tea if you haven't brought any with you. Have you bread with you?'

Frankie shook his head.

'Jazes man! Did you think it was a picnic you were coming on?'

Frankie remembered the threepenny-bit Sally had given him. 'I'll buy some buns,' he said.

'And where are you going to get buns here? This is a residential district. There are no shops here.'

There was a silence.

'You can't expect what tea I have in that paper to do for two.'

Another silence.

'If you go about it nicely, maybe you could scrounge some tea and a bit of bread from the mistress. Knock on the door that leads to the kitchen, and wait until she asks you in. Go on.'

Flushing hotly at the thought of having to ask the lady for bread and tea, and fearing he would stammer and she might not understand what he wanted, he knocked timidly at the door.

He could hear singing: 'We strolled the lanes together, laughed at the rains together.' He knocked louder on the door. It was opened quickly, and there was a wave of perfume.

'Yes?'

A cigarette hung from her lower lip and as she cocked her head, her hair spread over her shoulder.

He tried to tell her what he wanted, but his face was hot and he saw the quick movement of her hair as she turned away from him.

'Take it slowly, very slowly; don't rush it,' she said, walking towards the scullery. 'A deep breath, and you'll find easy does it, easy does it.'

He rocked from foot to foot, pointing to the gas stove in the scullery. She understood. 'Bread and tea, you want. Of course, it's twelve o'clock; your lunch time.'

Then she lit the gas and put the teapot on and prepared a tray with a white cloth. She looked around for something. 'I'm only keeping house today for my sister. Pardon me if I just cannot put my hands to things I want; I'm looking for milk.'

She bent to search in a cupboard, shaking her hair back from her face with quick impatient jerks. She was wearing dark blue trousers with red slippers. Her finger nails were red, like the colour of the pullover she wore.

She was a lovely girl, the nicest he had ever seen. She was nicer than Sally Blair.

'Is there a man named Sylvester Haig working in your firm?' she asked.

He told her that, this being his first day, he did not know. He had the feeling she wanted to talk more, but already he had made a move towards the door, carrying the tray with great care, fearful of dirtying the cloth.

She held the kitchen door ajar for him. 'If you want some hot water, come and get it. . . .'

Crawford eyed the tray. 'Well, here's style and no mistake. She didn't do that for me the other day; you must have a way with women.' Crawford stretched himself on the floor, resting his back against the wall. He took out his false teeth. 'Bloody ornaments,' he said loudly. 'I paid a botch of a dentist ten quid for them, and they're like lumps of bloody concrete in my mouth. They cut the gums off me.'

34

Frankie sat with his back against the piano.

'I heard her talking to you. What was she saying?'

'She was asking about somebody called Haig.'

'What about Haig?'

'If he worked here.'

'Holy God! Don't tell me she knows him. Beau Brummell to the life. You'll meet Haig before you're much older. A lout if ever there was one.'

Frankie was silent. He was glad that the piano hid him from Crawford, for his hand trembled worse than it ever had before.

'Do you hear what I am saying? Come out from behind that piano and be sociable. . . .'

Frankie moved out. Crawford lifted the teapot and left the room. When he returned he said: 'That's not the same woman was here on Saturday. That isn't the mistress of the house.' He sat down and when he had refilled the two cups, he said, 'Imagine a posh dame like that asking for a fool like Haig. It's a hundred to one he has met that dame at a flash dance. That's what he does; goes to these posh dances with a waiter's outfit on him. No tanner jigs for him. I bet you anything he has spun that dame a yarn. Isn't it rich! If she's any relation of the woman who owns this house, then she must be a friend of the boss. Jazes! isn't it a good one! Haig maybe telling her he owned the bloody firm, and then she turns out to be a friend of the man he's working for.' He lit his pipe and as he blew the smoke, he said thoughtfully:

'Imagine a bloke like Haig, setting himself up for a girl like that. That girl has class. You could see that from the way she walks.' He looked at his watch. 'Time we started again, better take those cups and things back to her,' he said.

'Had you enough to eat?' she asked, as Frankie brought the tray to the scullery.

'Ye — yes, thank you. . . .'

'Did you say you didn't know Syl Haig?'

'Ye — yes. . . .'

'Do you smoke?'

He shook his head.

'No bad habits? Not even got a girl?'

'No.'

'You're too serious, young man, that's your trouble.'

That afternoon Crawford told him to arrange a plank on two trestles to start washing the ceiling. Now he was afraid, for the ceiling was high and to reach it he knew he must put the plank right on the top step of the trestles. Crawford helped him arrange them.

'Now my lad, up you go and start sponging the ceiling.' The trestles were close to the wall. He was able to catch the picture rail, but what would happen when he had to move to the centre of the ceiling when there was nothing to catch?

He rubbed and rubbed, until he felt he must have softened the plaster.

'What the hell's keeping you? Are you going to rub in the one place all the bloody day?'

He hurried down the trestle, and Crawford helped him to a new stretch.

'Up you go now, and break a record. Let me see how little time it will take you to finish the ceiling.'

This time he caught the window frame, but soon he would have to move from the window and there would be nothing to grip. Why was he afraid? Why couldn't he walk along this plank? What was in his head that would not let him do it? Crawford was watching him . . . Oh, God! if only there were something to catch hold of. He could jump now and be safe if he landed on the floor. The chain that hung from the electric light fitting in the ceiling centre — could he get to that? Slowly he moved along the plank, with his eyes on the ground. He felt his head touch the chain, and he lifted his hand and clutched it.

'You're a bundle of bloody nerves, kid,' said Crawford, 'that's your trouble. Don't lean too much on that chain or you'll pull it out of the ceiling.'

He held the chain tightly and washed around it with his free hand. Another stretch would bring him to the picture rail on the other side. There was triumph within him, his chest burned and sweat oozed from his brow, running in tears down his nose.

When he finished the ceiling, Crawford told him to take his sponge to the scullery and get her permission to wash it clean.

He knocked the kitchen door and listened; she was still singing:

> 'You're gone from me but in my memoree.
> We always will be together. . . .'

He knocked louder, and she opened the door, motioning him into the kitchen. He passed through into the scullery and began washing the sponge. On the drain-board he saw her cigarette, tipped with lipstick. A girl like this would never look at the pointy-chinned prefect. She was like a flower. She was close to him now, reaching for her cigarette. He lingered with the sponge, not wanting to leave.

'You're back? You shouldn't have bothered coming back at all,' Crawford said with sarcasm.

The door bell rang and Crawford looked through the window. 'There's the boss,' he said in a loud whisper. 'Take that duster in your hand and not stand there gapin' like a corpse.' Frankie picked up the duster, fell to his knees and started dusting as the room door opened.

The boss and Crawford talked quietly. Frankie heard him ask how the new apprentice was doing and Crawford replying, 'God help him, he's doing his best.' The boss called him. He stood up.

'Bring your overalls and tools with you to the office in the morning.'

'Ye — yes, sir.'

'I am sending you to a country job. Have you ever been away from home before?'

'N-no, sir.'

'You won't be homesick?'

'No, sir.'

Turning to Crawford, the boss said: 'I'm sending him down with Haig to the Kilmourne job.'

When the boss left, Crawford told Frankie to ask the lady of the house if she had made up her mind what shade of green she wanted on the woodwork.

Frankie knew he would stutter the message in such a way that she would not make top nor tail of what he was saying. Yet he wanted the excuse to go into the kitchen again. But it was a different woman he saw this time.

She had a hard face, with a big nose, and there was too much powder on it. She understood what he was trying to say, for she took a shade card from the mantelpiece. 'I don't see any colour on this card that I like. But wait . . .' She went to the scullery and returned with a cup.

'Tell your foreman this is the colour I want.' She pointed to the green rim of the cup.

'How the hell am I going to match the colour on the rim of that cup? Jazes! my name's Crawford, not Michael Angelo . . .' Crawford reached for the cup, and Frankie, feeling sure Crawford had it in his hand, withdrew his fingers. The cup fell to the floor and was smashed.

'You bloody butter-fingers! What the hell are we going to do now?' Frankie looked down at the pieces of cup, annoyed that Crawford should blame him for it. Unable to speak to defend himself, he rocked from foot to foot trying to beat out what he must say.

'Quit your bloody crying. That's not going to help matters. Here, for Christ's sake pick up the bits and fly like hell into the city centre and see if you can buy one to match it.'

Frankie was on his knees picking up the fragments when the room door opened. Crawford was saying: 'I'm awfully sorry, madam, but we have had an accident.'

'What are you going to do about it?'

'It was the brat's fault,' Crawford said. 'Look up, boy. Look up when you are told. Get to your feet. Do you hear me, get to your feet . . .' he shouted.

From the stairs came a voice: 'We strolled the lanes together' and a moment later the first woman entered the room.

'What do you think, Pearl?' said the other, 'they have broken one of my cups, one of the best set too.'

'Well, if it's a gonner, there's nothing we can do about it,' Pearl said.

'It's all very well for you to take this attitude, Pearl.'

'What other attitude is there to take? The cup's broken and all the king's horses and all the king's men can't put it together again.' Frankie felt her hand on his head. 'Don't cry, sonny, don't cry. In a hundred years no one will know or care a damn about it. . . .'

'I'll report it to the boss, that's what I'll do.'

'I'm sure the kid didn't deliberately throw the cup on the floor, did you sonny?' Pearl kept her hand on his head.

'No, no, no. . . .'

'Stop your howling, will you,' Crawford shouted.

'Now, now, don't let's all lose our heads,' Pearl said. 'Try to think what's best to be done. . . .'

'I'll report it right away, that's what I'll do. I'll go to the 'phone right now. . . .'

'Don't be silly and fussy, Margo. Think for a minute,' Pearl said, but the other woman left the room.

Frankie still felt the hand warm on his head. She bent and whispered into his ear. 'Don't take her too seriously, she's impulsive and quick-tempered.'

'What kind of a fingerless prig are you?' Crawford asked, when they were alone. 'Dry your eyes, man, dry your eyes. Your bladder must be high up. Do you hear me, dry your eyes and take a sample of this into Hogg's in Donegall Square, they might have one like it.'

Frankie hurried away, glad to be out of the house.

When he got to Hogg's, the shop was closed. He stared into the bright windows of the shop. Delph ducks and geese and hens and delph apples and oranges were shining in the light, and a delph dog slept peacefully on a delph mat.

Should he go back to Crawford? The Assembly clock chimed six, then it played a hymn. He knew the opening words: 'There is a happy land, far, far away'. There were profane words for the second line: 'Where you get ham and eggs three times a day.' He sang the rest of it: 'Oh, how the niggers yell when they hear the dinner bell. Oh, there's a happy land way far away.' He wondered if Heaven was like that: lots of food, hundreds of eggs with bulging yolks. . . .

His aunt could beat him for the wrong things he had done, and after the beating he felt relieved; the guilt was away. The new fear he had was something that his aunt could not settle with the brush, the poker or her shoe. He wanted to cry out he had broken a cup, but that breaking a cup was not such a serious thing. He was stupid, as the schoolmaster had said: what he had for a head was full of grey jelly.

He hurried home.

'Well, how did you get on today?' He must answer her questions with lies. Perhaps by this time the lady had telephoned to his boss and he was saying: 'We must sack him; we can't have a butter-fingered lad like that working with us. . . .'

'Are you deaf? I am asking you how you got on at your work today?'

'I got on well.' Now he had lied. Perhaps in the morning he would be sacked and would have to come home and tell her.

'Take this supper,' she said.

It was a herring with two potatoes frosted green. He used his knife to scrape the green away.

'What's wrong with the potatoes?'

'They are green.'

40

'I had them for my dinner and there was no green on them.'

Couldn't she see the green on them? But she was not looking. She was arranging a hole in the fire for the teapot.

'I'm going to the country to work,' he said with effort.

'Will you be in lodgings?'

'I d-d-dunno. . . .'

'If you are, see you behave yourself. Don't turn up your nose at good food the way you do here. Going into lodgings will make you know your driver. It'll learn you to respect a good home, which you don't.'

She was cutting bread. He watched her, eager to know how much she would give him, now that he was working. She cut two slices, one of which she took to toast for herself. No, it was just going to be the same as before. Yet he was glad it was baker's bread she gave him. Usually she baked bread herself, but it was always soft, with lumps of baking soda in it. He looked again at the slice of bread. The crust was thick. Hunger was painful, but if you chewed a little of the bread, and swallowed it slowly, you could kill the pain, no matter how small the slice was. At school he had had to write: 'Never make two bites of a cherry.' He knew this was bad advice: if you managed to make four bites, and swallowed them slowly it would ease the pain of hunger. Hunger was worse at night. It was like a trap in the mind that snapped and held sleep, not letting it into your eyes.

'You haven't been doing much work today by the look of those hands.'

He told her that he was washing walls most of the day.

'Aye, well that yard needs washing. When you finish your tea, go out and see to it.'

He had imagined that now he was started to work, she would let him out at night.

'The men were here today to fix the spouting and they've left the yard like a pig sty, go at once and clean it up. Hurry, will you. You're making sounds there like a horse

41

at a trough. Hurry, it will soon be dark night, and not a finger laid on the yard yet.'

In a corner of the yard stood the old brush. It had no hair except three tufts in one corner, and these crushed flat to the ground when he tried to sweep. He opened the back door and asked if he could have the kitchen brush.

'Use what you've got. If you use it properly, it'll do all right,' she answered.

He took a sack from the door of the W.C. and wrapped it round the head of the brush.

'Let me in quick. We are playing hide and seek.' Sally Blair had rushed in and closed the entry door.

She was breathless as she stood with her ear tight to the door, listening for sounds of her seekers. Footsteps were loud outside, but they passed on, and Sally relaxed.

'They don't know where I'm hiding,' she said, brushing back her hair. Opening the door slowly she looked out. 'There's not a chance of them finding me.' She looked at him and then to the wet yard. 'Why don't you come out and play?'

He pointed to the brush.

'Won't you come to play when you have it finished?'

He made no answer.

'Will your aunt not let you out?' He shook his head.

'Couldn't you slip out, and we could play in the next entry? She would never know.'

'She would, Sally.' Yet the temptation was suddenly strong in him to tear up the entry for one hour's play.

'I broke a cup today, Sally, at work and the woman was very angry.'

'What's a cup,' she laughed with a shrug.

'But this was a special cup.' He had difficulty with the word 'special' but Sally understood.

'Ach! what odds about it. My mother says you need hands to make, so there must be hands to break.' She stooped to pull her long black stocking up her leg. He saw the white

42

elastic garter, and heard its faint smack as it flew back to hold the stocking. Then the back door rattled and he touched Sally on the arm, unable to utter a warning. His aunt saw Sally before she left the yard. Sally ran up the entry shouting, 'Here I am, come and catch me,' and a voice in the distance answered back, 'Where are you hiding?'

'Close that entry door and put the bar in it,' his aunt said. He obeyed her. 'What was that one doing in my yard? Answer me before I throttle you. I'll bring the priest on you. I caught her and you . . . Pulling up her stockings . . .' She had the brush now, beating him where she could. He rushed to the dustbin and got behind it. He reached up for the lid to use as a shield, but the brush was brought down heavy on his hand. He pulled the bin towards him to shield his body. Now, she could only poke the brush at the bin. She kept repeating: 'I'll beat the dirt out of you. I wouldn't have believed that if I hadn't seen it with my own two eyes.' Exhausted, she threw the brush away, and left the yard exclaiming: 'I know what I'll do. I'll go straight to her mother and complain.'

He listened at the back door. She was in the kitchen winding the clock. He opened the door slightly. She breathed wheezily and he heard her shaking a medicine bottle which she kept for her chest when the days were foggy. If she made to go out to tell Sally's mother, he would rush after her and try with all his might to stop her. Sally would never think of the things his aunt accused them of. Sally, Sally, if you only knew what she thought you were doing . . . Oh! Sally, Sally, if only you were my girl!

Sally was lovely. Sally never called her mother anything but 'Mummy' and got everything she wanted, from a bun from the baker to a real whole banana from the fruitman. She had a bicycle and would let everyone in the street learn to ride on it. Oh! Sally, that was so good and kind. . . .

He opened the door wider and tiptoed into the hall. Through a crack in the partition that separated the kitchen

43

from the back part of the hallway, he could see her sitting by the fire with the medicine bottle on the hob. Her skirt was above her knees. She was changing her stockings. He waited until she had fastened the ragged garters then he tiptoed into the yard again.

She called to him and he came into the kitchen quietly. 'I'm going up to Sarah Ryan's. If you budge one foot from this house, it won't be telling you. Do you hear me?' He said 'Yes,' rather quietly, suddenly surprised that she was going to Ryan's.

'I haven't finished with tonight's episode, I can tell you. I'll make it my business to see the priest about you and that one. Do you hear me?'

And again his 'yes' was quiet.

'You're not so quiet when you're behind the entry door. . . .'

There were so many things he could do now that he had the house to himself. He could take off his boots and stockings and toast his feet; or if there was any raw meat he could roast it on the tongs as he had seen Simon do.

He crossed to the cupboard and took out the half loaf. Yet he knew he would never be able to cut it as evenly as she had done; she was sure to know if he had tampered with it. No, he dare not touch the loaf; it would mean another beating, maybe when he was in bed, with no chance of defending himself.

The light from the gas did not reach the cupboard; he had to grope gently among the articles. He knocked over the tea packet and it made a noise like fine mortar rushing down behind wallpaper; but he was able to stand the packet upright again, and he knew it had not spilt out. His fingers felt the edge of a tin plate, and as they moved over it touched something soft. He took the plate out and saw a bit of steak glued in the centre of the plate in its own blood. If only he could spread it over the tongs and have one glorious gorge! But the shiny bulb-shaped handle of the poker gleamed in the

44

firelight, and on the hearth the black shaft of the hearth brush stuck out like a dark warning. They were her allies . . . If she came in and caught him with the plate in his hand! Quickly he pushed the plate into the cupboard and closed the door. He stood with the ticking of the clock loud in his ears. Then the gas went out. The blazeless fire lit the outside of the hearth; the rest of the kitchen was dark.

He heard sounds of running feet, and went to the door. 'Are you there?' It was Sally's voice.

'Here, take a handful.' She was forcing fried potato chips into his hand. 'Tear a bit of this paper and put them in it. And here's some fish. Take it, go on: I got it from Bruno and he always gives me good value.'

She was away, tiptoeing until she felt it was safe to run up the street. He hurried to the yard to eat the chips, turning them over and over again in his mouth until they slid down his throat like milk.

A church bell played a hymn he knew:

> God of mercy and compassion,
> Look with pity upon me,
> Father, let me call thee *faaather*
> 'Tis thy child *reeturns* to thee,
> Jesus Lord, I ask for mercy,
> Let me not implore in vain,
> All my sins I now *detest* them,
> Never will I sin again.

To think about Sally was a sin. But it was a sin he did not detest. In all his misery, when he was hungry, and cold, and sore from her beatings, there was a part of his mind where Sally always was, giving him hope and promise.

High above him the sky was filled with stars. Behind the stars there must be great brightness, shining up on God's throne. How did God pass His day? Was He looking through the silver stars at Devlin putting out the lamp so that he could kiss Sally?

It was a sad hymn the bells were playing, a hymn that made you cry when it was sung after the priests and missioners had preached about hell. Hell must be an awful place; the missioner had told them that to hold your finger over the flame of a candle was great agony, so what must the agonies of hell be like?

It was nearing his aunt's time for getting back. He must listen for her coming, for she was always afraid in the dark kitchen, and if he made a noise she would say he was trying to frighten her.

'Is the gas out?' she asked as she walked unsurely up the hall.

'It is.'

'They're not good that like to sit in the dark.' She put a penny in the gas meter. 'Take yourself up to bed, and not have me bawling my lungs out of myself at you in the morning.'

6   WHEN HE ARRIVED AT the office, the next morning, the boss was supervising the loading of a lorry. Frankie kept looking at him, waiting for something to be said about the broken cup.

From the men's conversation as they piled the steps and ladders he gathered that Haig was to be foreman on the job they were going to. He was pleased; Haig must be a nice man if such a lovely girl were interested in him. . . .

'See and don't break any more cups where you are going . . .' Had the boss actually said that? He could have shouted with joy. Breaking a cup could not have been such a terrible thing after all. The lorry was now loaded and they waited for Haig to come from the office.

Frankie looked up the yard at the tall man coming towards them. He had black, wavy hair and large brown eyes.

'We've got to call for the pastor,' he said.

'This is gonna be fun,' said one man, climbing on to the lorry. 'But I'm warning you, Haig, if he comes any Bible thumping with me, I'll throw a pot of paint about him.'

'Shut up, Toby. If you'd let the pastor alone and not taunt him about his Bible, you'd get on much better.'

The four of them were now on the lorry. Haig made room for Frankie beside him.

'What's your name?'

He stammered it out, pleased because Haig looked away.

'This is Tobias Mackin,' Haig said pointing to a fat man. 'And this is Doggie Turnbull.'

'This fellow here with the gut answers to Toby,' Haig said.

Toby laughed, and patted his huge stomach. It was covered with a waistcoat that had paint spots all over it. 'When I pup, I'll keep you a black and white one.'

The other man, Doggie Turnbull, was thin and miserable-looking. He had a long neck with strings of flesh reaching up under his chin. He smoked a pipe, and as he sucked it his jaws trembled a little. It sounded like someone supping soup.

'You'd need a pump for that pipe of yours,' Toby said. Doggie took the pipe from his mouth, and covering the head with his hand, shook it violently.

'That's it. Give us a bloody shower bath. Every time you shake that pipe I get the full of my face of slobbers.'

Doggie said he was sorry, and added that Toby was getting a 'great oul' nark!'.

The lorry stopped, and Toby looked out, shouting at the top of his voice: 'Come to prayer, come to prayer. . . .'

'For any sake, stop bawling, Toby,' said Haig, 'and let the poor sod alone. He'll pray in heaven for you when he gets there. So let him alone now.'

The newcomer climbed on to the lorry, but Toby continued to declaim: 'What does it profit a man to pass the two backs and skim the goalpost.'

The man known as the pastor sat opposite Frankie, who could not help laughing at what Toby was saying.

47

'Tell us about the night you picked up the brass nail in Atholl Street?'

The pastor drew his lips tightly together. He took a Bible from his pocket and opened it.

'Well, what does the form book say today?' Toby asked. 'He who sits on a hot brick shall rise again. . . .'

The pastor took no notice of him; he merely blew the pages of the Bible until he found his place in it.

The lorry quickened its speed. They were passing a farmhouse and saw a woman scattering food to hens. Doggie and Toby began arguing about how much money could be made by keeping hens.

Turning to Frankie, Doggie asked who got him started. When Frankie said it was Simon Clarke, Doggie sighed a very long sigh: 'I see . . .' Frankie felt that a great mystery had been solved. Doggie talked on about Simon, saying what a good tradesman he was, the best grainer in the British Isles or any other isles; he could have a job teaching in the Technical School if he wanted; but that Simon had great independence. After a pause, Doggie nudged Frankie to look at the pastor who was reading the Bible aloud to himself. The pastor caught them looking at him, and he moved up the lorry, covering himself with part of a dust sheet.

'Don't trust the pastor. He tells the boss everything,' Doggie whispered loudly. 'Don't let him see you doing anything you shouldn't. It won't be so bad on this job, for Haig's in charge, but if you are ever out on a job with him alone, watch him; he's an informer. Tell me son, are you a Catholic or a Protestant?'

He told Doggie he was a Catholic.

'I'm one myself,' Doggie said.

'Less dirty stories,' Toby said.

'I'm not telling dirty stories, am I son?' Doggie protested.

Frankie looked at the pastor. He was holding his Bible close to his red-rimmed eyes. His face was grey and hungry-looking. It was a face that never smiled. The lorry turned a

corner quickly and the pastor was flung from his seat and his
Bible knocked into a bucket of distemper. He snatched up
the book as quickly as he could, but its black cover was now
green. His hands trembled as he looked about for something
to clean the book with. Seeing nothing, he took the ragged
cap from his head and doubled it to wipe away the distemper.

'Hold on, hold on,' Haig shouted. The pastor looked down.
'Don't get fussed or panicky, gimme the book and I'll clean
it for you.'

From one of the buckets, Haig took a damp sponge and
cleaned the covers of the Bible; 'There now,' he said, 'if you
had used your cap, not only would you have ruined the Bible,
but your cap along with it. Try man, not to be so slovenly
and throughother. Have a little thought and patience. Look,
your book is as if nothing had happened to it. You can take
it to church and no one will ever know that it fell into a
bucket of distemper.'

'I don't go to church,' the pastor said, quickly snatching
the Bible from Haig.

'Of all the ungrateful bastards! Never a bloody word of
thanks to Haig,' Toby said.

'He'll pray for me; won't you pastor?' Haig asked, after
a pause.

'I'll pray for all sinners,' said the pastor.

'Well, wouldn't that get your bloody goat,' Toby burst
out. 'If there's anything makes me see red, it's the smugness
of these Bible-thumping bastards. Everybody's going to hell
but them.'

'Less bad language, Toby,' said Doggie.

'Bad language? Listen, Doggie, there's not a bad word I
use that you won't find in that Bible the pastor's reading.'

'Yes, brother, the devil can use the good book and quote
from it for his own purpose,' the pastor said.

'Less of the brother stuff, pastor,' Toby bellowed.

'Cut it out, cut it out, will you, Toby,' said Haig. 'There's enough misery in life without starting to quarrel over something written a hell of a long time ago.'

Frankie pitied the pastor. It appeared that the other men were always making fun of him.

The lorry stopped and Haig was first off.

'Nothing of the suburban salt-box about that,' he said, standing back to admire the house.

'Other people are crowded into slum houses where you couldn't whip a cat . . .' the pastor said.

'Cut out the street corner socialism,' said Haig.

'I wouldn't call what he's after saying street corner socialism,' remarked Toby. 'I'm a socialist and proud of it.'

To Frankie, the house in which he now stood was nothing short of miraculous. Never before had he seen anything like it; not even at the pictures. He crossed over to where the pillars reached to the ceiling, real stone pillars like those in the church.

'Look at the sweep of that staircase,' he heard Haig saying.

'I bet this belongs to one of them barts,' Toby said.

'It does. It belongs to Sir Robert Wosnam.'

'Wosnam the rag merchant?' Toby asked, astounded.

'The very man.'

'The war put the arse on him,' Doggie said.

'Aye, and the belly too.'

'Go on, go on, get the stuff from the lorry, and less scandal,' said Haig. 'I just can't get over the sweep of that staircase. It's magnificent. God! I'm an aristocrat at heart. Let them have their terrace slums and suburban salt-boxes; but this is the house for me. Look at it.' With a sweep of his hand, he continued: 'Morning room, dining room, library, study, ballroom. God above me, everything a man wants!'

Frankie thought of his own home, of the number of times it might fit into this one. He knew now what Crawford meant when he called Haig a 'swankpot'.

When they had the lorry cleared, Haig took them and showed them their respective jobs. Down in the kitchen,

Frankie heard Toby say: 'Listen, don't give me the pastor for a mate, or there'll be murder. He sings hymns all day; and if there's anything in this world that would drive a sane man into the madhouse, it's working with someone singing hymns all the time.'

'All right, take the nipper here with you.'

'I hope you don't sing hymns, do you?' Toby asked.

Frankie shook his head.

But Haig suddenly changed his mind and said: 'No, Toby, better take Doggie as a mate. I'll let the kid here stay with the pastor.' He left them, saying he was going into the village to see the lodgings and tell the landlady they had arrived and would be there for lunch.

The pastor took Frankie upstairs and they started to scrape the old distemper from the walls.

> This is my story, this is my song,
> Praising my Saviour all day long . . .

Frankie wanted to hear the words, but when the pastor caught him listening his singing got quieter; Frankie did not know what to do. When he scraped hard it spoiled the singing, but if he stopped the pastor might tell the boss he was slacking.

Someone was coming up the stairs singing loudly, as if to drown the pastor's voice.

Toby looked in. 'Is Syl not back yet?' The pastor did not answer. 'Are you both deaf? I'm asking is Syl not back yet?'

Frankie understood it was Haig he was asking about. It was the first time he had heard Haig's Christian name since the girl mentioned it.

'Not yet,' he managed to stammer out.

The pastor continued singing.

'You'll not be lonely while you've got Carooso here. Get him to sing the old maid's serenade to a soldier for you.' The pastor took no notice. 'It's a parody on Mother Machree: "Sure I love the brass buttons that shine on your spare . . ."'

Frankie laughed. 'Aye, you're laughing. Get the pastor to sing it for you, he knows it all. He's very hot on these dining-room songs.' But the pastor continued with:

> This is my story, this is my song,
> Praising my Saviour all day long . . .

Toby looked at the wall where Frankie had been scraping. He felt it, and said: 'Listen, son, if you go at it like that you'll ruin these walls. You're digging your scraper right into the plaster. Look, this is how it's done; run your scraper over the wall as if you were shaving it. You've seen a man shaving? If he dug into his face with the razor what would happen? He'd ruin his face, wouldn't he?'

Frankie nodded agreement.

'Well, that's what you are doing with the bottom of this wall. I'm surprised Jehovah here didn't point that out too. But I suppose he's wandering somewhere near the Pearly Gates and isn't interested in mundane affairs.'

Toby left the room, and Frankie eased his scraper over the walls, imagining he was shaving them. The pastor went on singing, only now he was inaudible. From the next room came the loud voice of Toby:

> When I wore the khaki, the dark coloured khaki,
> You wore your civvy clothes,
> I fought and bled at Loos,
> When you were on the booze, as everybody knows.
> You stole the wenches, when I was in the trenches,
> Facing an angry foe,
> You were a-slacking, when I was a-whacking
> The Huns on the Guillemont road . . .

Frankie walked to the lodging house with Haig and Toby, the other two dallied behind.

'What's the kip like?' Toby asked.

'Just the usual country house. I didn't ask to see the beds.

But I am sure they'll be all right. There was a clean smell about the place; and that's a fairly good indication of what the place is like. I'm taking the kid here as a sleeping partner. There are just the three beds, two doubles and a single. The single and one of the doubles are in the one room. If you like, Toby, you can have Doggie as a bedmate.'

'Damn the fears of me sharing the same kip as Doggie. He snores like a hog. I had one experience with him; never again. Did ever you sleep with a heavy snorer?'

Haig shook his head.

'I may be fat and ignorant-looking, Haig, but I'm sensitive about a lot of things. I don't mind snoring if there's some sense and reason in it; I could stand it if Doggie would snore in and out with rhythm; but no, he puffs and blows and grunts and groans like a dog dreaming on a mat in front of the fire. You'd swear somebody was choking him. But I think he's troubled with his heart. He gets purple at times; and that's a sign the heart isn't the best.'

Frankie was excited when he entered the lodgings. Here was a white tablecloth, such a change from the grey, shiny one he was used to at home. Knives and forks and spoons were around every plate.

Doggie sat down beside the pastor.

'What about washing the hands?' Toby said. Haig had already gone to the wash basin in the scullery. The landlady brought Frankie the towel, and he held it for the others as they dried their hands. She was an oldish woman with several hairs curling from her chin, and a dark shadow on her upper lip, like emery paper.

They had soup first, then meat and cabbage. Toby kept passing potatoes to Frankie, saying: 'Ate up, son. You're in your granny's.'

The pastor pushed his meat to the side of his plate.

'Can you not ate it?' Toby asked.

The pastor shook his head without looking up from his plate.

'Then give it to the kid,' and before the pastor realized what was happening, Toby had the meat from the plate and was sharing it with himself and Frankie.

Tapioca followed. It was sweetened with jam, and Frankie thought it was the most delicious thing he had ever tasted. Then there came tea with large 'stomach' cakes. The pastor could not eat his cake, he said he did not like the carroway seed in it. Again Toby reached out for it, and breaking it, gave the larger piece to Frankie, who was beginning to feel that he had never had so much food in all his life. Surely he would never be hungry again. He had eaten three times as much as he had ever got the chance of doing at home. He hoped they would be on this job for years.

For tea that night they had lettuce and red stuff that Frankie had seen often in the fruit shops. He never knew the name of it, but as Toby sliced it on his plate he said; 'Beet-root's good for the blood.' There was a whole egg on each plate. The pastor motioned to Frankie. 'Eat mine,' he said, 'hard boiled eggs don't agree with my stomach.'

The landlady asked the pastor if he could eat a potted herring, but he said if there was vinegar on the herring it would be as bad for his stomach as the hard boiled egg. She gave him more tapioca. The pastor spooned it quickly down.

'What's to do at night in a village like this?' Haig asked the landlady.

'Well, there's a picture house for them that likes it, and I think there's a hall where they squander their money playing cards; and there's a mission hall for believers.'

'Where is the mission hall?' the pastor asked.

'I'll take you there if you are interested. I'm a believer myself.'

'I am too,' said the pastor.

Frankie saw Toby wink at Doggie.

Haig was first to leave the table. Frankie followed Toby and Doggie up the stairs.

'The old hussy's a bible thumper too,' Toby said when they reached the landing.

'I don't give a damn she's a Dipper, if she feeds us well and has clean beds,' laughed Doggie.

'This is our room,' Haig said to Frankie. He turned down the blankets and examined the beds, muttering, 'They look clean enough.'

As he put his attaché case on the bed and removed the contents, he asked, 'Where are your things?'

Frankie was silent. He watched Haig stuff his blue sleeping suit under the pillow.

'Where are your things?' Haig repeated.

'I haven't got any,' he answered slowly.

'Do you mean you've come to lodgings without pyjamas, even a shirt, or a clean pair of socks?'

Frankie saw himself before his aunt asking her for these things ... but he knew he could never explain to Haig why she would not let him have them. These things belonged to another world, he had never had them.

'Are you really here without as much as a second shirt? Surely you know you can't sleep in the shirt you've been working in?'

He was suddenly afraid of Haig. He felt that Haig thought there must be lice on him, that he was dirty. He wanted to beat out that he could sleep with Toby, or even Doggie or the pastor. He was sure Toby would not mind about his shirt. He could even sleep in his bare pelt.

'Did you not tell your mother you were coming to a country job?'

'My mother's dead.'

'Well, what about your father?'

'He's dead too.'

'And who do you live with?'

Frankie looked over at the bed, at the white sheets; if he stained them with yellow piss. . . .

'Who do you live with?'

55

'My aunt. . . .'

Frankie felt that he was alone for the first time. He was away from the familiar smells and things that formed his world. At this moment he longed to be back with his aunt; even if she had the poker in her hand and was beating him. Before he could say more Toby entered the room and made straight for the window.

'Give us a mouthful of fresh air for God's sake,' he said.

'What's wrong?' Haig asked.

'The pastor's after changing his socks, and the whiff from his feet would poison you. I've landed myself in for something I can tell you! The snores of Doggie, and the reek of the pastor's tootsies. If I had the money I'd go out and get drunk.'

Frankie wanted to say that he would go and sleep with Doggie if Toby came in with Haig; but Toby was now fussing about the room. 'Not a bad doss at all,' he said, feeling the bedtick. His eyes lit on Haig's case. Picking up a blue shirt, he read aloud what was inscribed on the neck band. 'Guaranteed pure silk.'

'What about it?' Haig asked quietly.

'Silk shirts? How the hell do you do it on your wages?'

'Listen, Toby,' Haig said, facing him, 'Do I go into your room to examine your wearing apparel?'

'Now, now, take it easy . . . Don't get ratty. Jazes, man, life's too short to pounce on every skittery thing a man says or does wrong. Good luck to you Haig. Believe me, I hope you'll always be able to buy and wear silk shirts.'

'Thank you,' Haig said, and Toby laughed as if nothing had happened, and left the room.

Haig picked up the shirt, and throwing it to Frankie, said, 'If you've nothing to wear in bed, you'd better have this.' He left the room with a razor and shaving brush in his hand. Frankie looked at the shirt, at 'Guaranteed pure silk' printed on the neck band. Crossing to the mirror, he held the shirt against his body.

I'm Bert, Bert, I haven't a shirt,
But my people are well off you know,
I've just had a banana with Lady Diana,
I'm Burlington Bertie from Bow . . .

He knew it was Toby, but the fat man had only looked into the room, and then moved away, still singing. Frankie sat on the bed examining the shirt. He liked its colour and knew that he suited it.

When Haig returned, he said, 'Do you like the shirt? If you behave yourself, I'll make you a present of it . . . I forgot to bring boot polish. Would you ask the landlady if I might borrow hers?'

Frankie was out of the room before Haig had spoken the last words. The landlady gave him a boot box with polish and rags in it.

He picked up one shoe. 'What are you going to do?' Haig asked.

'To clean them.'

'I don't want you to clean them. Just because I gave a shirt doesn't mean you must sell your soul. I don't want you to do things like that.'

Frankie stared at the ground. He wanted to help Haig, and he saw nothing wrong about polishing his shoes. He wanted to be friends with him.

'I think you'd better go and wash; the bathroom is just next door and you'd better take this towel.'

He let the water run in the basin. It looked yellow, recalling his fear of the night.

Someone knocked the door and a voice said: 'Can I come in?' It was Toby. 'Move over a bit, till I get some shaving water.' Toby's shirt sleeves were rolled over his elbows. Frankie stood back to let him get closer, looking at the same time at Toby's massive arms, and at the tattooed figure of King William on a horse.

'Are you looking at William, son?'

Frankie nodded. He knew it was William from the painting on the gable in the street where Simon lived.

'They say King William was a fruit merchant. . . .'

Frankie looked puzzled.

'Aye, he was a "poof" so they say. I got that on my arm over twenty years ago; I was in the Navy then. I had little sense. Nothing short of a blow lamp would take it out.' As he washed, he sang:

> I don't know why I love you, but I do, do, do,
> This world is full of girls the same as you, you, you,
> There's something in your spell, tells me straight to go to
> I don't know why I love you, but I do, do, do.   [hell,

Frankie loved Toby. He had only met him this morning, but he knew there was kindness in Toby's fat face, and he liked the way his head moved when he sang. Toby could make you happy with the songs he sang and the way he sang them.

'Do you think, son, we could carry the pastor in and give him a bloody good bath? You know, baptize him all over with soap powder and then into the bath with him, and let him steep there overnight . . . He's the dirtiest hallion I've ever met. . . .'

When Toby had gone Frankie closed the door, pushing the bar into its clasp. Hurriedly he took off his boots and socks, and taking the towel, he wet a corner of it and quickly rubbed it over his toes and heels. On the landing he could hear Toby talking in to Haig. Frankie looked at his feet, at the backs of his heels; they were clean now, and he put the boots and socks on again.

Haig was standing before the mirror when he returned to the bedroom, fixing the curls above his forehead. Frankie looked at him, but Haig continued to arrange his hair as if no one was in the room. He was good-looking, and unusual. He wore green corduroy trousers with a sports jacket the colour of gold. His shirt was green, with a yellow tie.

Toby sauntered into the room again. 'Doggie's not going to the pictures,' he said.

Frankie's heart sank. 'Well, aren't you coming with us?' Haig asked.

'I have no money . . .' he got out.

'Who's talking about money? Comb your hair and come on.'

He ran his fingers through his hair.

'Whoa, whoa . . .' Haig was saying, 'here's a comb. That's the way the wild man from Borneo would arrange his hair; the way you are doing; with his fingers. There, keep that comb, and put a nice shade in your hair.'

At the picture house, Haig took his pocket book and flicked a pound note from it. Frankie looked at him, pleased that some day he would be able to do this. It was strange to sit in the picture house, knowing no fear. He was so excited that his mind wandered from the picture. It was an unbelievable experience for him. Here he was, sitting in the pictures; not frightened to go home; even when he got home there would be food waiting for him. No, it did not seem true. His heart beat loudly. He glanced at Toby, at the fat belly, and the smiling face; then at Haig, with his long fingers holding his cigarette, every now and then tapping the ash away from it. He was with these two men; no need for him to be frightened; his aunt was far away and could not touch him. This was freedom. He could go straight to bed with no one to say a word to him. This was escape.

'I wonder what's for supper?' Toby asked on the way back from the picture house.

'Forget your belly,' Haig said.

'I hope it's cheese. There's nothing I like better than a couple of cracker biscuits and a bit of Gorgonzola . . . Do you fancy Gorgonzola?'

'I like it on occasions,' Haig answered.

'There's nothing to beat it. Give it to me with a couple of cracker biscuits and a glass of good fresh milk, and Bob's your uncle,' Toby said.

'And do you think you'll get Gorgonzola here? What do you expect for twenty bob a week? The Savoy menu?'

'Aye, I suppose you're right. Shocking thing to be poor.'

'You've said it,' Haig laughed. Then after a pause he said: 'I'm not fussy whether I eat or not. But maybe the kid's hungry. Are you?'

'Of course he's hungry. Did you ever know a kid of his age that couldn't ate the legs of the table?' Toby said.

When they entered the house, the pastor was sitting with the landlady at the fire, his Bible on his knee. She told them they could have porridge or hot milk. Haig had milk, and Toby spoke for Frankie; 'Give the wee fellow and me the porridge.' The pastor left the kitchen, humming a hymn which the landlady took up. Toby winked at Frankie, and whispered; 'How would the old maid's serenade to the soldier do her?'

As they went up to bed Toby halted: 'Listen,' he said. 'Listen to the snores of Doggie. Imagine me having to sleep in the room with that?'

'Sure if you are asleep, you won't hear it,' smiled Haig.

'Aye, but I have to get to sleep first.' Toby moved along the landing, and at the bedroom door beckoned with his forefinger. He opened the door and switched on the light.

'Look at him,' he said. 'Look at his face, it's the colour of purple. That's the heart that does that. Some night, Doggie will pass out just like the flame of a match.' Quickly he pulled the bedclothes down and smacking Doggie's stomach with his palm, shouted: 'Get up there, and stop snoring.'

Doggie wakened, his head trembling.

'What hell has you snoring so loudly?' Toby said.

'What, what, who was snoring?' Doggie asked, his eyes blinking.

'The woman next door was snoring and I woke you up to hear her. You're groaning and grunting there like a bloody hog. . . .'

'I wasn't snoring.'

'If there's anything I hate it's a liar. Ask Haig and the kid if you were not snoring. . . .'

Doggie, now wide awake, was smiling. 'Was the picture any good?'

'No. It was a murder picture. About a man killing his bedmate. He killed him because he couldn't sleep with him snoring . . .' Doggie laughed loudly and reached out for his pipe.

The pastor came into the room.

'Doggie, don't smoke will you. It upsets my chest,' he said as he put the Bible under his pillow.

'Listen, pastor, if Doggie can't smoke, there's gonna be no light kept burning for you to read the "form" book. So make up your mind, no smoking, no light for the Bible. . . .'

Doggie nodded approval.

'All right. No light then. I won't read,' the pastor said in a huffed tone.

Doggie fondled his pipe, then put it slowly back on the chair. He was his old pathetic self again, his cheeks sunken because his false teeth were out, wrapped in a red handkerchief on the chair.

'Fight it out among yourselves,' Haig said good-humouredly, as he left the room.

'Good night, Haig. Good night, son. If the fleas bite, squeeze them tight. They'll never come another night.' Toby recited this as he pulled off his shirt, and scratched his hairy chest.

'Good night,' Frankie stammered.

Haig was sitting before the mirror again when he got to the bedroom. 'Frankie, go down and ask her to waken us at seven thirty . . .' Pleased that Haig should call him by his Christian name, 'Yes, yes,' he stammered eagerly, and hurried down the stairs.

'Why were you at the pictures tonight?' asked the landlady.

61

Frankie, startled, had no answer.

'Why were you at the devil's picture house?' She came towards him quietly and caught his hand, whispering loudly into his face: 'I love Jesus. Do you hear me, I love Jesus . . .' Her breath was terrible, as if her teeth were rotting.

Haig was not in the room when he arrived. He could hear him in the bathroom. He undressed quickly, feeling no cold, not even when he put on Haig's shirt, and got into bed. Reaching down he caught the ends of shirt firmly between his legs. He prayed a little prayer asking God to keep him from wetting this clean white bed.

Haig came into the room. He stripped, then he opened the window and began some exercises, rising on his toes as he took each deep breath. He bent and touched his toes with his hands counting twenty as he did so. Turning, he brought his head back until it nearly touched the ground. Frankie pulled the clothes up over his eyes, lest Haig should catch him looking at his naked body. Haig put on blue pyjamas, and got into bed. Frankie noticed he had not said any prayers. He lay on his back, breathing heavily.

'You told me tonight your parents were dead?'

'Yes.'

'This your first time away from home?'

'Yes.'

'And you are not homesick?'

'No.'

'Something wrong when a kid like you feels like that. Who got you started here?'

'Simon . . .' he could not get the rest of the name out without moving awkwardly in the bed.

'This isn't your first job? You were working yesterday?'

He sat up in the bed to answer this question. 'I worked in a house and the girl asked about you.'

Haig smiled.

'She was a lovely girl.'

'What's that?'

62

'A lovely girl. She gave me tea ... and I broke a cup and she laughed and patted my head.' He got this out with tremendous effort.

'A lovely woman,' Haig said quietly. He reached to the chair beside the bed and lifted two magazines. 'Here you are. Like to look at one before you sleep?' Frankie opened the magazine. It contained photographs of naked men and women. One page had big letters telling of a man who could add two inches to your height. Haig sprang out of bed. 'Let's dowse the glimmer. It doesn't suit for reading.'

They lay quiet. Frankie crushed against the wall, praying silently to God for nothing to happen in this warm, clean and white bed.

7   IN THE MORNING, he felt the bed. It was dry. Haig was awake.
'Did you sleep well?' he asked.
'Yes....'

Haig yawned, then threw the clothes back and got out of bed. Frankie examined the bed when he got Haig in the bathroom; there was nothing to show he had even slept there.

They had bacon and eggs for breakfast, with fried soda bread stacked on a plate. Toby said: 'Ate up, my lad, it's out of your belly you grow.'

Frankie was happy. Every time Toby came in contact with the pastor there was always a laugh. Haig seemed to keep aloof. He gave them their jobs, and Toby said that he was a good foreman and knew his job well; he was not a slave-driver so long as the men did the decent thing. Frankie did little jobs for him, like cleaning his shoes and fetching cigarettes from the shop.

He was only four days on this job, but it seemed like a

month. He wondered why Doggie was longing for Saturday and home.

During one meal hour when the five of them lay on the grass in the warm sun, Toby spotted a red hen left behind by the previous owner. Frankie and he chased it, for Toby wanted it to take home, but it flew through the thicket, and as they tried to follow it, pheasants cried out and rabbits skidded on the dead leaves and darted from sight.

The pastor spent most of the time talking with the landlady about the Bible. Toby referred to him as 'the gloomiest come-to-Jesus merchant' he had ever met. Haig maintained that he was happy even though he looked miserable.

When Saturday came the pastor told them he was staying, and sure enough when they were on the way to the bus they passed a gospel hall with a placard: 'Special service tonight. How I found the Lord. A house painter will (D.V.) tell the amazing story of his conversion.'

'I wonder will he tell them about picking up the "brass" in Atholl Street?' Toby laughed.

'Don't be so hard on him,' pleaded Haig.

'People who get religion like that are to be pitied,' said Doggie. 'I mind hearing a doctor saying, when I worked in the asylum, that religious cases were the worst. They needed strait waistcoats for them.'

'You're right, Doggie,' Toby agreed.

Frankie wished he was not going home. After a happy week, the old fear was creeping on him again. He longed for Monday morning.

As they waited for the bus, Haig told them that this job would last the best part of six months. 'Frankie,' said Toby, 'if you are here for that length of time, you'll have a belly on you like a poisoned pup.'

In his pocket Frankie had the magazines Haig had given him. If he practised the exercises he might become as big and strong as Haig . . . Now there were the red trams, the cars, the noises and the smells of the city. Soon the bus would stop and he would be on his way home. He felt Haig push something into his hand, his fingers closed on the nickled edge of half a crown. 'That's for yourself. Take yourself to a show with it,' Haig said. And when the bus stopped Toby gave him a shilling, saying: 'Here, don't get drunk on that. Keep out of it what will buy you a curer on Monday morning.' Doggie gave him sixpence. Four shillings! It was a fortune. He could take Sally to the pictures, if she would come, and if his aunt would let him wear his Sunday suit. He felt his pay packet with the folded ten shilling note pressed inside it. He did not expect she would give him pocket money. He must be careful about the four shillings; if she knew he had it she would take it from him.

The old fear was swelling inside him. The wet tick, and the library book under it, the talk of his aunt about Sally and the entry, the smells of the home . . . He knew he had been away for a week and she would surely have thought up things to beat him for.

The first person he met was the long-chinned prefect from the confraternity.

'You were not at your meeting on Tuesday night,' he said.

Frankie wished Toby had been present. Toby would have the right answer for this fellow.

'Why were you not at your meeting?'

'I am working on a job in the country . . .' he stammered.

The prefect moved his chin, but said nothing.

'I love the brass buttons that shine on your spare . . .' Frankie could not help laughing when these words strayed into his mind. 'What's the laugh for?' asked the prefect. But Frankie moved away towards the house.

As he entered, he coughed warningly.

His aunt turned from the fire: 'Oh, it's you,' she said.

He took out his pay envelope and put it on the table.

'What's that?'

'It's my pay.'

'Well, can't you reach it into my hand like a Christian. Am I a beggar to pick it up off the street?'

She snatched it from him, poking her long fingers under its flap, ripping it open. She took the ten shilling note from its belly, straightened it, and crammed it in her purse.

'Near time for you to start working and pay back to me something for all my trouble.'

She made tea, and put before him the usual two slices of bread. 'When you eat that, go out and clean the yard. There hasn't been a finger laid on it since last week. And if I hear the entry door opening and that bitch Sally Blair near the place I'll go straight for the priest.'

It was just as he expected it would be. No pocket money; no changing into his Sunday suit, no freedom; out into the yard as before. The kitchen floor was dirty, and by the way she fussed over the kettle he knew she was boiling the water for him to scrub it. She would complain of the pains in her back; say she had been unable to move her legs all week with these dreadful pains, and could hardly stoop to lace her boots.

He had not minded scrubbing the kitchen floor when he was at school; it was the hall floor that embarrassed him, for some of the other boys in the street always looked in at him. She would never let him close the front door when he scrubbed the hall; no, he must always keep it open, on the pretext that the floor dried quicker with the breeze.

He gulped the meal and hurried into the yard. If he could only go to the pictures! Dare he tell a story about having to see Simon Clarke, something about tools? He swept the tiles, wetting the brush to wash away the few blobs of pigeon dung that reminded him of sea shells.

She was at the back door, looking out. 'I've hot water here for the kitchen floor when you have finished the yard.'

'I have to go to Simon Clarke's.'

'What for?'

'About tools,' he stammered.

66

'Tomorrow is Sunday; you can see him then. He neither darkens the door of church, chapel or meeting.'

He took the bucket from the nail, and put a handful of washing soda into it. She gave him a shaving of soap, thin as a leaf, and with this she expected him to lather the scrubbing brush every time he dipped it in the water.

She sat at the fire with her feet resting on the fender. Her evil eyes were fixed on his every movement.

'Come now, buckle up your sleeves, and don't be afraid to scrub; scrub man, scrub the dirt away.'

The water was too hot; she maintained the hotter the water, the easier it washed away the dirt. She pushed the point of her finger into the bucket and quickly drew it out again.

'Nonsense, man. That water isn't too hot.'

Inwardly he cursed her, cursed her to hell, to where the red flames would burn and torture her. Five long years he must wait until he finished his time and got away from her.

He started the floor at the sofa, crouching under it.

'That's right. Bend your back. Is there a bone in it?' He scrubbed loudly, knocking the brush against the wall, for he knew that under the sofa he was defenceless and if she felt like it she could beat him with the poker. She stared at him as he wrung the water from the floor cloth.

'That's right, wring it out dry, I don't want the water lying in puddles.'

He twisted the cloth until his hands trembled and sweat oozed to his brow, and moved on his knees to the table.

'Put plenty of weight on the brush when you scrub under the table. It's the dirtiest there.'

It was impossible to please her; when he had the kitchen floor finished her verdict was: 'It's not half done. If I was able myself, I wouldn't see you in my way. You use too much soap in one place and none in another.'

The jobs to follow, he knew, were cleaning the fender and the knives and forks; then there was the cleaning of her shoes, a job he hated if they were wet, for no matter how hard he tried he could never get them to take a polish.

He looked at his hands and arms, already the dirt had formed a lace patterned mark just below his elbows. He was glad to see this for it looked as if he had been working hard.

There was also the cleaning of the stair rods. He had to be careful lest he cut his fingers on the ragged edges of the scabby-looking brass plating. The right thing for him to do was to face up to her and say: 'Look aunt, these stair rods are finished. The brass skin is worn off them, I can't get them to shine. How can I, when there is no brass on them.'

But he knew she would never listen to him. All these jobs were forced on him just to torment him.

'Get some fresh water now, for the hall. . . .'

'I'll need soap for the hall.'

'Is the soap finished and not a hand on the hall yet?'

He moved the two mats and fell to scrubbing the hall floor. He kept the front door closed; he did not want any of the boys to see him — washing floors was a girl's job.

'Open the front door wide and let the air in to dry the floor,' she said.

But now he did not care for he was working towards the kitchen and could not be seen as easily from the street. His knees were cold and pained him when they crushed into the grit on the floor. Looking into the kitchen, he saw she had her two pairs of shoes on the fender and was searching in the bottom of the cupboard for the polishing brushes. On the newel post his coat hung with the magazines which Haig gave him neatly folded in the pockets. He took them out and stuck them between the oilcloth and the front of one of the stairs. Tonight he could buy a candle and a box of matches.

The hall now finished, he emptied the water and hung the bucket on the nail in the yard.

'I have these shoes ready for you,' she called.

It was nearing dark and he saw she was getting ready to go out.

'Is this your Communion Sunday?'

He said that he did not know.

'If it was what picture was in the Palace you'd know. Wash your face and hands and go to confession. You would know all right if it was concerning that Sally one up the street. . . .'

She left the house, and he sat by the fire, looking for a moment at the damp patches on the floor. It was nearly three weeks since he was last at confession. He had told the priest his usual sins; that he had cursed and told lies and that he was disobedient and that he had thoughts at nights about a girl. He had said he was sorry for these sins and had recited loudly the Act of Contrition. 'Oh my God, I am sorry and beg pardon for all my sins. . . .'

He knew all this was a lie, for he was not sorry — not sorry in the way he wanted to be, for to be sorry was to cry about something he had done. He knew he must go on telling lies, he must go on being disobedient, he must go on thinking about Sally. Sally could soothe him. When his body had suffered pain, and his eyes burned with tears and his mind was warm, the image of Sally would come to him, and he would think of her lovely face, her laughing eyes, her fat lovable hands. He knew he could be sorry if he disobeyed Sally, and sorry if he told her lies, and he could cry when he was sorry for anything he had done to Sally.

On the chair opposite him lay the *Messenger*, a little red book. He picked it up and opened it, and there was a story in it about a boy who told lies, who lied even about going to confession. 'John Harper was fifteen years of age. His mother insisted on him going to confession every week, but John deceived his mother by telling her . . .' The bright flame died in the fire and he could no longer see to read.

Would it matter if he missed confession? Just this once? It was not his confraternity Sunday and there would be no one able to tell his aunt whether he had been at Communion or not. It was all very puzzling, these questions and answers about religion. It was puzzling to him when he heard the priest saying that if he or anyone else sinned it made God suffer. But why should God suffer? God who made the sea and the sun and the flowers and the trees: why should God suffer over lies? How could God suffer? If he went to the pictures tonight, and told his aunt he was at confession, would God be upset in heaven and not be able to sleep? Or what pain could God suffer?

The fire sprang to life again, lighting for a moment the red picture of the Sacred Heart on the wall opposite. He could see the upraised hand and imagined himself saying: 'Hello, God. I want to love you, God. Why don't you make me love you? Why must I live on with my aunt? I am very unhappy with her. One time I was going to put the gas tube in my mouth and turn the gas on, and it would hiss down my throat and then I would be dead. That was the way Matthew Farley up the street died. But then the neighbours said it was a great sin for him to take his own life, and that he might go to hell for it. Why God? Why is it, that when people are unhappy, to take gas is to commit a sin? You God, could make everyone happy, just as you make the flowers come and the birds sing. Wouldn't it be great, God, if every summer people were singing in the streets, just as the birds did in the mornings? You could make it one season when everyone was happy. You could do it God, if you wished. You could stop people from being hard on each other. You could stop my aunt from beating me with a poker. You could make people kinder if you wanted to. The long-chinned prefect from the confraternity loves you. He goes to Mass every morning and to communion every week, but everyone in the street dislikes him; yet he is good. Sally Blair's father gets drunk very often and the priest says it is a sin for a man to get drunk. Sally Blair's father must be a sinner and the long-chinned prefect near to a saint; yet all the people in the street seem to like Sally's father. It is all so very hard to understand.'

The flames died and the picture became a square of darkness on the wall.

70

He washed himself, treating his face to hot water, allowing himself the luxury of the white towel which she kept for herself. He was tempted to use the scented soap, but its aroma was strong and she was sure to smell it when she got back. He took her blue comb from behind the tea canister, feeling its broad, open sweep through his hair.

He left the house, dallying up the street, hopeful of meeting Sally. It was not hard to tell where she lived; light filled the window, making the drawn blind like bright butter, and behind the blind was the outline of a bird cage. Sally's house was a happy house. Her father never looked like a working man. He had always a bright sports coat, light grey flannels, and a little red bow in his collar. He would get drunk on a Saturday night and arrive home in a taxi. Everyone said he was a good workman. Once he made an altar for a priest and it was so good that people paid money to see it in St. Mary's Hall.

Sally was not to be seen. Probably she was out with Devlin. At the top of the street he hurried, turning just for a moment to look into the fish and chip shop, and went on to the picture palace. It was a heaven of warmth, of bright lights and coloured pictures of girls and cowboys on the walls. A boy with a tray hanging from his neck wandered up the aisle crying: 'Apples and Lotus toffee.' The audience were waving and shouting to one another. Three members of the orchestra appeared. A voice called out: 'Come on now, rattle up the old buckets. Give us Sheik of Araby.'

But the crowd did not want to hear the orchestra, and there was such a stamping of feet that the lights dimmed and the picture started.

He kept his eyes on the screen as he tried to sit down. A woman's voice said, 'Watch where you are putting your arse. The child paid its money as well as you.' He was confused, but a sudden change of lighting in the picture showed him a vacant seat in the next row. The woman's words were hot on his neck, every moment he expected her to reach out and hit him. On the screen a cowboy with a gun in his hand was creeping up a rocky bank. He pointed the gun at the driver of the oncoming coach. He fired and the coach-driver tumbled from his seat, dead. The dead man seemed to be smiling as the dark blood trickled from his mouth. But in a moment his death was forgotten, and the scene was a pub with a piano playing. Then there were palm trees and great stretches of desert.

Bells were ringing when he left the Palace. They sounded their warning in his mind; another sin was to be stamped on his soul — the terrible sin of telling lies about going to confession. He moved slowly down the road. All around and about him people were laughing, and boys of his own size were talking excitedly about the day's football.

His aunt would ask him what priest had heard his confession. He would say it was Father Markey; this would strengthen his lie. Father Markey was a cross priest; even if you confessed the simplest sin, he would make you promise never to commit it again. She would think he had been good if he said he had gone to Father Markey.

The bells stopped; he was within the long shadows of the tall spires. The doors were closed; one showing its bright yellow varnish face to the lamplight, the other faded and dim. He turned the corner to the small calvary, where Christ hung on the black stone cross. He stuck his head through the railings and stared at it. That was Christ, and Christ had died to save everybody. On top of the cross were two blobs of bird droppings, and at its foot a cat was scraping. He could see a cobweb in one of the folds of the cloth that circled the body. It must have been terrible for Christ on Calvary; if He had lurched forward His hands might have pulled the nails, and He would have hung there by the feet. . . .

He hurried away from the dark church, feeling that the few moments he had stared at the figure had lessened his guilt. He had felt sad when he looked at the nailed hands, sadder than he had ever felt when leaving the confessional.

He slowed down when he reached his own street, again hoping that Sally might be about. But there was not a sign of her. Where could she be at this moment? Sitting in an ice cream shop with Devlin? Or maybe down in North Street where the hobby horses and the swing boats were.

His aunt was standing at the fire when he looked into the kitchen.

'Where were you?' she asked.

He must tell the lie boldly. But supposing someone had seen him at the Palace?

'Where were you? Can't you answer me?'

'I was at confession . . .' He waited, confused, two awful thoughts burning into his mind: that God might strike him dead for the awful lie; and that his aunt would use the poker, if she knew he had been to the Palace.

'Come in here,' she called.

She wanted him in the kitchen. Upstairs there was no light, and if he dashed into the yard, she would not be able to reach him.

'Do you hear me talking to you? Come in here at once.'

Always in a situation like this, he would ask God not to let her beat him; but what could he do now? He had told the awful lie about confession. He moved towards her slowly.

'Where did you get these books?' She held up the magazines Haig had given him. 'Where did you get these black-guard books? Look at that. Full of naked women. You're a dirty low corner boy, that's what you are, bringing filth the like of that into my clean Christian home. Where did you get them?'

'I got them from a man . . . I have to bring them up to Simon Clarke . . .' He forced this out in terror; fear had now almost paralysed his effort at speech. Her mouth moved quickly, and her hand trembled as she held the magazines above her head. She had intended them for the fire.

'Next time, get the sender to do his own messages. I

73

don't want dirt like these in my home. If any decent body came in here and found those books, what would they think of me; or the type of home I kept? They're just what you would expect a heathen like Clarke to be reading. He's never forgotten his soldier's habits.'

She flung the magazines at his feet. He picked them up, and rolled one into the other.

'Were you at confession?'

'I was.'

'What priest were you with?'

'Father Markey.'

'Upstairs with you now, and rise for communion in the morning. Go on. Waken too, when you are called.'

He said his prayers loudly, thinking at the same time of the crucified Christ, and hoping that he might feel sorry. But his triumph over his aunt was uppermost in his mind.

He turned on his side, hearing his heart-beats. If they stopped he would be dead and standing in front of God. Would God know about the Palace? Did God keep hundreds of thousands of angels with books writing down every sin? Did the angels look out through a star and say: 'There's that fellow Frankie at the Palace and he told his aunt he was at confession; that's a bad mark against him. He told another lie about those books Haig gave him by saying that they were for Simon Clarke. He's a terrible liar that Frankie. He'll burn down in hell surely enough.'

He was never able to rid his mind of fear and guilt. His mind was never at peace. If he had not offended God he had offended his aunt. And to offend the One appeared to be linked with the other ... He had forgotten about the money — the three and ninepence he had in his pocket. He sprang out of bed to get the money from his trouser pocket in case she searched his pockets during the night.

'What has you out of bed?' Her loud voice came up from the kitchen. He stood still. His trousers were on a chair at the far side of the room.

74

'What has you out of bed?' This time she was coming up the stairs. She had a lighted candle. He crept into bed again, crouching against the wall. Her shadowed head was picked out witchlike on the ceiling. She was bent looking at something.

'Where did you get this money?'

'It's change from the magazines for Simon Clarke . . .' Forcing this out was agony.

'You're not stuttering when you are behind the back door with Sally Blair. I hope you're telling the truth. If I thought you were paid more than was in the envelope you gave me!'

'No, no, no. . . .'

'A thief you can watch, but a liar you can never watch or trust. If I thought you were keeping money from me after all I done for you!'

'No, no, no . . .' There was nothing else he could say. He would suffer whatever she wanted to do.

'I'll write to your boss and find out what they are paying you. . . .'

There was a smell of burning hair and a sudden movement. Her hair had trailed near the candle flame as she searched his other pocket, and there was a cracking sound.

'Sacred Heart, I'm burning . . .' she cried, beating her head with the palm of her hand as she hurried downstairs.

In the morning she wakened him. 'Hurry now, or you'll be late for Mass,' she said.

In the church he sat in the front seat, looking round him every now and then, making sure no one from his own street was present. The crowd for communion was big. He saw that if he joined it he could move along the altar rails and down the other aisle. He got into the crowd, pushing his way until he felt himself hidden. He knew now there was no chance of him being seen. He walked down the side aisle and into a seat. He knelt down and recited an act of contrition. The church was emptying and the bells were chiming for the next Mass. He pushed his way out and hurried home.

From the Grosvenor Road came the sounds of the Salvation Army band playing 'This is my story, this is my song . . .'

He looked forward to his breakfast. Usually on Sunday she would fry him a slice of bacon, and at times, if they were cheap and plentiful, she would give him an egg. A smell of soot greeted him in the kitchen. Soot had fallen in the pan, and shreds of it combed a pattern in the gravy on his plate.

The strains of the band came to the kitchen. He knew some words to the tune:

> Salvation Army free from sin,
> They all went to heaven in a corn beef tin.
> The corn beef tin was made of brass,
> And the lid fell down and skinned their arse . . .

'Are you sleeping on your feet?' On the table lay her prayer book and rosary beads. Her prayer book was called 'The Key of Heaven', and it bulged with holy leaflets and pictures. She loved this prayer book, because it was given to her by her boy who everyone said had died for Ireland. The only time he remembered her being kind to him was when she lost this book. She had left it behind her in the church, and she told him she would give him tuppence if he found it for her. He got the book but there was no tuppence. But the money did not worry him for it was one errand he knew he could dally over, as he did, stopping to play football on the way back, knowing he had found the prayer book for her.

'When you finish your breakfast, take those blackguard books up to Clarke. And I'm warning you never to bring the like into my Christian home again.'

He swallowed the tea, and, taking the slice of blackened bread with him, rushed upstairs for the magazines; then quickly from the house. Looking about to make sure no one was watching, he darted into Kelly's yard and threw the bread to the scraping fowl.

76

As he turned into the street where Simon lived, he noticed a car outside the door. A woman came out of the house, got into the car and drove away. He knew it was the woman who had asked him about Haig.

'Come in, Frankie son. Come in quick, son, until I close the door. We want to get that din they call religion out of our ears,' he said as he pointed towards the main road. 'Do you know, Frankie, God must often have many a good laugh to Himself when He looks down on the city of Belfast. God's idiots, that's what I call them. Will you, Frankie, or any other sane man, tell me where the beauty, or dignity or poetry of feeling is in an empty mouthful like "The wages of sin is death". Yet these mugs are bellowing out platitudes of a like nature Sunday after Sunday. I was up in the park this morning, Frankie, and I saw God's greatness in a meal-chested thrush that was dancing about on the grass, and in a white duck swimming in the pond, and in a twisted oak tree . . . Tell me, son, had you any breakfast yet?'

Frankie pretended not to hear him, but his eyes wandered to the covered plate on the table.

'That's an apple cake, I bet you would like a slice.' Frankie felt ashamed that Simon had caught him staring at the plate.

'Boys like you are always hungry,' he said as he uncovered the plate and searched in the drawer of the table for a knife. 'A good friend of mine baked this for me. We'll have it together with a cup of tea. I was never married, Frankie, but I have women friends.'

Simon laid two cups on the table. 'Now, Frankie, to what do I owe this visit?' The boy told him about the magazines, and Simon laughed loudly. 'God help your aunt and may He forgive her her great ignorance.' But all he said about Frankie's not going to confession was, 'I cannot advise you on that, son. I steer my barque from organized religions. Is there anything else on your mind?'

He was glad to hear that Frankie liked the job he was on now.

'And you would like to remain on it?'

'I would.'

'Well, I'll have a word in the proper quarters and see what can be done. You say you like the lodgings?'

'Yes, the food is good and you can ate as much as you like.'

'You know, Frankie son, I envy you. When you become a journeyman you are going to get a hell of a kick out of the simple pleasures of life. You'll appreciate a good home for one thing.'

It was good to hear Simon talk like this. 'Do you like Haig?' he asked. Frankie nodded.

'A good boy, a lad of breeding. Now don't ask me to define breeding. It means what I think it means in the case of Haig. Watch him, Frankie, in a few years' time he will have his own business. I'd bet my last cent on that lad; watch him, he's going places. He has brawn, and what's more important he has brains; that combination, Frankie, is rare, very rare. There are many with brawn who need to use brain and vice versa. I have met dockers that should have been doctors, and doctors that should have been dockers. I have met bookies' touts that should have been clergymen, and clergymen that should have been bookies' touts. I've met servant girls who should have been in the place of the mistress and vice versa. But Haig, to my mind, is the perfect blend, and what's more, he likes his trade. Young as he was when I first met him, I heard him tell an architect off, and the architect went off with his A.R.I.B.A. between his legs. He has one weakness: he would like to live a Rolls Royce life on a Ford income, but still, that's a minor fault and one easily cured by a mild attack of bankruptcy. But I am talking now out of your depth.'

Frankie cupped his hands about the slice of cake, for the apples spewed out. Simon laughed. 'Sweet as a maiden's kiss that fruit is. When you pick a wife, Frankie, make sure she can bake. The woman that baked this . . .' But Simon stopped suddenly, and his eyes went to the cat. 'Well,

McCusker, are you in for your breakfast?' The cat, at the sound of Simon's voice, put its forepaws on to his knee. 'Why don't you wash yourself, you're a dirty looking devil, McCusker.' As he spoke he tickled the cat under the chin with his forefinger. He poured milk into a saucer, adding a little hot water.

'You know, Frankie, this cat is very fastidious. Damn the milk he would lap unless it was heated.' Frankie could not understand why Simon was so fond of the cat, nor why he should wash the saucer before he poured the milk into it. His aunt would hardly clean the saucer for him, never mind for a cat.

'Another slice of apple cake?' But Simon had a way of asking questions and not waiting for answers.

'Yes, Frankie, keep your eye on Haig. Be obliging if he wants any little thing done; don't hesitate to show your willingness when he asks you to do something. It'll pay dividends. That's what you need most — friends. We all need friends, but you of all folk need them most. So give loyalty to Haig, and he'll help you along, for you have many handicaps. And listen, Frankie, it would be a good thing if there was some wee girl that you could take to the pictures now and then; say once a week. Someone, too, that does not live near you, so that your aunt wouldn't get to know about it. You know she's a frustrated old hen. It takes a nice wee girl to give a fellow the right idea about things. It's wonderful how a nice wee girl can make a fellow use a tooth brush and keep his hair neatly combed and his shoes polished. She can make him save a sixpence or two to take her to the pictures and maybe to a café afterwards for a snack, and she can make him keep his face and neck and hands clean. Those things are not taught in Sunday school, Frankie, but they are the right things; the things a young fellow like you needs. I mind when I was about your age there came a family to live beside us, and there was a daughter called Ray; and let me tell you I was the sort of youngster that

79

thought the cuff of his jersey was just as good if not better than a handkerchief. I thought the comb should only be used once a week; but a couple of smiles and a nod from Ray, and I was saving my pennies to buy a threepenny bottle of hair oil, and I was plaguing my mother for a white handkerchief. Now, I don't want you to involve yourself in a street corner courtship, or a back entry rendezvous, but just a wee girl that you can take to the pictures once a week. Do you know of anyone?'

All the time Simon had been talking, Frankie was thinking of Sally.

'Do you know of anybody?' Simon repeated.

Frankie answered that there was a girl in his own street, and that her name was Sally.

'No, no, not from about your own doors,' Simon said warningly. 'Your aunt is not the type of woman to agree with what I have been talking to you about. It's the sins your aunt won't let you commit that would be your salvation. See her attitude to these magazines you have.' Simon reached for one of them, and opened it at random. 'Take that droop from your shoulders. Get health into that chest. Develop those biceps . . .' He put the magazine down. 'Frankie, you could profit a lot by buying these papers regularly and reading them intelligently. Why not get them from Haig as he finishes with them and you can leave them with me and pop up here any time you like to read them. You need to develop your body, Frankie. It is cramped, held in the clamp of fear. When you get the fear from your body, then you must try to purge it from your mind; but you must first learn to straighten yourself as you walk. You alone can cure yourself. Do you hear me?'

Frankie nodded.

'Remember that. Only yourself can cure yourself. As soon as possible you must get away from your aunt. You are fourteen now?'

'Yes.'

80

'Struggle on, boy, another five years and you'll be free. You'll be a journeyman with any city you like in the British Isles in front of you. That's the beauty of being a tradesman, you can go where you like. A doctor, if he means to earn his living must settle in one place and stay there for keeps; so must a lawyer and a banker or a civil servant. But a tradesman can spend a year in London, then move to Manchester, Glasgow, Dublin, or any other town or city he prefers. In the meantime do all you can to grow up; and remember, you have a friend in me and regard my house as Dr. Barnardo's, "the ever open door".'

PART TWO

1 ON MONDAY MORNING Haig sat beside Frankie in the bus. 'Were you up seeing Simon yesterday?' Haig asked. Frankie nodded. 'You would like to stop on this job?'

'I would.'

'Very well. As long as I am in charge you shall stay.' Frankie looked at Haig's long fingers, at the careless way he flicked his cigarette.

The bus stopped and a woman got in. Haig stood up and offered her his seat. This annoyed Frankie, for it meant now he was unable to talk to him. Turnbull and the pastor were in front, Turnbull sucking his pipe, the pastor's head bent over his Bible. When they arrived he learned that Toby had been sent to paint a big warehouse, over the week-end.

'There was a message for you too, pastor,' Haig said.

'I don't work on the Sabbath. I would not have obeyed the message even had I been at home,' the pastor said quietly.

'Did you stay here all day Sunday?'

'I went home on Sunday night. God made the Sabbath for rest and there should be no work.'

'Can it, Calvin, can it,' Haig said sharply. He put the pastor to scraping the outside sashes. The pastor sang all the time: when he came down the ladder he would chant: 'Into hell I would go, O Lord, but for you,' and when he climbed up the ladder he would shout with joy, 'Halleluyah. Praise the Lord!'

At lunch time there was a telegram for Haig. He opened it and smiled as he read it; then he put it in the fire, crushing it down with a poker. Frankie looked at the pastor who sat staring wide-eyed at Haig.

'Not bad news is it?' the pastor asked.

'No,' Haig answered lightly.

'That's good. Usually when people like ourselves get telegrams, it means bad news.'

'How come?' inquired Haig.

'Well,' the pastor began hesitantly, 'people like ourselves only get telegrams when there is somebody dead or when somebody belonging to us is sick.'

'What do you mean by people like ourselves?'

The pastor seemed lost for an answer. 'Well . . . working-class people . . .'

'Why must you people generalize? And why the apologetic note in your voice when you speak of working-class people?'

The pastor remained silent, but when the landlady came from the scullery with food, he said: 'All people are working classes, or should be. The Master Himself was a worker.'

'And no one worked harder,' said the landlady.

'Forget about it,' Haig snapped, and Frankie saw anger in his eyes.

'We must all work to earn our bread in the sweat of the brow,' said the pastor, looking up at the landlady.

'Didn't I tell you to forget about it.' Haig was angry. 'Look, pastor, I'd like you a lot better and so would everybody else if you weren't so bloody dogmatic, so damned cocksure you are right, so sure of your entry into heaven.'

'You can enter the Kingdom as well as him, Mr. Haig, if you'll be born again,' said the landlady.

'Would you please finish serving the meal, missus. My spiritual life is my own concern and no one else's.'

The landlady lingered about the table. 'You're all right for tonight at Ballymoy?' she asked the pastor.

The pastor nodded.

'There will be a car for the both of us at half past seven.' She sat down and removing her shoe adjusted the paper that peeped from underneath the toe of it. Frankie saw

83

Haig watching her. She fondled her foot with her hand before putting the shoe on again. Then she moved to the scullery and cut some bread.

When they finished eating, the pastor remained at the table. Frankie walked with Haig back to the job.

'That landlady suits the pastor,' he said. 'Did you see her caressing her foot, and then cutting bread without washing her hands? But look, Frankie, you heard the pastor's going out tonight. I am going out too. I am meeting a girl friend, so you'll be on your own tonight. If I am late getting in, and the pastor should ask you at supper time where I am, tell him you don't know.'

'Yes, yes,' Frankie said eagerly.

'You are little more than a kid, Frankie, but always remember the story of the three monkeys; they saw nothing, heard nothing, and spoke nothing; and they got on well with all their friends. Remember that, Frankie. You will hear many tales about me; they will tell you I am a snob, because I don't go about ragged and unshaven like the rest of them.'

'Crawford said that . . .' began Frankie. But Haig cut in: 'There, you see, you are guilty of the very thing I have just warned you about. I don't want to know what Crawford says about me. All I want you to do, Frankie, when they talk about me, is to remember that I have a point of view too. If I am anti-trade unionist, as they say, it is not because I do not think they ought to belong to a union, or that they ought not to struggle and fight for good wages and conditions. I am an individualist, Frankie, as far as one can be that in this set-up. I don't want to be called brother by every man. I don't want to go to a trade union meeting and be called brother by the man who, maybe the following night, will plot my downfall at an Orange or a Republican meeting. I am not a misanthropist, Frankie, but I want to be able to pick and choose the man I call brother. Only one man was able to call everyone brother: Christ.'

Haig lay back on the grass shielding his eyes with his hand and smoking.

The red hen appeared from a rhododendron bush, and Frankie got to his feet. 'The red hen,' he shouted. But at the sound of his voice, the hen turned into the bush again and was lost.

'I wonder how she is making out with feeding? We should have brought her some bread,' Haig said, getting to his feet.

Haig inspected Frankie's work, warning him not to score or dig his scraper into the wood. The pastor worked above him, and when he was singing, 'There is a happy land, far, far away,' Frankie found himself joining in, because he himself was happy that Haig had talked so much to him. When he went inside he heard Haig singing too: 'Your tiny hand is frozen, let me warm it into life. Our search is ended, in darkness all is hidden.'

That afternoon, the owner of the house arrived. As Haig walked round with him, Frankie heard him say: 'Yes, Sir Robert . . . Very good, Sir Robert. . . .'

Sir Robert! Was he actually a real Sir, this man in a worn and ragged coat? He did not conform to Frankie's conception of a baronet. When the car moved off Haig waved to it.

'That's Sir Robert off,' he said. 'You wouldn't think to look at him he's as near being a millionaire as makes no difference.'

'Easier for a camel to pass through the eye of a needle than for a rich man to enter the Kingdom of Heaven,' said the pastor, moving his ladder.

'Well, of all the cynical devils, I have ever met, you take the biscuit.'

The pastor was fixing his ladder in position. Haig looked at him. 'I suppose the fact that the man has bought this house and is indirectly responsible for giving you employment has never entered your head?'

The pastor climbed up the ladder singing: 'This is my

story, this is my song. Praising my Saviour all the day long.'

'I think, pastor, you have a grudge against everybody. Nobody envies you your spiritual wealth.' Haig stood waiting for a reply from the pastor, but none came.

At tea-time there was cooked ham and lettuce. Frankie had seen ham in the shops in Belfast, but this was the first time he had ever eaten it. The soft red meat on the plates looked luscious and juicy, but was salty, and although he ate it with relish, he was somehow disappointed in it. The pastor offered him his slice. 'Here, ate this.'

'Don't you like it?' Haig asked.

'I like it well enough, but I can't chew it. I have no back teeth.'

'You'd better see about those teeth of yours. If you can't chew anything, you'll kill yourself with indigestion.'

'It takes a lot of money to get false teeth.'

'It will cost you more money if you don't chew your food. You will finish up in hospital with stomach trouble.'

Frankie thanked the pastor for the ham. The pastor was kind. He gave you things in the same way that Sally Blair gave you things. He pushed them at you, never looking at you. He took little interest in food. The others always looked curiously at the meal prepared for them. The pastor just sat down, muttering a grace. Sometimes he seemed unaware that the food was there. He looked pathetic, with the hair uncombed, reaching in tails down his brow. Now he left the table and went upstairs.

'I won't be in to supper,' Haig told the landlady.

'If you are going to be late, I can give you a key,' she said.

Later, through the window, Frankie, who was cleaning Haig's shoes, saw the pastor and the landlady get into a car.

There was a knock at the front door. 'Well, well, look who's here. Are you breaking any more cups? And are you going to keep me standing at the door?' The girl entered and sat down by the fire. 'Is Syl about?' But Haig had heard her and now appeared with his face lathered. 'Hello, Pearl. Make yourself at home. I'll be ready in a couple of minutes.'

'How do you like it down here?' she asked Frankie. He stole a glance at her red slacks and the hair spread about her shoulders. Her hands were thin and long, her nails varnished scarlet.

Haig came down the stairs, two steps at a time. She stood up and kissed him. 'Easy, easy,' he said; 'you'll have me covered with lipstick.' He laughed, and she took from her bag a powder puff and a lipstick.

'Well, Frankie, we are off. Now that you have the house to yourself, see you don't make off with the family heirlooms.' Haig closed the front door. Frankie crossed to the window; he could see them at the car, arguing who was going to drive. He saw her turn from the car and come towards the house.

'Syl tells me there's a picture house here. Take yourself off . . .' She gave him half a crown. 'Go on, take it. Go on. . . .'

He climbed the stairs to the bathroom and washed his face. In the bedroom he was tempted to use Haig's hair oil. Haig might not object, but it would be best to ask him first. On the bed lay the shirt Haig had been working in, and near it was a pair of socks. On the end of the bed his coat hung. A letter peeped over the pocket opening. Frankie felt a sudden urge to take the letter and read it. As he moved to the coat a board in the floor creaked, and seemed to echo all over the house.

'Darling, I am leaving this note with Uncle Simon. I could not get telegramming you today, but will meet at the Classic six-thirty tonight, Saturday. God bless and love, Pearl.'

With trembling fingers he put the letter back. He was ashamed of what he had done. He left the house and walked towards the cinema. On its door a bill advertised a dance to be held that night, from eight to twelve; admission one-and-sixpence. Old and new music would be supplied by Tommy M'Fettridge and his rhythm kings. Meanwhile the cinema was closed. He turned away with his mind made up — he would go to the dance. It would be fun to sit hearing the music and watching the others. Passing the Gospel Hall he saw that the bill announcing that a house painter would give his testimony was torn and flapped against the board with the wind. Somehow it expressed the unhappiness of the pastor. The pastor wanted to be unhappy. Toby had called him a 'whinger' and said he would always whinge his way through life. 'There's isn't enough sin in his life to make a good man of him,' said Toby. How could sin make a good man of anyone? The priests said that sin was a sickness that killed the soul just as sickness killed the body.

The feeling of shame came on him again, and yet he was glad in a way that he had read the letter, for he had learned that Simon was her uncle. It made him happy to know that Simon, her uncle, was a friend of his.

He found himself looking into a blacksmith's shop. Some men were standing near the hearth, the red glow of the fire lighting their faces, and one of them came to speak to him.

'Aren't you one of the painters that's working at the big house?'

Frankie nodded.

'Could you tell me what to do with a door that has been tarred. I have tried to paint it, but the tar always comes through. What am I to do with it?'

Frankie managed to stammer out that he did not know as he had only just started to work.

He walked away from the man, elated. Even if he had not been able to answer the man's question, he had a feeling that already he was becoming important. He would ask Haig this question tonight.

People were gathering outside the cinema now. A dozen or so paid their money and went in. The music started. Inside the cinema three men were shaking powder on the floor, and

88

others were sliding to spread it. On the stage four men with accordions and a fifth at a piano, were playing 'Happy days are here again'.

They wore grey flannels and blue blouses. Frankie recognized the pianist as the man who asked him about the tar. There were more girls than men in the hall. They were knotted in a corner, powdering their noses, patting their hair, and one hid herself behind another to fix her stocking. The man at the piano stood up and said the next dance would be a quick-step and he wanted everybody on the floor. One of the accordion players nicked his cigarette and put it behind his ear. The pianist made another announcement: 'As there aren't enough men as yet in the hall, there will be no objection to "Stagging" in the meantime; so ladies and gentlemen, get swinging to the strains of "I'll see you in my dreams".'

Frankie was more interested in the band than in the dancers. He gathered that the pianist was Tommy M'Fettridge, and the others were the rhythm kings. He was disappointed: these rhythm kings were just ordinary men, and the king himself was wanting to know how to keep tar from coming through paint. There was nothing kingly about these fellows. He could see that one of them had shoes that badly needed cleaning, and his socks were wrinkled and curled in folds about his ankles.

The music stopped, and the leader said the next dance would be 'a Ladies' choice'.

A girl approached Frankie, a little fat girl about the height of himself, with a blouse the colour of a mouse. She was pushing a crumpled handkerchief up her sleeve.

'Ladies' choice,' she said, stretching her hands out to him. 'I can't dance,' he protested, but he had already taken her hands and was on his feet. The girl giggled and said she was not much of a dancer herself, but that they could walk round the floor like the rest of them.

The music was lively, and Frankie did not want to walk around the floor, as she put it; instead he wanted to make some movement with the music. Turning the corners he found most difficult, and his feet touching hers, sent her into a giggling fit. When she was not giggling or telling him how well he was doing, she nodded and made eyes at her companions. The pianist shouted down to her, 'You are doing well, Susie . . .' She giggled again and asked Frankie if he knew Tommy M'Fettridge. 'He's a bit of a boy, is Tommy.' The rhythm kings were working hard; sweat was showing dark blue under their arms.

'Are you staying in Essie's? she asked. How did she know he was a stranger in the place? He supposed country people took an interest in every stranger. He nodded his head.

'It's a wonder she isn't trying to convert you? Are you religious?' She did not expect answers to these questions, for she continued to nod and make faces at her companions.

'Is it true that she sings her lodgers to sleep every night? Does she sing, "If ever I loved you be Jazes it's now"?' She stopped dancing to laugh, this time so loudly that the other dancers looked towards her.

'Are you religious?' she asked again. 'You mustn't be or you wouldn't be at this dance. I wouldn't like to stay in Essie's house. They say she never got a man because she was so religious. Could you get me a job in Belfast? I was at service here with the schoolmaster, but I left him last week; a parcel of dirt both him and his wife. I was better reared than either of them. I wasn't going to let dirt like them order me about like a dog. All they ate was stew. It sickened me. If it wasn't stew it was roast rabbit. Do you like rabbits? I don't. My father warned me against rabbits, he said they bred with cats. Is that true? Just think of it, ating cats?'

She shuddered. Frankie was aware of her sweating hands. The music stopped, and he went towards the seats. She was following him, rubbing her fat hands with a handkerchief. He did not want her to sit beside him. One of her companions passed by.

'I'm for the Ladies', Susie. Are you coming?'

She hesitated, but followed.

Frankie looked up at the platform, at Tommy M'Fettridge mopping his brow. The accordion player took the butt of the cigarette from behind his ear and lit it. The others lighted cigarettes from the butt. Frankie turned to find the girl beside him again. 'The next dance will be a waltz, not that I can waltz.' He saw she was smoking, sucking the yellow end of a cigarette between her finger and thumb. Her cheeks were fat and red, and they bulged, making her eyes look very small. She was not like Sally. Her fat, stumpy hands had nails almost like the pastor's. You would want to buy chocolates for Sally, but not for this girl.

The band started again and one of her companions dragged her to her feet and they started waltzing. Near the bottom of the hall they stumbled and fell on the floor. Her clothes were above her head, showing her blue knickers. Determined not to dance with her again, Frankie left his seat and moved to near the door. In the porch he met Haig and Pearl.

'Well, well, how did you get here?' Pearl asked.

As best he could he explained there had been no film to see. 'So you came to the dance instead? Sampling the night life of the town?' He had no answer, and she laughed and said, 'Well save a rhumba for me, will you?'

He was glad they had arrived. As Pearl moved into the hall someone whistled at her but stopped when Haig came in now and followed her to a seat. Frankie stood, not knowing what to do, for the moment disappointed that he was left alone. 'That's a smasher,' he heard one man say.

Haig stood up and took Pearl in his arms. She had a way of holding herself with her head slightly tilted back, her hair falling from her shoulders. She glided, as if the music were playing for her alone. Once or twice she brought her head forward and rested it against Haig's. There were few dancing now, and the sitters stared at Pearl as she moved up and down across the floor.

The lights in the hall dimmed and the red lamps began to blink. Frankie was happy now — far away from his aunt and her brush and poker. The lights went up again and the music stopped. Haig took Pearl's hand and led her to her seat.

'I didn't know you could dance,' she said to Frankie. He told her he could not. 'Couldn't you shuffle through a quick-step with me?' He blushed. 'Come, you must try. You'll never learn sooner.'

Removing the small coat she was wearing and throwing it across Haig's knees, she took Frankie's hands. He was aware of his damp palms, and his feet felt tied together. She was much taller than he. Yet, never once did he look up at her face. He heard her laughing and felt her pushing him forward. Where her pullover failed to meet her skirt, he saw her white flesh. A chain bangle she was wearing slid against his wrist. It felt cold, and the little stones in the links glistened.

Confused and warm, he felt the sweat trickle down his back, but at last the dance was finished, and she took his hand, leading him to the seat.

'Time I was calling it a day,' she said to Haig.

'Let's have one more dance, then you can hit the trail.'

She put her coat about her shoulders.

'What about you, Frankie? Are you staying until the end?' Haig asked. It dawned on Frankie that outside it would be pitch dark, and he might not find his way back to the lodging house. 'I'm going back,' he stammered.

As he was leaving the hall one of the girls called after him that Susie was asking for him, but he took no notice.

The sky was clear, although darkness hung about the houses. The strains of 'Ramona' got fainter as he walked to the lodgings. Suddenly the street was lit up by a car. It passed him slowly and the horn was hooted three times. He watched it until the tail light faded and all was dark again.

A light showed dimly in one of the windows of the house. He touched the handle of the door lightly and pushed at it.

It was locked. He wished Haig had been with him. But the landlady could not beat him for being out late.

'Who's there?' He recognized her voice. 'It's me.' The door was opened quietly. As she turned the lamp flame higher, he saw she was wearing a black coat over her long nightdress, and a man's cap sat flatly on her head.

'Don't think it unmannerly of me to bolt the door, but I was warned that Red Rufus, the grocer, is on the drink again. And when that man is on the drink he's not particular whose door he opens. He would land into your house and plank himself on your sofa and sleep there without a word of invitation. Your other friend is not in yet.'

Frankie sat down near the fire. Her words banished his fear. He wanted to thank her.

'Would you like a cup of hot milk, or some cocoa?'

He told her the hot milk would do.

'There was a dance on in the cinema. I heard the music when I was at the pump for water. Was that where you were?' He nodded. 'It's a wonder one so young as you would take to the sinful habits so soon. I think if your mother and father knew you were dancing they would be annoyed. Out of sight, out of mind, that's what it is.' She gave him bread, a small square of cheese and the milk.

'Were you up dancing at all?'

'Yes,' he said.

'Well, well, you city ones acquire sinful habits when you've hardly quit the cradle. Was it a girl from this town you had as a partner?'

He said it was someone called Susie.

'A wee, fat bit of a thing, no higher than a duck. I know her well. I tell you it won't be her fault if she doesn't get a man. It won't be for lack of cheek and push. That lassie was at the powder afore she left school. She was up to all the dodges; she used to spit on the red back of the rent book and rub it on her cheeks to give them a splash of bloom. She was at service for a while in the employ of the schoolmaster, but he had to get rid of her. She's throughother about her appearance; and there's something wrong with her blood. She can't keep her head clean, would need to be fine combing it every hour . . . and then the cheek of her looking for a man. I hope now, for your sake, you didn't make a tryst with her. For it you have truck with her, I'd ask you to seek bedding and kitchen elsewhere. Did you ask to meet her again?'

'No.'

'That's good. Have no truck with her at all. I suppose she struck up to you without as much as knowing your name?'

'Yes.'

'Didn't I know it was something like that happened. Well, be warned about her. Her people keep a kind of model lodging house, where tramps and tinkers get a shakedown bed and a mug of tea with a slice of bread for about eight-pence or ninepence. And they are not particular whether their lodgers are clean or not. Put your empty glass in the scullery when you are finished: I'm away to bed, and you might rinse the glass when you are at it.'

She left the kitchen. Frankie crossed to the grey fire. He was excited. The events of the night jumbled in his mind. He was pleased. Pearl had danced with him, and the land-lady had warned him against Susie. He was getting confidence. He was growing up. What did it matter that he was small or that he stammered? People liked him.

Haig came in and threw himself on the sofa. With a smile he said quietly: 'Christ, Frankie, but it's a great old life.' Frankie looked at him in silence. 'Why hasn't a man got money? Why must he be condemned to a life of bloody poverty? Look at me, the soaring of an eagle in my yearn and can fly no higher than a tame hen.' He opened his shirt and ran his hand impatiently across his chest. 'Oh damn! Damn it all . . .' He laughed. 'Don't look so terrorized, Frankie. Come on, let's go to bed.'

Haig climbed the stairs, humming to himself. 'Mustn't do that. Might wake the landlady and the pastor,' he said under

94

his breath. Frankie wondered if he had taken drink. He made for the pastor's bedroom, striking a match before he opened the door. 'Come, Frankie, let's have a looksee at the sleeping saint.' He tiptoed into the room and Frankie followed. The pastor was asleep. The Bible was on the chair beside the bed and near it was a bottle of stomach mixture with hard, white tears around its mouth. . . .

2   HE HAD NOT BEEN six months on the country job, and most of the neighbours said he was getting fat — his landlady must be feeding him like a fighting cock. He knew he was not growing taller, for he still measured himself with the aid of a pencil-marking on the closet door at home. Haig showed him the exercises he must do to add height, but they had no effect. Haig had also taught him to wash not only his neck and feet often, but the other parts of his body as well. He had declined Haig's offer to take him to the baths, because he was frightened to wet his hair lest his aunt should see it. He was always on his guard against her.

He heard that Sally had won a scholarship and there was a rumour she was going to a convent as a result. When she was studying for it, her father had made a bargain with her. If she got the scholarship he was to stop coming home drunk. He had now taken a shed in Kelly's yard as a workshop, and had his name painted on the gate outside: 'T. G. Blair. All classes of joinery work carried out. Estimates free.' Everyone said he was a changed man — as sober as a judge. Devlin was starting with Sally's father as an apprentice joiner, though his mother wanted him to be a civil servant up in Stormont.

'She says a civil servant gets a good pension whenever he's sixty and he doesn't have to dirty his hands.'

95

'Well isn't that typical of the Irish. They never take a chance. Look at you, Devlin, a young fellow, are you looking forward to the day when you're sixty and have a pension? You might never see sixty. And listen, promotion in the civil service is slow. You're a Papist, and there's as much chance of you rising in the Ulster civil service as there is of me flying in the air. Do you want to be glued in an office for life?'

Frankie could see that Devlin did not know what to say.

'Look at Frankie there, when he finishes his time, he can either open up for himself, or if he likes he can work one year in London, the next in Edinburgh, the next in Glasgow; he can get about and see the country.'

Devlin started with Sally's father, but he told Frankie it was because he knew he would never pass the civil service examination.

One morning the boss arrived and took Haig to lunch in the local hotel.

'That should please Haig well,' Toby said, 'he loves the atmosphere of hotels. I'll give him my share of hotels. I worked in one and we happened to be doing the kitchen apartments. There wasn't a bloody scrap of meat left on the plate in the restaurant that wasn't brought back to the kitchen and dumped into what they called the "stock pot". Give me the honest-to-God fish and chips any day. Just imagine having soup in one of those kips, after everybody slabbering and sucking the meat . . . Oh! Christ!'

'Something serious when the boss takes him to a hotel,' Turnbull said.

'Fair play for oul' Bonzo, he's not bad about a drink,' Toby said.

'I never got anything from him only what I worked for,' said the pastor.

'Cold ballocks, you're there! Do you ever say a good word about anybody?' Toby shouted.

'I am only speaking the truth, that I never got anything from him only what I wrought for,' repeated the pastor.

96

'Same here,' agreed Turnbull.

Returned from the hotel, Haig said nothing concerning his business with the boss. Frankie saw very little of him at night. He guessed that he was meeting Pearl. The others were not interested in Haig's movements. Toby had discovered a pontoon school and reported that the card sharpers in the village would beat any in Chicago. The pastor would sit reading his Bible, waiting for a chance to talk 'scripture' privately with the landlady.

Frankie was left with Turnbull, a pathetic figure. He was a Catholic, haunted by one fear. He had once denied his religion during a riot in the shipyard. When one of the mob had kicked him in the privates he yelled out that he wasn't a Catholic. He felt that God was angry with him for this and had punished him by afflicting his youngest daughter with sleeping sickness. At times when Frankie looked at Turnbull, he almost cried. But there was another Turnbull, a man who knew the names of flowers and trees, and would stop on the road to cock his head and listen. 'Is that a curlew whistling?' He would poke and probe and fall on his knees on a grass bank to discover whether a bird he heard was a robin or a stonechecker. He would talk about Canada as the land of trees, and tell stories of the strange places he had worked in and the people he had met.

Toby could only talk about pubs and women. The women were either wanting Toby home with them or were willing to leave their husbands for him. Never once in their walks did women enter Turnbull's conversation. Toby would taunt him every Monday morning with: 'Well, Turnbull, were you on your face at the week-end?' For a long time Frankie did not know what he meant by it. Turnbull would laugh lightly and say: 'Is there nothing else in your head Toby, but women?' 'The first person I ever slept with was a married woman,' Toby declared. 'Don't look at me like that, Frankie, the first person I was ever in bed with was my mother, and wasn't she married and a woman?'

But for all his taunting, Toby did not dislike him. He said to Frankie: 'God help the poor bastard. I think it's little sleep he gets when he goes home at the week-end. That daughter of his must be a heavy handful.' And Turnbull did not dislike Toby: 'He isn't a bad sort, but as full of ignorance as an egg was full of meat. Mind you, he has reared a fine family. One of his daughters works in the government office at Stormont, and another is married to a police sergeant. At one time Toby was well up in the Orangemen; did you not see King William tattooed on his arm? But he's given all that up. He was working down in the shipyard one time, and he mated with all the "red flaggers" down there. I heard him say myself that if he had his way he would blow every church, chapel and meeting house in Ireland sky high. Toby's a good man for the rights of the workers. There's some bosses in Belfast wouldn't employ Toby because of his trade union principles. He's big in the mouth at times, and when he opens it to mention women, he doesn't know when to stop.'

Turnbull was curious about Haig's interview with the boss. What could it have been for? 'If you find out, Frankie,' he said, 'let me know. I'm frightened of a pay-off. You're just an apprentice and know nothing about these things. You will, one day. I'm worried; I've exhausted my unemployment benefit, and I need another ten weeks' work to get back my full quota of employment stamps. There's work and plenty in England, but family reasons force me to stay at home.'

That night Haig returned earlier than usual. In bed, he said 'I'm leaving you soon, Frankie. I'm going to Liverpool and Manchester to take charge of a few picture houses. That's what the boss was down seeing me about.' There was a pause. 'I bet you'd like to come, Frankie?' The boy nodded.

'Sorry, son, it couldn't be worked. You're just an apprentice, but it would cost as much to keep you over there as it would a journeyman. Besides you have no experience of climbing. Work in picture houses is dangerous and ugly, and I've noticed, Frankie, that you are not the best of climbers.' Frankie wanted to ask him who was coming as foreman in his place; but he couldn't. Haig's talk about his not being a good climber alarmed him. He slept very little that night. Haig tossed and tumbled and three times lit cigarettes. He had never smoked during the night before.

In the morning he told the others as they sat at breakfast. Toby said he was glad that *he* was not going; he had had his fill of knocking about English cities. The pastor and Turnbull both hoped they would not be sent. Frankie wondered why anyone could refuse the chance of going to England.

That afternoon a car drove up. Pearl was driving it. Somewhere in the house Toby was singing: 'Oh, Mr. Porter, what am I gonna do? I wanted to go to Birmingham and you've carried me on to Crewe.'

Haig did not return that night. At lunch time he announced he would be leaving them. He called Frankie upstairs, and as he took his belongings from the drawer and flung them on the bed, said:

'Here's a shirt, Frankie. Get your aunt to tuck in the collar. And here's a vest and a couple of pairs of socks. You can use what's left of my hair oil next time you go to a dance. And, wait, here's something else. I'll see you when I get back from England.' He gave Frankie five shillings.

Leaving the job, Frankie walked with Toby and Turnbull. They were making for a pub, and Toby insisted on Frankie coming in for a lemonade.

'Don't be like the bloody pastor. You are part and parcel of the honourable and diseased fraternity of bug blinders.'

'Well, if it isn't my granda,' said the barman.

'Away and bury yourself. You were wetting the bed long before I was pupped,' laughed Toby.

Frankie joined in the laughter. Wetting the bed could not be the awful thing he thought it was; here was Toby joking about it.

'Is it the usual for you, Toby?' the barman asked.

'Aye, a pint and a half'un for me, a pint for this other gent, and a bottle of lemonade for the kid.'

Toby poured his whisky into the pint of stout, and lifting the glass said: 'Well, chaps, here's thanking God the Pope's a Papist.'

Turnbull ordered the same again, and said: 'Well, Toby, to show there's no ill feeling, here's thanking God the King's a Protestant.'

'I don't give a damn if he's a Calathumpian. Do you know what a Calathumpian is, Frankie?'

Frankie looked puzzled.

'He's a fellow that studies his navel . . .'

'Now, now, Toby, keep the party clean,' said Turnbull.

The door was pushed open and two men entered. Toby looked up. One of the men, as he sat down, recited:

> Bring your chair up to the table,
> Stay as long as you are able,
> We're always glad to see a man like you.

Frankie knew they were painters. He could see their overalls crudely parcelled, and their hands were red.

Toby introduced Frankie. 'This is Frankie. And these fellows, Frankie, are Barney Google and Crippen. Wouldn't you know to look at that fellow that Crippen was innocent. That fellow couldn't look you straight in the face.' Toby pointed to the smaller of the two men. His face was wrinkled and his eyes did not look as if they belonged to his face at all. The other man kept nodding and smiling as if he could do nothing else with his face.

Toby ordered them a drink, and as he talked to them, Turnbull whispered into Frankie's ear: 'All the painters gather here. But you must be well in the know to get into the circle. I don't belong to it. I am only here because Toby asked me in. But if you are accepted into the circle, that meets here, you're landed.'

'I bet you, Frankie, this fellow has his pockets filled with paint?' said Toby.

'He's working in the shipyard.' The man called Crippen playfully made to hit Toby.

Toby squared. 'Any time, Crippen, you fancy ten rounds, I'm your man,' he said, amid laughter.

Crippen pressed the bell to order another drink. Turnbull stood up, telling him not to order another for him.

'You're going to have another drink,' said Toby. Turnbull explained that he wanted to be home early to take his daughter to the first house of the pictures.

'That's the one that has the sleepy sickness?' Toby inquired, and Turnbull nodded.

'That poor bastard there carries his daughter to the pictures every Saturday night. You'll get to heaven for it, Turnbull, if there's any such place.'

'Why don't you get some of the boys to run a concert and get her one of them wheel chairs?' Crippen asked.

'We couldn't get a wheel chair next or near the place. It's a kitchen house we live in,' Turnbull said.

'One of them salt-boxes,' Crippen spat.

'If I got her a wheel chair I'd have to get a garage to store it in.'

'Christ help the poor, for the devil looks after the rich,' Toby said.

'I don't like taking too much drink,' Turnbull said, as he left the pub with Frankie. 'You couldn't get into that pub on a Saturday night, with painters and plasterers and tailors. Them lads we've just left, their fathers and their great-grandfathers were all at the trade. They would regard me as an outsider. But it was Toby brought me in. There have been painters in Toby's family since anybody minds. The others are the same. They don't want you if you have no background. They've been going to that pub for years, and when anybody belonging to the circle dies, they all stand up and drink to his memory; then they whip around with the

cap for money to buy a wreath. I've seen them at it myself.
Did you see the fellow Toby called Crippen? A tragic case.
That man, in my own hearing, cursed his own mother.
Why, I don't know. He thinks he's ugly, and when he's
drunk, he'll shout and call himself an "ugly so and so". He
blames his mother for it. My girl might as well blame me for
her sleepy sickness, mightn't she?'

Frankie saw that Turnbull did not expect an answer.

'He's not that ugly. If he went about it the right way, he
could get a woman to marry him. He's good at the piano,
so he is. I mind one time we were on a job in Barrow-in-
Furness, and in nearly all the English pubs there's a piano.
He would sit down and play it, and the women coming in
would ask him if he knew such and such a tune, and he
would play it for them. I tell you, Frankie, I seen stacks of
drinks piled on top of the piano that they bought for him.
I bet you he could have got any of them. I heard him playing a thing one night; it was called "In a monastery garden",
and be dammit, to hear him doing the birds on the piano, it
was better than anything I ever heard in the music hall. He
could nearly make the piano talk. But there he is, living in a
bad temper all the time because he thinks he's ugly. He's
very touchy, but, as you see, Toby can say anything to
him.'

They crossed the road. Turnbull resumed.

'The other man is a harmless soul. Barney Google's not his
name at all. Toby calls them anything that comes into his
head. He's a bachelor, but they say he does a line with some
woman that comes in to clean for him. He's wild about
pigeons. He bred birds for the War Office, so you can see he's
no dozer. He would go without food himself to get it for the
pigeons. So there those men will sit all evening, and others
will join them. They'll send round the corner to the pork
shop for roast pigs' knees and ate them. Them lads know
how to enjoy themselves. I tell you, Frankie, there'll be
more houses papered and more doors grained there tonight

than they'll ever see. But painters are not their lone in talking shop. If you watch the tailors taking off their coats, you'd swear they were going to fight; but you'd be wrong, for they are only showing each other how to sew a vest. And the plasterers are as bad. I've watched them spill drink from their tumblers to the counter, and then with a finger, make movements through it to show how they worked a cornice or a centrepiece. But them lads we've just left have no worries. Two of them are not married, and Toby has his family all reared. Their crack is good, and laughter is always the keynote, but take my advice, Frankie, now that you have started to work shun the pubs. The publicans are like the bookies; you never see them poor. A poor publican is a rare thing. I know when to stop. Three pints of beer was always my limit . . .'

Turnbull suddenly stopped and looked into a window of a second-hand clothes shop.

'Dammit, there's a right-looking pair of subs there. They look just about my size.' He pointed to a pair of shoes in the window. 'Come in with me, Frankie, and we'll price them.' A fat woman was sitting behind the counter.

'That pair of shoes you have in the window, could I see them?'

'Certainly you can. That's what I have them in the window for.' She fished them out with a pair of tongs. 'If they're for yourself, why don't you try them on.'

Frankie saw that Turnbull was slightly ashamed of his heelless socks, for he tried to turn his body towards the wall. He forced his feet quickly into the shoes, stood up and walked to the door.

'Do they fit you?' the woman asked eager to make a sale.

'Aye, they feel comfortable enough.'

'They were hand-made those shoes. Look at the rat pad running around the sides of them.'

'What's the price of them? Now, don't open your mouth too wide.'

'Gimme eight-and-sixpence for them and you can wear them home.'

'Would you not take three half-crowns?'

'I would not. I'll take eight shillings and if you don't like that, you can lump it.'

Turnbull looked down at the shoes. 'All right, I'll take them. Wrap them up.'

As the woman looked under the counter for the paper, Turnbull was searching among a pile of vases and jugs in a bath. He took out a pair of ornaments.

'They're like angels, Frankie, aren't they?'

He held them up. 'What would you be asking for them, missus?'

'Give me half a crown for the pair of them and they are as good as on your mantelpiece.'

'I'll give you one and sixpence.'

'You will not, for I won't take it. If you are keen to get them, I'll not take a penny less than two shillings.' Turnbull looked at her.

'All right, all right,' she said. 'It's not hard to get the better of big-hearted Lizzie. Put them in your pocket and gimme one and six for them. Quick with them; I'll shut my eyes, I couldn't bear to see you getting them for nothing.'

'Wouldn't them dealers sicken you with the poor mouths they put on?' said Turnbull as they left the shop. 'Although I think I got a bargain in the shoes. And I like these wee angels. They'll look well on the mantelpiece upstairs.' He was suddenly silent. At length, he said: 'Wouldn't you think, Frankie, after all these years of married life that I would have a home stitched together. That's what the wife and I often say to each other. Aye, it takes a poor man a long while to gather a home. Now, goodbye, Frankie. I'll see you Monday morning.'

Frankie watched him hurry away, his thin figure drooped at the shoulders, the clothes hanging on the body. He saw him take one ornament from his pocket, stop and examine it, then the other. He felt in his pocket and took out his pay envelope to have it ready for his aunt.

As usual she held it to the light before she ripped it open. She put the ten-shilling note into her purse, and eyed the parcel he had left on the table.

'What's this?' she asked as she opened it.

The shirt and socks fell to the floor.

'Who owns these?'

'One of the men gave them to me.'

'A shirt and a pair of socks. Were you putting on a poor mouth to him?'

'No, no, no.' He shook his head.

She examined the shirt, then let it fall to the sofa. 'God alone knows who wore that. If you want to wear it, take it outside and wash it. I don't want any dirt in my house.'

That was like her; always the hurtful 'my house', making him feel the stranger.

'Go on, wash it before I touch or handle it.'

He darted into the kitchen, snatched the shirt from the sofa and the socks from the floor.

In the yard, he plunged the shirt into a basin of water. The water flooded the shirt, and it lost its bright blueness and became inky. The little white tag on the neck with 'pure silk' written on it, remained bright. He spread it on the line, looking at the water that ran from it to the purple tiles of the yard. He heard the yard door open.

'Mrs. Denver up the street wants to see you. She wants you to put in a pane of glass for her.' His hands trembled, and for a moment his brain clouded. He did not know the first thing about putting in a pane of glass. He examined the scullery window, the ragged ridge of putty running round it. How did you put the glass in? Midway he felt a tack. He wished he could put the pane in — it would set all the neighbours in the street talking. They would say how smart and clever he was.

He knocked on Mrs. Denver's door.

'Have you come about the pane, son? It's the front window. Brats of children playing football, and they not from about these doors at all; that's how it was broken. I dunno what we pay peelers for; scratching their backs against the warm walls of corner houses is all them black bastards are good for. Do you think you could put the pane in for me?'

The doubt in her voice discouraged him. If he broke the new pane . . .? If he pushed at it and it cracked in bits . . .?

'Yes, I can put the pane in for you.' He stammered that he would come back in a little while.

Simon could tell him how to put a pane in.

His heart sank as he knocked on Simon's door for the fourth time. He listened with his ear tight against the door. It opened and Simon bade him enter.

'Were you long knocking, Frankie? I was in bed. Stretched myself for an hour or so on top of the clothes. Nothing like rest, son, for the chassis when you are my age. Chase that cat off the chair and sit down.'

Frankie sat down, feeling the seat warm, and looking at the cat stretching itself lazily.

'Now, is your visit social or professional?'

He told the old man about the pane.

'Well, Frankie, I don't think you'll get an O.B.E. for putting in a pane of glass, nor do I think Queen's University would confer an honorary science degree on you for it. But I see your point, son. It is an important thing for you; Your stock will go up in the street one hundred per cent. The wee bit of pride will swell in you; a good thing, Frankie, a good thing. I often wonder why your church made pride one of the seven deadly sins. Come with me to the yard and I'll show you as best I can what to do.'

Simon took a knife and scored the putty from the glass in the window. 'Now,' he said, 'see how the glass is in. Pushed right against a filling of putty, with a tack hammered in but don't let your tack get off the plumb; keep it straight and everything in the garden will be rosy.' For ten minutes or more, the old man demonstrated. 'Now, are you sure you have the idea clear in your mind? Better borrow these tools of mine for the job.'

He hurried away from Simon, but when he reached his own street, he found he had no rule; but even had he had a rule he could not read it.

Perhaps Mr. Blair would lend him a rule, and show him how to read it.

Mr. Blair was stretched on a sofa, facing the fire. Above the fireplace a large mirror showed apples and oranges and bananas, and the top of the cabinet that held the dish they were in.

'What's your trouble? Don't get excited now. Take things cool and calm.'

He managed to tell Mr. Blair what he wanted.

'But, Frankie, you don't need a rule for that. These sashes are all a standard size. Here, I'll write it down for you.'

Frankie's eyes wandered round the kitchen. Everything in it was shiny, the paint on the walls, the fire-irons, the oilcloth, the tiled hearth. . . .

He cleaned out the old glass working slowly, always remembering Simon's instructions. The pane was a good fit, and now his worry was to get the tack in; his hand trembled with excitement. Now all he had to do was to run the ridge of putty round.

It was finished. He had done his first job, his first real job. He felt like shouting it to everybody. Mrs. Denver gave him two shillings, which his aunt took from him without as much as a 'thank you'.

'Get some water,' she said, 'and wash this floor for me. I haven't been able to bend all week with the pains in my back.'

He could have cried. After the triumph of putting in the pane, she tells him to wash the floor! Mrs. Denver had patted his head and said: 'Well done, Frankie. It will be well for the woman that gets you.'

Going to the yard for the bucket, he saw that Haig's shirt had ceased to drip, and the inky blueness was gone from it. Patches of it were almost dry. His aunt was the one to talk about Haig, and about dirt. She ought to go to Blairs' to see what a clean home was like. Everything in her own house was miserable and gloomy and greasy. The only bright object was the picture of her boy who had died for Ireland. It was painted green, white and orange.

'Take your time and do it well,' she commanded as he knelt to wash the floor.

'I must go to Simon with his tools,' he lied.

'You can bring them up to him tomorrow. It's Sunday, and you have nothing else to do.'

'He's going to Bangor, tomorrow.' Another lie. How easy the lies came to him. Was it the devil that put the lies so easy and quickly into his mouth?

He was frightened of these lies. But maybe God could see that she was forcing him to tell lies. He wished his aunt dead. He wanted her to burn in hell. He looked at her sitting by the fire, with his two shillings in her purse. There was nothing the matter with her back. She was lazy and just wanted to torture him. His temper gave way to self-pity, and he cried. He plunged the floorcloth into the bucket so violently that japs of water leapt to her legs.

'Careful, careful, you brat. Take your time and do the thing right.' She stood up, and as he moved, frightened she was going to beat him, he knocked the bucket over. It flooded the kitchen. She caught him by the collar and lifted him to his feet. He brought his leg up and caught her shin with the toe of his boot. She fell back to the sofa, still holding his collar. He tore himself free, looking down for a moment at her bare knees. She was crying out that he had broken her leg. He saw she was making an effort to rise, and he ran from the house.

3   HE GOT OUT at the city centre.
He knew that near the Albert Clock there
was a good café. He could get something to
eat and then go to the pictures. He ordered fish and chips.
A man opposite him put a penny into a little brass slit in
the wall and music started. He then took a red notebook
from his pocket, and began to write, mouthing the words
that were being sung. He nodded his head as he recited:
'I stood in old Jerusalem, beside the Temple there.' He
wrote quickly, and when the music stopped he put the red
notebook in his pocket.

'I'm doing a bit of busking tonight,' he said, in a deep
throaty, almost hoarse voice. 'There's a big fight in the
Ulster Hall.'

The waitress brought the food.

'Them chips look tasty, son. Would you mind if I ate one?'

Frankie saw the man's dirty fingers reach to his plate. He
pushed it towards him.

' "The Holy City" goes down well with the crowd. Much
better than "Nelly Dean" or "Baby Doll a year ago",' he
said as he helped himself to more chips. ' "The Holy City"
is always good for the doss money.' He lifted the fish from
the plate and crammed it into his mouth. 'I'm sorry, son,
but hunger knows no manners.' He stood up, and as he
left, he took the remaining chips.

Frankie drank the tea. Down the street, he could see the
masts and funnels of the ships. Haig would soon be sailing
to England in one of them. Suddenly he felt lost. Haig and
Toby and Turnbull, and even the pastor, had helped to form
the world he liked. His aunt was not in this world. She was
in no world; no world that he could claim as any part of his
life. He had kicked her and run away. He felt dizzy, and
leaned against the corner of the café. A policeman passed
by. 'Come on, now, hop it. No loitering.'

Walking slowly on, he was filled with despair. To jump
from the bridge and fall into the water, and feel the water

gurgling down his throat — no, it would be so hard to die in that way.

He could go to Simon's and ask the old man to let him sleep there. Simon had told him to come any time. 'Dr. Barnardo's. The ever-open door.' But Simon was not at home. 'The ever-open door' was closed. There was nowhere he could go but 'home'. He would not care now how much his aunt beat him. Let her use the poker, the brush, her boot. The pain would hurt, but once he got to bed he could sleep; the pain did not bother you while you slept.

He passed Mrs. Denver's house, looking at his greasy finger marks on the pane he had put in. The dim lamplight picked them out like large fish scales. That was his first job, the first time he had felt proud.

He knocked the door timidly. Looking through the keyhole, he saw there was no light in the kitchen. His aunt must be in bed. He knocked again, but not loudly. If the neighbours heard him and opened their windows, his aunt would beat him all the harder.

The window above him opened quietly.

'Who's there?'

'It's me.'

'Take yourself away from here, you murderer. It's a wonder you are not ashamed to put your neb near this place again. Do you hear me? Take yourself away from here. Take yourself away, before I get the police and have you locked up in a reformatory.'

The window closed again. He tiptoed up the streets. There was a light in the Blairs' house. On the buttercoloured blind was the shadow of the bird cage. Should he knock and ask for shelter for the night? But it seemed a stupid question, for here he was, walking away.

He walked on towards Millfield. Here there were houses with notices nailed above their doors: 'Lodging for men.' From one of the houses came the sound of music. He knocked, and a woman opened the door. A shawl hung from her shoulders, trailing its tail on the floor. A child was at her breast, its little mouth moving quickly. 'Come in and tell me your business. I can't stand here at the door all night. Can't you see the predicament I'm in,' she said, making an effort to draw the shawl over the head of the sucking child. He had difficulty telling the woman what he wanted. 'Here, Barney,' she called, 'take this child till I find out what this lad wants.' She went back to the kitchen and returned without the child. She covered her bulging breast, catching her blouse at the neck with a large safety-pin. 'To sleep,' was all he could stammer out.

'A bed for the night, you want?' He nodded. 'Well, come in.'

He followed her into a large kitchen, its walls distempered blue.

'Come in and welcome,' a man's voice said. 'Had you a row with the wife and left the house?'

The woman offered him a chair and he sat down.

There were three men opposite him. One of them was cleaning a cornet, blowing his breath on it, and rubbing the fog off with a khaki-coloured handkerchief. Another man who was holding the child seemed to be the owner of the house. His chest was bare and showed a lot of black hair. Beside him on the hob was a bottle of wine. The third man was bearded. He was searching his pockets, taking out fag ends to make into a cigarette, with the slip of white paper carefully placed on his knee.

'Did the wife give you a hammering, or did you give her one?' This came from the man with the child.

'No, I er . . .' he made to speak.

'Now, now, we don't want to know the whys and where-fores,' the bearded man said.

The man with the child laughed.

'No disrespect to your hospitable home, sir, but this, son, is a doss house. . . .'

Frankie looked at the bearded man as he spoke.

'No, son, no questions asked in the doss house. Christlike, that's what it is, Christlike. Come to me . . .' He reached to the hob for the wine bottle, held it to his mouth, then offered it to the man with the cornet, who declined it. The owner of the house took it. As he was about to drink, the bearded man said: 'Don't kill it, Barney. Leave what'll wet my lips in the morning.'

'Jazes, sure it's half full yet.' He placed the bottle on the hob again, and said to the man with the cornet, 'Give us something cheerful, mate.'

'Do you know "Whispering"?' asked the cornet player; but he put the instrument to his lips without waiting for an answer.

'Chuck that music. Do you want to wake the child again?' The woman had entered the kitchen. The cornet player put the instrument into the wide pocket of his raincoat, and from the other took a parcel of sausages. 'Anybody like a fried sausage?' The bearded man shook his head. 'Not for me,' he said. 'What about you?' the cornet player asked Frankie.

Frankie stared at him, unsure what to say.

The woman suddenly started singing: 'Pale hands I love, beside the Shalimar . . .'

'Never mind the bloody Shalimar,' said the owner, 'if there's gonna be any tea made, get the cups on the table.'

She put mugs on the table. The cornet player, when the sausages were ready, spread a newspaper on the table and set the pan on top of it. Then he took two soda farls from his pocket. The bearded man had tea, taking buns from a paper bundle he had tied to his waist.

Frankie was given a mug of tea. 'Have you nothing to eat?' the cornet player asked. He tore a farl in two and scraped one part around the pan and handed it to Frankie. 'Ate a sausage with it. They're not very good, but they weren't expensive, so I suppose you can't have it both ways.'

When they had finished the meal, the owner said: 'Well, gents, you know the rules. I collect in advance.'

The cornet player pushed his hand into his pocket and pulled out a handful of coppers. He spread them on the table and counted out twelve.

'There you are,' he said, 'a bob.' The bearded man turned to Frankie. 'You have the money, son?'

'One shilling,' the owner said.

Frankie offered him half a crown. 'A millionaire in the house. Did you rob a bank, or hold up a rent collector?' He counted Frankie's change, using the cornet player's money, and two of the threepenny bits the bearded man had paid.

'You're in the room with Gladstone here,' the owner said, jerking his thumb at the bearded man.

'Well, if you're coming to bed, I have a candle here. I'm not a crank but I hate latecomers in my room. They invariably waken me.' The bearded man walked towards the stairs. Frankie followed him.

The bearded man lit the candle when he was half way up the stairs. In the room he tilted it until grease fell on top of the mantelpiece, then he stuck the candle in it.

'When you're ready,' said the man, 'put the light out. I can't sleep if there's any light.' He turned his face to the wall and sighed loudly.

Frankie took his coat off. He looked at the bed. A brown army blanket was the only covering. He decided to keep his trousers on, but then the old fear of wetting the bed came back to him. If he wet his trousers . . . He took them off, pushed them under his coat, then removed his socks and got into bed.

From the other bed came heavy breathing. Who was this man? He did not know. He felt he would never know. He was in a strange world himself. Yet, not far from here, Toby was at home, and maybe Haig was with Pearl; and his aunt would be in bed. Would she be wondering where he was?

There was no pillow and he found it hard to sleep. Suddenly a voice was calling out from the next room: 'I've lost my job. I've lost my job. I've lost my bloody job.'

'Shut your mouth up there. If you can't keep quiet, get to hell out of this . . . ' Frankie knew this came from the owner of the house. The voice in the next room stopped, but he heard a low grumbling as if there was more than one person in the room.

A pigeon nearby coo'd in its sleep. A ship's whistle sounded and again he thought about Haig. Cats howling in the yard chased Haig from his mind, but his aunt came again when the cats ceased.

The voice in the next room cried out afresh: 'I've lost my job. What am I gonna do? I've lost my bloody job.' And from the kitchen came the final warning: 'Look, up there, if you don't shut your mouth, outside you are going.' Again the low groaning and muttering from the next room, then silence.

He thought about his aunt again. If he had drowned himself. The neighbours would take her part. They would listen to her and tell her how good she had been to him, and that he had not deserved a good home. He knew Sally was the only one who would understand. Sally would pray for him, would offer up prayers for the good of his soul.

The man in the next room began laughing, but the laughter died into a soft sobbing.

When Frankie awoke in the morning church bells were ringing loudly. When he dressed and went downstairs, the woman looked at him as if she had not seen him before. She was bruising bread with her fingers in a bowl of milk. The child was crying and she called out: 'All right, all right, I'm coming, I'm coming.' Her tones were weary and sleepy. She returned and placed a mug on the table in which she shook a spoonful of condensed milk. 'There,' she said, 'there's your breakfast,' as she poured tea into it.

'If I want a bed tonight, can I come?' he stammered out.

'Yes, if you want to.' The house was quiet now. The woman went upstairs. When he finished the meal he closed the door quietly behind him.

4   SIMON WAS AT HOME, and made him welcome. As usual he made for the scullery to get the teapot.

'I was up here last night,' said Frankie. Simon paused as he filled the teapot.

'I was out last night, Frankie. A friend of mine took me out to a British Legion smoker, and I spent the night with him.' He moved about laying the table, cutting bread and washing cups as Frankie told him what had happened.

'And where did you spend the night?'

'In a doss house in Millfield.'

'I see.' He poured out tea and motioned the boy to the table. 'You are a bit on the young side for that kind of life, Frankie. But I suppose must do is must do. I'm sorry now I wasn't at home, but wouldn't something like that happen? The night you wanted me, I wasn't here. Time will come, Frankie, when she might need you, and need you badly. Has she any relatives?'

'Not that I know.'

'Time, time will come, son. Great old boy is time. Did you ever see a drawing of him? His wrinkled face, his scythe, and his hour glass. He sees them all down; saints and sinners, kings and cadgers. If we could only get the Society interested in your case, but then that makes things worse, if the Society intervened. Tell me, are there any marks on your body?'

'They go away easy. . . .'

'I know. But that is not the point. I always say that it wasn't the soldier who lost a leg or an arm that suffered the most.' Simon stopped talking and lifted the cat to his knee. 'Wouldn't it be great, Frankie, if we were all animals. Look at this cat here, fed like a lord.' The cat wanted to play with him, but he put it down. 'You could come and live here, Frankie . . .' He got up from the table and went to the fire for the teapot.

'No, son. You mustn't come here. I told you before there would be all the fuss of religion. No, you can't come and live here.' He laughed. 'Time, Frankie, time. . . .'

'I wish I was like you,' Frankie said.

'No, no, you mustn't wish that. I'm soon finished with life, you are only starting it. But that's what happens. When we are young we want to be old, and when we are old we want to be young.' He prodded the fire with a poker.

'Tell me, Frankie, did you know Haig had made a mess of things?'

The boy stared at him, not knowing how to take the serious tone in the old man's voice.

'You were on that country job with him. Did you notice if he was tig-toyin' with a woman? Did she ever come near the job?'

Frankie remembered his promise to Haig. He guessed that Simon was referring to Pearl. He made no answer.

'You slept in the same bed with him. Was he ever away any night?'

'I don't know,' Frankie answered.

For a moment Simon looked into the fire, then he turned and faced the boy again.

'You're right, Frankie, you know nothing. Don't get yourself involved. Let that always be your answer — "I don't know".' The old man was silent again, then he spoke quietly: 'She's my niece, Frankie. ˉIt was in this house that he met her. I don't fault either of them, but the pity was that she already has a husband. I suppose in a way I was to blame. They had the key of this house when I wasn't here. Maybe I should have sent the pair of them about their

business. But I couldn't do that, Frankie; I'm just a senti-
mental old coof. I thought I was doing the right thing . . .
You like Haig, Frankie?'

'Yes, I do. He showed me things. Taught me how to use
a brush, and gave me shirts and socks.' He got all this with
an effort.

'With a woman like Pearl behind him,' said Simon, 'Haig
might tear the world apart. But there's a baby coming,
Frankie, after five years of married life, and it looks like Haig
is responsible. There will be a divorce, and of course that
means money and mud slinging in the papers . . . I don't
know that Pearl has any means of her own. She's my
brother's daughter. He was the only one in my family
that made good. He became a bookie, if you like to call that
"making good". I never asked him for a silver sixpence in
my life. Bookies are one race of men I despise . . . But there
it is, Frankie; time will smooth it all out, time will do that.'

Frankie had only a vague idea of what Simon had been
talking about. He wanted to question him about Haig, to
ask if he would not be back, if the talk about the job in
England was all an excuse. But the old man's tone did not
invite questions. Simon looked upset about it. He screwed
his mouth and puckered his brow, then he rubbed his hand
over his face impatiently and shook his head.

'Well now, Frankie, so much for Haig's trouble. What
about your own wee bit of bother? I think the best thing
you could do would be go back to your aunt. You could stay
here for a week or so, but sooner or later she would get to
hear of it, and I know she would have priests and politicians
of all kinds after me. So make up your mind, son, to go
back home. Could you not make up your mind to face her
outright, and let her know how you feel about everything?'
Frankie was surprised at Simon talking like this. It looked as
if he did not understand. 'Could you not go right down now
and face her?'

Frankie was silent.

'If I went down with you, and tried to reason with her, do you think it would help things?'

'It might.'

'Right, I'll come down with you.'

'She mightn't let me in.'

'If she turns you out, she must do it in my hearing. Then I'll put it up to her. I'll ask her straight if she has any objections to your coming to live with me. Isn't that fair? If she turns you out, I'll take you back with me?'

Frankie now hoped that his aunt would turn him out.

'Now, Frankie, if you don't mind, son, I got very little sleep last night, for I don't take kindly to strange beds; so I am going upstairs to stretch myself in bed for a couple of hours. Did you sleep well yourself in the doss house?'

He shook his head.

'If you like you can stretch on the sofa there, and if you want there is soup in a pot in the scullery and you can heat it for yourself.'

Simon climbed the stairs.

Frankie closed his eyes, shutting out the grey light that filled the kitchen. He slept.

'Come, Frankie, it is struck seven o'clock,' Simon was touching his shoulder. 'Come, son, it's time we were going on our job of reconciliation. Give your face a rub in the scullery and it will chase the sleep from your eyes.' While Frankie washed, Simon made more tea. As they ate he questioned Frankie about Haig's behaviour on the country job. To the answers he got he merely said: 'That's right, Frankie, you know nothing, that's the way it ought and should be.'

When they left the house, Simon stopped at the corner. 'I think that man over there is keeping an eye on my house.' Frankie looked across the street, but the man had moved away. 'I believe that bucko is a private detective. It's a feeling I have, for I could swear I have seen him in our street two or three times this past week. He might be a private detective, doing some spotting for Pearl's husband;

you just would not know. It's only now I am beginning to put two and two together.'

'He's wee for a detective,' Frankie ventured softly, afraid to sound as if he were contradicting Simon.

'He's not small for a private detective. You could be three hands higher than a duck and still be a private detective.'

As they neared the Grosvenor Road, he said: 'Frankie, we must brace ourselves for the affray. Enter with me now, as if you don't give one tinker's curse for her. . . .'

He tugged at Simon's sleeve as they reached the house and the old man knocked the door.

'Well, I have brought the prodigal back,' he said, with a laugh in his voice.

'You've brought the murderer back,' Frankie heard his aunt spit out. Simon turned to him. 'Come in, Frankie,' he said, 'no use in letting all the neighbours know our business.' Frankie followed him.

'We all have our little outbursts of temper. But believe me, I have cautioned Frankie, and from this on you'll find he will be a good boy.'

Frankie was hurt at the way Simon was talking.

'I wonder he dare show his face in this street again after what he has done,' said his aunt. 'He's left me a nice leg, I can tell you. A low, dirty murderer, that's what he is, that would lift his boot to a harmless soul like myself.'

She was crying.

'I was at the doctor with my leg and he said it was the work of a savage.'

'Well, he has promised to turn over a new leaf, haven't you, Frankie?' The boy dropped his head.

'Look at him, he can't even look anyone straight in the face. A bad sign surely.' She turned and walked into the kitchen. Simon followed her, taking the boy's hand.

Frankie pulled his hand away and remained at the foot of the stairs. She was sitting in her usual chair at the fire. He

looked at her leg. Through the black stocking he could see
the bulging of the bandage. Simon sat on the edge of the
sofa. He knew the old man would not stay long, and he
dreaded his leaving.

'Try to overlook his behaviour this time. As I say, he has
promised to reform, so like a decent woman, give him another
chance.' Simon stood up and edged towards the door.
'You'll find now that he will turn over a new leaf . . .'
Frankie sensed that Simon wanted to go. Now he was
leaving.

'Be a good boy, Frankie, and do as your aunt tells you.
Good evening, mem . . .' Simon was gone.

Simon had let him down badly. Simon helps Jesus to
carry His cross. Not this time. Simon was not kind any
more. Simon had not done what he had said he would do.

He moved away from the stairs out of her view. He knew
she was in one of her tempers. Through a crack in the
partition, he could see her untying the ragged garter. Her
stocking slid down her leg. She removed the white bandage,
her lips moved; she was talking to herself, but he could not
make out what she was saying.

'Come here,' she called. 'Come in here, you murderer,
you hangman. Look at that leg you've left me.' She shot
her leg out, and from where he stood, he could see the black
mark; the edges were red and swollen.

'I have been to the doctor with it and if gangaree or blood
poisoning sets in, you will be jailed for it. That's the thanks
I get for all I have done for you. But God will punish you
for it. God will surely punish you for using your boot on a
half-dying woman . . .' She started crying. 'Here I am, not
able at times to lift my hands or feet with the pains I suffer,
and to be left with a leg like that . . . But I'll leave you to
God and He will punish you and punish you severely . . .'
Her tears gave way to anger and she reached to the hob for
the poker. He rushed down the hall and into the yard,
holding the latch of the back door tightly. She was pulling

at it. He had not heard her come up the hall. He held tight, his hands trembling with the effort as they gripped the handle. He heard the bolt being shot in. The church bells rang out nine o'clock, then played a hymn.

> I rise from dreams of time,
> And an angel guides my feet,
> To the sacred altar throne,
> Where Jesus' heart doth beat.

It was now dark, but he could see the outline of the entry door. He could open it and get away. He had enough money for another night in the doss house. He crossed to the dustbin and sat on it. Above him the sky was bright with stars. God was up there. She said that God would punish him. The priests preached that it was a sin to lose your temper and evil would come from it. What was evil, the evil they preached about? They said, too, it was a sin. What is sin? 'Any transgression against the law of God?' That was what the catechism said. But what did 'transgression' mean? God would surely not allow her to use a poker or a brush to beat him, without blackening her soul with the marks of sin. He had marks on his body, although he did not say it to Simon. He had the smooth mark on his arm where she had cut him with a knife. He had a dent in his head where she opened his brow with the poker. On the last day these marks would be there for God to see. He could say to God, 'This is what she did to me, this is why I kicked her, why I hated her.'

He pushed at the door. He shook it gently and listened, but no sound came from within. The closet door leaned forward, hanging awkwardly by one hinge. He could sit there, but he was frightened, frightened of the grey wood lice that moved and curled in the rafters on the roof. They might drop down his neck, or curl themselves in his ear.

He shook the door again, then tapped it with his knuckles. 'You are not the fine manly man tonight,' she called out.

'You are not kicking high tonight. The temper's cold inside you now. You have to crawl home to me, for there isn't one of your own friends want you. I'll cool your courage for you, my buck.' Now she was going up the stairs. Through the hole in the lath he could see the candle flame jump as she walked.

He sat down in the closet, leaning his head against the wall, feeling the whitewashed surface cold on his ear, and hearing the everlasting hissing of the cistern. He took off his coat and pulled it shawl-like over his head. Why was he such a coward? Why couldn't he run away? He had read stories of boys who had run away to sea. Why couldn't he do the same? He was afraid of the sea, that was why. He was a coward. He felt he was like a cat that Denvers had one time — a cat that was always being kicked about, and was starved and scabby looking. As often as they flung it out, it huddled against the door again and darted in when it got the chance.

It was late, very late. In an effort to warm his feet, he paced up and down the yard.

He counted his steps as he walked: over five hundred. That, he thought, should warm his feet, but they were still cold, and he took shorter steps, so short they were that he could not count them. Then he tried the short heavy taps of a dancer.

A light in the back bedroom made him look up. Through one of the broken panes her voice came in a loud whisper: 'What are you prancing about down there? Do you want to waken all the neighbours in the street?'

'My feet are cold.'

The light disappeared, and in a little while he heard the bolt drawn from the door. He waited until he felt that she was back in bed, then he opened the door. Inside all was dark, he reached the stairs and took off his boots. When he got to the top step she called out: 'If I was doing what was right, I wouldn't let you across my door.'

He got into bed. It was so very cold and he gathered his feet up against his hips. Down inside him he was warm, and it would soon reach his feet.

In a day or two she would forget her hurt shin. It could not be as painful as she made out; for often when she kicked him, the mark of the wound healed in a short time. To-morrow night he would be at home again, and that meant the confraternity, but he would go and let her see he wanted to be good. She would not bother him any more tonight; he could let his thoughts dwell on Simon, so worried over Haig and Pearl. Haig must be a great man with the girls when a married woman like Pearl was in love with him. And what a woman Pearl was!

His feet warmed and his eyes closed. He was pleased, pleased that he shared Haig's secret. Toby and Turnbull and all the others would think that Haig had gone to work in England, but he knew different.

5   HE FELT THE BED when he awoke. It was dry. From the kitchen his aunt was calling to him to hurry down.

'I'll need a lunch with me. I am not going back to the country job.' Hurriedly she cut the bread and spread the butter so thinly that it was invisible.

'I'll need some tea and sugar too.'

'God such carrying out! Take yourself to a lodging house and see how far your ten shillings a week will go on food and carrying out with tea and sugar.' As she moved, he saw she limped and caught at the nearest object for support.

At the office the girl handed him a little slip of paper. 'That's the address of the job you are to go to. You'll find Boal there.'

He showed Toby the slip of paper. 'I'm going to work with a man called Boal,' he stammered.

'Watch Boal. He's an arse-licker of the first degree. You know the type; washes the boss's car and cuts the hedge of the house for him. A belly-crawler, he's lower than a snake, so you know what that means. I'm marking your cards for you now, so remember.'

Frankie disliked Boal from the moment he first saw him. A tall man with a crooked mouth and a nose that seemed to curl, his eyes were light blue and he had a great expanse of cheeks. A perpetual smile on his face exposed his mouthful of rotten teeth. His laugh was ignorant, as if it did not come from inside him, and he did not control it.

Boal set him to wash the paintwork of the room. Toby could curse but he cursed in a way that you could laugh; you could not laugh at Boal when he cursed — he cursed with a snarl on his face. He inquired about the last job Frankie was on.

'Was Haig in charge of it?'

'Yes.'

'Thon snobbish bastard. He'll play with fire too long, the same bucko, and by God! I'll be glad to see him getting burned. Did he even speak to you?'

'Yes.'

'Huh. Thon's only a pishpot. Rudolph Vaselino . . .' A clock struck twelve and it was time to get the tea made.

'Have you tea and sugar?' Boal asked.

The boy was surprised. On the job it was always the apprentice that attended to the tea-making. He handed Boal his poke. Boal looked at it.

'You'll get fat on all the tea and sugar that's in that packet,' he said.

Frankie heard him talking to someone in the kitchen. The voices died and the handle of the door moved. He looked up and the maid entered the room with two cups.

'I'm coming in to have a look at you,' she said. 'Your man in the kitchen tells me I should make a date with you.' Turning, she called back into the kitchen: 'If I was to court

this fellow, I would need to carry a soap box about with me.'
She laughed loudly at this.

'But wee dogs have big tails,' Boal shouted from the scullery.

She passed Frankie the tray, he thanked her, and she called back to the scullery: 'He has good manners anyway.'

She surveyed the room in expectation. 'You haven't the wallpaper on yet,' she asked.

'What do you think we are, flying machines,' Boal shouted back.

She was small and wore glasses. One of her eyes turned in towards her nose, as if it did not want to look straight out at all. She took her glasses off and wiped them with her apron. Her face changed completely. It looked old and her eyes were flat; no shine from them at all. It seemed to Frankie that her face came alive when she put the glasses on again; it was like a light being switched on.

Boal came into the room and put his arm around her waist. She giggled. His cheek touched hers. 'Did you shave this morning?' she asked awkwardly.

Boal laughed and Frankie saw him move his hand until it flattened over her chest.

'Now, now . . .' she said, pushing his hand away.

'Easy tickled, easy courted . . .'

'I'll let you get your tea before it gets cold.'

When she was gone, Boal said: 'I fancy I could go to town with that one. . . .'

Frankie did not answer. Boal had his sleeves rolled up. A lion was tattooed on his arm with 'God Save the King' underneath. That meant Boal was a Protestant.

About four in the afternoon the girl made their tea and gave them cheese sandwiches.

As they ate, Boal said: 'It pays to be nice to slaveys. You see what happens — tea, scones, and all your orders. Haig isn't the only man that gets away with women. I mightn't be a hulluva lot to look at, but I have a way with the wenches just the same. That dame in the kitchen there, I never set eyes on her before till this morning, and what happens? She's atein' out of my hand. Quick work, what?'

Frankie returned the cups to the kitchen. 'Had you enough to eat?' the girl asked. He thanked her and said he had.

'Is your workmate married?' she asked quietly.

'I dunno.'

She seemed disappointed with his reply. 'Is he a Protestant or a Catholic?'

Frankie wanted to repay her kindness in some way. He remembered the tattooed inscription on Boal's arm. 'I think he's a Protestant,' he said with an effort.

On the way home that night, Boal made him promise that he would never say anything to anybody about what happened with the servant girl. 'You'd get the sack for that,' he said ...

Mrs. Blair was at the door when he passed, looking in his direction.

'We're having a party tonight, Frankie. Will you come up for a while?' she said. He looked wide-eyed at her. 'Sally's going away to a boarding school, a convent, so we're having a party, just a few of her pals. We won't see her again for about six months.'

'Yes ... yes ... yes ...' He was moving from one foot to the other with delight.

'Your aunt won't object to your coming?'

'I'll not tell her ...' He stopped. Mrs. Blair might ask what his aunt had against Sally.

'I know ... I know ...' she said. 'I know how things are; I'm not sleeping. If you care to come up, we'll leave the entry door open for you. Just slip around in your own time.'

'Yes, yes. ...'

'Don't get excited now. Just come up in your own time and enjoy yourself.'

In front of him he saw an ambulance and he heard the children shout, 'Hold your nose, there's the ambulance.'

It stopped outside the prefect's house. Frankie hurried down and learned that the prefect had been suddenly taken ill. Two men were carrying him out on a stretcher.

Seeing the prefect lying there with a red blanket covering him, he was not sorry for him; he hoped he would be in the hospital for years.

Now he could tell his aunt that he was going to the confraternity. His sudden good luck puzzled him. Was it the devil who had arranged all this as a reward for his telling so many lies?

Tonight he was not worried about the small amount of food she had left for him. There would be lots to eat at Sally's party.

'What's your hurry?' his aunt asked.

'The confraternity . . .' he managed to stammer out.

'Well, see and pray for your prefect. He's just been taken away to the hospital to get his appendix out. Say a prayer that he'll come out of the operation all right. He's a good boy, and a credit to the street. . . .'

Frankie knew he was a good boy.

'He kept his eye on you for me. . . .'

Frankie knew this too. But he could not pray for him. If the prefect had died it would not worry him in the least.

'So say a prayer for him, do you hear me?'

'Yes . . . yes. . . .'

If his aunt only knew! Here he was promising to pray for the prefect, and all the time was filled with joy at the prospect of Sally's party. What did it matter if his aunt found out about it later on? He could suffer the hearth brush, the poker, the shoe on his shin; he could and would suffer anything for the party.

Outside there was the noise of the neighbours. He could hear their voices and he knew the talk was about the prefect going to hospital. His aunt left the kitchen, pulling her coat over her shoulders. She was joining the others in the talk. When she was gone he hurried to Simon's house.

The old man sat by the fire. He lit his pipe and stretched his legs. 'Remember the small man, that I thought was a private detective . . . Remember the other night . . .?'

Frankie nodded.

'I was right. But he's away now, his job is finished. Pearl has gone to England, to join Haig . . .'

There was a silence. Simon puckered his brow and looked into the fire.

'I dunno,' he said with a sigh, 'I wonder is it the right thing? Her husband's in a terrible state about it. No matter how you look at it, Frankie, she has left him . . . left him . . . That's a simple statement, son, a very simple one; but it can mean a helluva lot. I feel partly guilty . . . They used to meet here . . . I told you all that before . . . Still, it worries me. It isn't the first time it has happened, I suppose, nor will it be the last time . . . Still there's little comfort in platitudes . . .'

Frankie wanted to go away. The thoughts of the party excited him.

'I only hope they're happy for their own sakes . . . Still . . .' Simon was worried.

'But Frankie, say nothing about it, to anyone. I like Haig, I wouldn't like indecent tittle-tattle about him. They are two people in love. That may be hard to understand.'

Frankie stood up, wondering how he was going to get away. If he could only explain to Simon about the party.

'You want to be away,' Simon said suddenly. The old man rose and went towards the front door.

'I wish I were like other men, Frankie. I could go down to some pub or club and get stinking drunk and forget all about it; but that's not the way I am made. Well, good night, son. Come again any time you like.'

Frankie rushed away. At the Blairs' Sally greeted him.

'Ach! Frankie. We never see you this weather at all, since you have started to work . . .' She put her arms around him, forcing him from the threshold of the door.

'You're lovely, Sally. . . .'

'I'm not. I'm getting too fat. But I'll lose it all when I go to the convent school. I hear they don't feed you well at these places. But I'm going to like it, I know I am. I couldn't stick the typewriting school. Daddy's doing well since he started in business for himself, so he's gonna try and make a lady of me . . . What a. hope . . . ' All this she said with her arms around him, hugging him, her legs warm against his own, her cheek soft against his.

'Come inside quick. You're just in time for tea.' She took his hand, leading him up the scullery.

'Here's the working man himself,' said Mr. Blair. The others laughed.

'Don't be making the wee fellow shy and embarrassed,' said Mrs. Hinds. 'Sit down, Frankie, beside me, and don't heed that man.'

It seemed to come as a surprise to her that he was working. She had a son who was going to be a priest; everyone said he was clever and talked about the scholarship that was taking him to Rome, right to where the Pope himself lived.

'You working, Frankie. Child dear, you should still be out enjoying yourself with the other children.'

'He'll be a credit to the street yet,' Mr. Blair put in.

'Don't be making fun of Frankie, Daddy,' said Sally.

'I'm not making fun of him. I mean what I say. Nobody knows what's in store for Frankie. He might die a millionaire . . . I'm serious.'

'That's right,' agreed a woman named Tully. Her son was studying to be a schoolmaster.

'You never know what's in front of you.' This came from an old woman called Breen. 'I often wonder what changes there'll be in this street in another ten years. You, Mrs. Hinds, your son will be a priest; maybe with God's help a bishop. Your son, Mrs. Tully, will be a schoolmaster, maybe in charge of a great big school. And your daughter, Mr. Blair, will come from the convent school and have a nice way of talking and maybe marry some rich man. And then you'll all leave the street, and take yourselves off to live in them grand houses beyond the tram lines. You'll forget all about the old neighbours and the folks that haven't done so well as yourselves.'

'That won't happen,' said Mrs. Blair.

'But it will,' prophesied the old woman. 'I know. Go up beyond the tram lines on the Falls road, the Malone road, the Antrim road and you'll find the old, old story . . . they had all their startings in the kitchen house. . . .'

'True, very true,' assented Mr. Blair. 'And where would you like to live, Mrs. Breen?' asked Mr. Blair.

'Not at the end of the Falls road nor the end of the Malone road, but back in Kintaugh, where it's wild and lonely. But everyone to their taste. It's where I was born. There's nothing of it now. I was the last of my breed, and God didn't bless me with brothers or sisters nor children of my own. The house now is in wreck and ruin, but the graveyard is still there. But children, dear, this is a party and not a gathering listening to the rantings of an old woman the likes of me. What about Frankie giving us a song?'

He blushed and dropped his head.

'He must get something to eat first,' said Mrs. Blair. 'A bird can't sing without seed. Isn't that right, Frankie?'

He did not look up, and the others answered for him.

'If you can ate any more, there's lashings here,' said Mrs. Blair, as she brought him a dish of pears and ice cream.

'Don't ask him if he can ate any more, keep on feeding him till he refuses,' laughed her husband.

'That's right,' said Sally.

'Give us something on the piano, Sally,' coaxed her mother.

Sally protested: 'I can only play with music in front of me. My teacher won't let me play by ear. All the music I have is "Won't you buy my pretty flowers".'

'Well play that,' said Mrs. Breen.

Frankie ate his pears and cream, his hand shaking. No

one was looking at him. His eyes rested on the sideboard with its dish of fruit and bright bottles of lemonade. He could see Sally's books, her bicycle pump and tin of paints; everything to suggest the comfort and pleasure of a home.

She was now at the piano and her father was singing in a comic way, pretending he was drunk: 'Won't you buy my pretty flowers?'

'Maybe we shouldn't be singing and playing the piano,' said Mrs. Blair suddenly.

'Why?' Mr. Blair stopped singing.

'On account of the sickness in the street.'

'You're right, dear. It perhaps isn't proper,' said Mrs. Hinds.

'He's away to hospital, and I suppose his life is in God's immediate hands, but I must speak the truth, I never liked him . . .' said Mrs. Tully.

The others remained quiet. Frankie wanted to agree with Mrs. Tully. It was clear that nobody liked the prefect very much.

'Maybe there would be no harm in the magical lantern,' said Mr. Blair.

'What slides are we going to show?' Devlin asked.

'Show the ones about the hunted deer.'

'Ach! I'm tired looking at them.'

'That doesn't mean that everyone else is tired, does it Frankie?' said Sally.

He was shy about answering her. But from the way she fussed about the lantern it looked as though no reply was needed. Devlin offered to assist her, but she said, 'I'll do it myself. You'll only break them. Tell you what you can do, put out the light when I'm ready.'

They crouched in a corner, behind the chair on which the lantern was placed.

Now Frankie was close to Sally. The slant of light picking out her knee, as she pulled her skirt up her legs to give her more freedom of movement. He longed to touch her leg.

He could see her white garter, and the curling end of her knickers.

Sally had shown the first slide upside down. 'Put the light on again, till I arrange them properly,' she said.

The light was switched on.

'Quiet in there,' came a voice from the kitchen.

Sally opened the door. 'What's the matter, Father?'

'Just take things a wee bit easier. . . .'

'He's dead,' Mrs. Tully cut in. 'Peritonitis, I'm sure that's what it was. It must have burst before they got him on the operating table.'

'I'd better go and see his mother,' said Mrs. Hinds, 'see if there's anything we can do. She's leaf alone now, and she might need someone to see to the body, the burial and all that.'

One by one the neighbours left until only Mrs. Blair and her husband remained.

'I'm sorry, children, this has spoiled your evening's fun,' Mrs. Blair said.

'We used to make fun of him too, call him chinny chin chin. . . .'

'You'll make fun of him no more. He was just as God made him. He couldn't help his chin.'

Frankie made for the door. 'Good night, and thank you.'

Sally came with him into the hall.

'I'll see you again at Christmas,' she said, 'and we'll have a better party, for tonight's wasn't a party at all.'

'Yes, Sally . . .' What was there to say? 'You're lovely, Sally. . . .'

'You're the only one ever says that to me, Frankie. But I'm too fat. Fatty Arbuckle, that's me.' She laughed and caught his chin in her hand, and for an instant he felt her soft warm lips on his own.

'There now, I'll give you another kiss when I come home at Christmas; that is if the nuns don't know about it. I'll write you a letter some time, Frankie. . . .'

'Will you?'

'Uh-huh. Would you write one to me?'

'I would, I would.'

'You couldn't put kisses at the bottom of it; you know "xxx's" and "o" for hugs.'

'Why?'

'The nuns wouldn't allow it. They read all your letters. I'm sure they would throw me out of the convent if you started "x"ing and "o"ing.'

'Goodbye, Sally, goodbye . . . Oh! Sally, you're lovely. I wish you were my girl . . . Oh! Sally, I do, I do . . .' His eyes were blurred, even if there were no tears.

'I'll write you a letter, I will Frankie, you'll see. There now,' she said, and kissed him again. 'I'll see you at Christmas.'

And now she was gone. He turned and walked from the house towards the top of the street. The bells for nine o'clock had not gone yet. He would have to wait for them, for that was the time he usually arrived home from the confraternity. They played a hymn:

> O turn to Jesus, mother turn,
> And call Him by his precious names,
> Pray for the Holy Souls that burn,
> This hour among the cleansing flames.

He knew that hymn was for the Souls in Purgatory. The words made him sorry now that the prefect was dead. He could imagine the prefect being buried in the flames in Purgatory and his long chin wriggling with terrible pain.

His aunt was waiting for him. 'They're looking for you to distemper the front room before they bring home the body.' He was pleased, very pleased that he should be sent for. He would be talked about in the street. Already he had put in a pane of glass; now a room to distemper. . . .

The prefect's mother was crying loudly as she pushed the strands of hair from her wet cheeks. Mrs. Hinds was there.

'What's your trouble, Frankie?' she asked.

He stammered out about distempering the room. 'She has changed her mind. She's letting the body go to the church.' She tied up the hair of the weeping woman. 'His remains will be better in the church for the two nights. If you bring them home what will you have? Spongers in at the wake, looking for drink and food, and behaving like people not civilized.'

'Yes, yes, you're right, you're right.'

'Of course I'm right. His remains will rest in the church in the company of Christ.'

'Yes, yes.'

'You haven't got a whole fistful of money to spend on drink and food.'

'I haven't, no I haven't.'

'Thank you all the same, Frankie. It was a Christian act you were about to do, but it won't be needed now.' He remained for a moment looking at the prefect's mother. Never once had she addressed him.

All over the world there must be millions of people praying. How did God know about them? He would have to keep a note, too, of the others who did not pray.

He loved to think about things like these. They could make him forget his stammer, his smallness, his shaking hands, his hunger and poverty. There were times too, when thinking about Sally, he could forget them. But then he would suddenly become aware of his appearance, and see himself beside Sally. God if He liked had only to blow a tiny breath or move His wee finger and He could have made him like Haig. It was strange when you thought about it; that God had made birds, and flies, and cats and dogs, and He made them perfect. But when He made human beings He gave them noses too big for their faces; and lips too thick; and red maps on their faces; and funny eyes; just as if He enjoyed making them, for the fun of it. He made the prefect with a big long chin, and everyone had made fun of this chin.

And look at the way He had made Frankie himself? God sometimes must have a good laugh to Himself when he looked down from heaven at all the queer shaped human beings. . . .

Next morning Boal was on the job when Frankie arrived. He was sitting on the covered settee, smoking a cigarette.

'Close that door tight.' His tone was suddenly aggressive. 'Close the door tight,' he repeated. He spat angrily into the grate but missed it. 'Clean that up at once.'

Frankie rubbed his foot on the spit until it was just a dark stain on the white timber. What was wrong? What had he done now? He had broken no cups. He had worked hard. He was in time. What was wrong? Boal stood up and came slowly towards him. He suddenly gripped him by the chest and pulled him close.

'Listen,' he said. 'Do you want to stop stuttering? I'll tell you how. Keep your bloody mouth shut. If you don't I'll shut it for you. For two pins, I'd ram your bloody teeth down your thrapple.' He bent his head and talked into the boy's face. His breath was unpleasant, and flecks of spittle peppered Frankie's cheeks. 'Why did you tell the dame in there that I was a Protestant? What hell business of yours is it what I am? You have no right to be blabbing out what anybody's religion is. How did you know I was a Protestant anyway? You're the sort that creates disturbances. Keep your mouth shut in future. If you open it any more to discuss my affairs with anyone I'll bloody well close it for you; and I'll close it tight.'

He pushed Frankie away from him. The boy trembled. He tried to recall what the row was all about. He remembered then the servant asking him about Boal's religion. All that day he was terrified. Why could he not have told Boal how it all started? He had tried, as they sat at their lunch. But Boal shut him up by asking him what he was trying to say. This accursed stammering made his attempts at explanation hopeless.

Boal mentioned the incident to the Protestant members of

the firm, and while they did not speak about it to Frankie, he knew that their attitude towards him had changed. He tried to explain to Simon, but the old man shook his head. 'I despair of this country, Frankie. Fifty years of atheism is what Ireland needs, just fifty years of it. A Dutchman by the name of William, and a Pope, an Italian by the name of Gregory . . . What's the use, son, what's the use? You'll find your world will change, Frankie, it must change. As you get near to manhood you'll discover that men fight over childish things.'

Simon's eyesight was failing. 'I've been with an eye specialist. He says he won't look at my eyes if I bathe them in cold tea any more, but the ointment he gives me for them I might as well rub it on the handle of the floor brush; the cold tea clears them best of all. But I need to be doing them every half hour, especially at night when I am trying to read.' He screwed up his face as if he were trying to force his eyes to widen. Frankie wondered what would happen if Simon went blind. He saw himself leading Simon about. Perhaps he could come and live with Simon.

―――――――

PART THREE

1   HE HAD NOW been four years at the trade.
Turnbull had told him that it was not a good
thing for a boy to learn his trade with a firm
like St. Clair's; while the work they did was good, it had
little variety. For general experience it was better to get
into a small firm where you limewashed a yard on a Monday,
and were sent to wallpaper a drawing-room on a Tuesday.
Not that St. Clair's did not take on an occasional 'rough
job'.

Such jobs were usually done by what was known as the
'awkward squad'. Frankie had now seen enough of the
workmen to tell the good tradesmen from the not so good;
the tidy from the untidy; the clean from the careless. Toby
was foreman of the awkward squad when they were sent
out to clean up a factory, a foundry, or the interior of a
cheap cinema. Turnbull, too, belonged to this group. The
good tradesmen had various other names for them, like the
'hole borers', the 'fifty minute cleaners', the 'do or die
merchants'.

Frankie discovered that Toby could be a tyrant when he
had power. If he did not like a new workman all he had to
say to the boss was: 'That new man you sent me. God help
the soul, he's doing his damndest, but he didn't get the eggs
nor the beef when he was young ...' That was enough.
The new workman would be sacked. On the other hand, if
Toby liked you, you could do almost anything, keep bad
time, even bring drink to the job. Friends and enemies alike
seemed afraid of Toby. He was strong and fearless and was
famous for the amount of food he could eat and the number
of drinks he could consume. When they were working at

the abattoir, Toby astonished everybody by drinking a can full of bull's blood as it flowed from the dead animal.

Frankie appreciated Toby's kindness, but was aware that he learned little from him. Simon said: 'Try and keep from Toby's jobs. Toby's all right, but he's too coarse. He knows nothing himself, and when a man knows nothing himself, how can he teach others? Toby's all right for the type of work he does, but he's a sow's lug and a sow's lug he will always remain; and you can't make a silk purse from a sow's lug.' But if he was sent out with Toby he just had to go. He wanted Simon's advice. The old man was not nearly so talkative as he used to be. He was still worried about his eyes. He said that the doctors in London helped them just a wee bit, and reaffirmed his belief in cold tea.

'My mother, God rest the good woman's soul, always believed in cold tea for anything wrong with the eyes. She got that cure from her grandmother. When you tell this to the modern doctors, they say that it's an old wives' tale and has its origins in witchery. Maybe it has. The witches had the power to heal. What odds if, as people say, they got it from the devil? The devil is God's foreman, God's favoured; if he passed on power to the witches, where did he get that power from? From God of course. . . .'

Frankie got the impression that Simon did not want to talk about work now. When a notice board was sent to him to do for the University, he returned it with the message that his eyes would not allow him to continue his sign-writing. Any sight he had left he was saving for reading. He was worried about having to learn Braille. He never once mentioned Haig, although the whole report of the divorce was in the papers. It had angered Frankie when he heard the men talk about it.

Toby stood up for Haig. 'He has to pay three hundred quid damages. So he's bought his woman; that's love for you. I bet you there isn't one of you here that would pay three hundred for your woman . . .'

'I'd give mine away for a fiver,' shouted one.

'And a hell of a lot more of you would do the same,' said Toby.

Haig's divorce had made him more popular in the firm, because the men associated divorce with the upper classes; they all said that Haig was aiming high in life.

It was remarkable what changes had taken place in the past four years. How right Simon was when he said: 'Frankie, never be afraid of the day you might never see.' He could think about this advice, but found it hard to live by it. How he had worried about Boal! Now Boal was no more; at least as far as the firm was concerned. He was lying in bed permanently, with a back that the doctors could do nothing for. He had fallen over sixty feet from a ladder. The other men never spoke of him, nor did they visit him. Turnbull was bitter about Boal:

'Many's a man he crucified. He can lie in bed now and count all the good turns he done his fellow men on the fingers of one hand. And he can pull a feather out of the tick for every bad turn he done. When one tick is plucked naked he can get another.'

It frightened Frankie to hear Turnbull talk this way about Boal. He was sorry for Boal, and he could not dismiss from his mind the thought of the ladder, the long seventy foot ladder, that swayed as Boal was climbing it, the slow, sliding, scraping noise it made as it began to leave the wall — and Boal looking right and left, and up and down, just seeing space, or below him the seats on the floor . . . then the ladder leaving the wall, and Boal jumping from it, trying to save himself, yelling with a voice that only the fear of death could force from him, and landing on the seats below on the broad of his back.

Perhaps his main reason for liking Toby so much was that he would never let him climb very high. Twenty feet was about the limit, and even then Toby made sure the ladder was firm and strong, with no spring in it. 'You weren't made for the "Flying Trapeze", Frankie,' he said. But this kindness caused Frankie to wonder whether Toby pitied him. Perhaps he said to himself, 'Frankie's useless. He can't climb any higher than a broomstick. He can't go up on a plank unless it is just about four feet from the ground. Every job can't be only four feet high. What's the use of trying to teach him anything?' Perhaps that was why Toby kept him cleaning the floors and removing paint spots from furniture, or windows.

What could be his future? In another year his term would be finished, and his chances of being kept on in the firm were slight. Other boys, he knew, had been sacked as soon as they had completed their apprenticeship. It was the policy of the firm. You might be taken back after you had gained experience elsewhere. But who was going to employ him? There were so many things he could not do. Apart from his nervousness, his height was against him. He was so very small that when he was on a plank his end had to be so much higher that it almost made it impossible for the other man to work. Yet there were times he could be proud of his stature. If, as it often happened, there was some corner which machinery or some other obstacle prevented a normal-sized man from negotiating, he was always called upon. 'A wee man comes in useful sometimes,' they would say, or, 'No matter how bad you are, you are always good at some things.' The firm might keep him on for this kind of work, but he doubted it very much. Turnbull's advice to him seemed the wisest:

'If I was you, Frankie, I would try and get into the shipyard. The work isn't hard, and above all there's no climbing to do. If you are not a neat worker, as many of us aren't, God knows, they'll put you on the type of work that doesn't call for a lot of neatness. So, when you finish your time, try and get into the shipyard. It'll be hard, for they only employ Papishes when there's no Protestants available. If you only knew some of the big bugs ... like somebody well up in the

Freemasons or the Orange order ... That's the curse of Belfast. You could be a full cousin of the Pope or a half brother of the Duke of Norfolk's or the full brother of the King of Spain — all these people are influential and powerful, but if they lived in Ulster, a farm labourer who happened to be chairman of Ballydoodle Orange Lodge would have ten times as much power as them. You see that's what you are up against. Do you know, Frankie, I once heard a man saying that when he died and went before the gates of Heaven, he would have a hell of a debate with St. Peter if he wouldn't let him into Heaven. This man maintained that he was really a martyr for his faith. He had been refused five jobs, two houses, was shot in the arm, and kicked in the guts — all because he was a Catholic. And he had ten children. If that wasn't martyrdom, he used to say, he didn't know what the blazes else it was. He maintained that Peter was done to death, and that got his trouble over quickly. But then I suppose you can't fault the Protestant for trying to get high in the Freemasons or the Orange order. In this life it's the survival of the fittest. If I happened to be a Protestant myself I'd be in every bloody order from Catch my Pal to the Girl Guides if they'd let me in ...' Turnbull laughed loudly at his own joke and repeated it ... 'Aye, even the Girl Guides if they'd let me in.'

He knew Turnbull was right. The shipyard usually employed only Protestants, but when they were busy they took on Catholics. If he could once get in and prove to them that he was willing and anxious to work well, some foreman might take a liking to him. He had heard that men in the shipyard did not kill themselves. There were tales of their sleeping or playing cards during working hours, and drawing their wages all the same. If he could, as he knew he could, refuse to play cards and loaf, he might, by applying himself constantly to his work, do well in the shipyard. It could all be so simple. It really did not matter whether you were a Catholic or not if you knew the right person. It was so hard to get to know the right person. He heard how it was done. If you went to a pub where a boss or a foreman was in the habit of going, and bought him as much drink as he wanted, he kept you right about a job. Toby said that some men fell so low as to bring the bosses to their houses to 'have a go' at their wives. Turnbull did not believe this; but Toby swore it to be true and others backed him. That surely was a terrible way to get a job, Frankie thought. It could never happen with him, he said to Toby.

'Don't worry, son,' replied Toby, 'You haven't finished with life yet. Wait until you're unemployed; no dole; no work; no bread; wait son, for the dead fire, the empty bread-bin, the "no" and the banging of the door every time you ask for a start ... Do you think you'll thole all this while your wife's five minutes under the blankets with a boss or a foreman will banish it? Not that it ever happened to me, but I know them it did. Look at Blacker's wife? Isn't her last child the spitting image of Scaldy Shankers?'

Frankie felt he would die sooner than that should happen to his wife. Supposing it were Sally ... But there was no danger of that now. She was still at the convent and there was talk of her going to the University to be a doctor. Her father was doing well. He was building houses up at the end of the Falls road. He had a motor car now and was moving into a house he was building for himself — a house much different from the others. Sally had changed. She was thinner, her skirts were longer, and the last time Frankie had seen her she was wearing glasses. She still spoke to him, asking how he was getting on at his trade. Devlin told him she could not make her mind up about anything. One time she wanted to be a nun and another time she wanted to be a doctor.

'Will you marry her?' Frankie asked him.

'Me? No. She's cut all that out. She wouldn't let me put my arms around her for anything; anyway I'm not worrying. Girls are four a penny.'

Yes, they were four a penny for Devlin. He could go to the pictures any night and pick up a girl. Frankie knew that he had the key of Mr. Blair's workshop. He told Frankie he had brought girls there and wanted him to come along some night.

His aunt had changed a little. He was giving her more money now. He was doing minor jobs at night for the neighbours, and she did not care when he missed the confraternity meetings on a Monday night if he was out earning money for her. She beat him less, but still tortured him with questions. He longed to keep some of the extra money, but was frightened to do so, because she might ask the neighbours what he had charged.

He could take no chances with his aunt. She was aware that he was slowly becoming a man. He realized that on the night he brought in a little paper parcel containing a safety razor.

'What's that for?' From the way she stared at it he knew what she was thinking. The razor, as it lay on the table, presented a strange symbol. It seemed to say, 'Here I am to shave the soft hair from Frankie's chin. He's no longer the boy you can beat with the poker, the brush, or kick . . .' The whole outfit — razor, brush and soap — had cost him a shilling. The windows were full of them, with showcards saying, 'Never again can this great gift offer be repeated.' He needed to shave; Toby had poked fun at him one day by holding out a blow torch and saying, 'Come on, and I'll burn the hair off your chin.' That she accepted the fact of his shaving was evident. She never complained when he asked for hot water; and once she put a penny in the gas slot to heat the kettle; she had even given him a cracked cup for the water. But he had to be very careful where he went at night; she was strict about the time. 'Anyone out of their house at half-past ten at night,' she said, 'could be up to no good.'

Her anxiety was caused by the fear that he might go off and get married before she reaped the harvest of his full wages as a journeyman. One night he had heard her talking to a neighbour. They were discussing Devlin, saying he was the type that would get married as soon as he had his apprenticeship served. His aunt said, 'He wouldn't do it if he was anything belonging to me. I'd see that he paid back some of the money that was spent on him.'

Huh! she could talk as she liked, Frankie had his mind made up. As soon as he had finished his time he would look about for a girl and marry her. What had his aunt spent on him? She had provided the bare necessities — not even those. At school it had been humiliation all the time for him — begging for days for a penny to buy a jotter; or twopence for a composition or drawing book, and not getting it; forced then to borrow a page from another boy; going around the class like a dog begging, begging, all the time.

'Twopence for a writing book ... Huh! Twopence buys two soda farls.' That was her whine all the time. Any money spent on school books was wasted according to her. So she could talk as much as she liked about all she had done for him. She could rant and rave about giving him 'a good home' as she called it. It was not a good home and never was. He hated it. It was a house of fear; of cruelty; of poverty; a house that never once had the peace of happiness in it. As Simon said, when he told the old man he would get married as soon as he finished his time: 'That's it, Frankie. You can't kick a dog on a Sunday and get him to lick your hand on a Monday.'

'He wouldn't do it if he was anything belonging to me,' she had said. He would let her see he would do it. He would tell her too that he did not 'belong' to her. He did not want her as an aunt. He would have been much better in an Orphanage. She could worry about his soul if she liked. He did not even know what a soul was. All he knew was that he was small and nervous, with trembling hands, and the pains of hunger and fear inside him. Simon was right when he said that she and she alone had made him what he was.

Yes, he would let her see what he would do when he finished his time and was earning tradesman's pay. . . .

If he was not learning his trade he was learning a lot of other things. At lunch time there was always a discussion of some kind. As the men sat around drinking their tea, Frankie could tell the sort of homes they came from by the way their lunches were wrapped or their sandwiches were made. Sometimes Toby would unwrap his lunch and spread it in front of him. 'Look at that,' he would say, as he pointed to the neatly-cut squares. 'That bloody daughter of mine thinks she's making sandwiches for the church bazaar. Look at them; as thin as bloody razor blades . . . And what the hell's this? Bloody fish cakes. She must think I'm like one of her cissy boy friends. Here Turnbull . . .' He would pass Turnbull a fish cake, then catching Frankie's eye, he would throw him one too. 'Those are civilized mouthfuls,' Turnbull would tell him. 'Jazes, Turnbull, you would get on well with that daughter of mine. There's a refined streak in you.' But Frankie knew that Toby was pleased and this was his way of showing off. Every day he would condemn his lunch; but he would eat it and usually finished by saying: 'Well, what there was of that lunch was tasty.'

Turnbull, on the other hand, usually kept his lunch so close to him that the ends of his coat hid it. Frankie could see that it was roughly cut, like his own. Sometimes there would be meat, usually on a Monday, but oftener there would be nothing but bread and butter. It was wrapped in newspaper; Toby's was packed in soft white paper that looked cool and fresh.

In conversation Turnbull appeared to know more than the others except when it came to sex. Toby, who in his early life worked for three years in a hospital, was able to talk fluently about all the diseases connected with sex. But Turnbull was more interesting; for he spoke of the mental cases he had seen during his spell of work in a mental home in England. Toby, when he talked about the sex diseases,

K   APP.   145

made the subject revolting; Turnbull would connect these diseases with some of the mental cases he had seen and make it interesting. There was sympathy in the way he told his stories.

Frankie found, too, that Toby was not very helpful when you asked his advice. On the question of marriage his only answer was to sing, 'I wish I had someone to sleep with, for I'm tired of sleeping my lone.' He did not seem to understand what Frankie wanted. It was not a woman to sleep with; that was a tiny part of it perhaps; the important thing was to get away from his aunt; to have a real home and enough to eat; a place where he could belong; where his fear might leave him; where he did not have to creep about mouselike; where he could live. All this was beyond Toby. He never talked about life as Turnbull did. Turnbull was always thinking about life. He said of Toby that he had it easy when he was young. His father had been a well-known contractor, but when he died Toby, who got the business, let it fall, through his own carelessness. Yet Frankie had heard Toby declare that if he had his life to live over again, it would be the same. In their songs Turnbull and he were poles apart, Toby's songs about drink and women, Turnbull's sober and sad — 'In the gloaming, O my darling'.

'Toby had the good times when he was young,' Turnbull said. 'That's why he has no regrets. He had the comforts early in life. That is the great thing. It's like training a plant; get it straightened early and when it grows up, it can stand up to whatever wind blows on it. Poverty or hard times can do you damn little harm at fifty or sixty; but get it when you are seven or eight or twelve, fourteen or sixteen and by God it leaves its mark. It tears a gap in the soul that you can never heal; it leaves its echo always there, Frankie, and the echo is fear; fear of want, of hunger, of no work, of sickness. Poverty, son, is cancer of the mind. I've known it, and I wouldn't wish it on my worst enemy.'

Frankie asked whether he had ever met Toby's wife.

146

'Of course I have. A fine woman; a woman of breeding. Toby broke the poor woman's heart with his boozing about. When he lost the business, she set to and opened a home bakery. That's why you see Toby with so many fancy things for his lunch. His wife's a great woman. She would have been on top of the world if he had given her half a chance. But it doesn't worry her. She thinks there's nobody like Toby. He calls her his oul' cigar. Toby could chuck working if he wanted to. But he's happy. I don't know of any happier man in the world than Toby. Nothing worries him.'

Frankie could picture Toby's wife. He could picture Toby slapping her on the back as he did with others and shouting, 'Well, and how's my "oul' cigar" the night?'

'As far as I know,' Turnbull went on, 'Toby always played fair with her. He was never one for other women, though you mightn't think that from his talk. It's never the dog that barks the loudest will bite. I've been in England and Scotland with Toby; been in the same digs with him often, and never once, not even in the pubs where the women were like flies, never once has Toby looked at another woman. I suppose his wife knows that. That's one thing about women, Frankie; they'll stand for a hell of a lot of drinking and gambling, but not for the other women. Always remember that, son. When you're married, shoot straight as far as other women are concerned; give them a wide berth.'

This was the opening Frankie wanted. Turnbull was the right man to advise him about marriage.

'Do you think a man should marry young?' he stammered out.

'It all depends. If you are restless and want to see a bit of the world, a wife can be cumbersome; and unless she's a bit of a rover herself she'll nag you blue in the face about settling down in one place and trying to get a home together. All women are great birds for building the nest. I suppose you can't blame them. But if you are the settling type, get married as young as you can and your children will be man and woman big while you are still young yourself. But it's hard to advise anyone about marriage. You meet a girl and you think there's nobody else in the world like her, and you marry her; it all looks so simple, and yet, Frankie, it's not. I suppose you would laugh if I told you my story.'

Frankie shook his head.

'Well, son, I wasn't rich enough to afford the luxury of love. When I was twenty-four or five, I used to frequent a pub in North Street. I met a woman there. It got to the stage when I would buy her a drink and she would buy me one in return. I had great affection for her. I took her to the pictures, but after the show she always wanted a drink. She was a whisky drinker — too fond of it. I let her go — I knew if I married her I could never get her off the habit of drinking whisky. I, son, couldn't afford a wife like that. But she still sticks in this old grey head of mine, and if I live to be a hundred she'll still be there. I suppose the right thing for me to have done would have been to go ahead and marry her; but my own mother, God be good to the woman, was fond of her whisky, and I knew too much unhappiness to inflict it on any children that I might have had. So I married another. A good woman, son, that tries to make one shilling do the work of three. She's good and kind and all that, but I haven't the same liking for her as I had for the other woman.'

Turnbull stopped suddenly, pursed his lips and looked up into the sky. 'But who knows, if I had got the first woman there might have been some other yearning in me ... Sometimes, Frankie, I think we have lived in another world and that we have died, and this world as we know it is the Purgatory we are told about. Look at the handicaps we have. Look at mine: a daughter twenty-two years of age useless with sleepy sickness. We can do nothing for her, and what worries me is what will happen to her when the wife and I are gone. I suppose the other three daughters will

148

look after her; I hope they do. They say that blood is thicker than water; that's all right where there are no encumbrances to thin the blood.' Turnbull shook his head and took his pipe from his pocket. 'You must come up some night and see us,' he said, in brighter tones. 'Why not tomorrow night?'

2   TURNBULL'S HOUSE was like his own. Two rooms upstairs, a kitchen and a wee room just off it. Turnbull appeared not to belong to the house at all. He looked about him for a seat, and finally sat down on the edge of the table. His wife was a small woman with a great mop of uncombed hair. Her eyes were large and her face very white except for the daubs of red on her cheeks. His daughter lay on the sofa, her eyes closed. She reminded Frankie of a dummy that had been left lying in a window awaiting dressing in the morning. The only signs of life were her outstretched, shaking hands. A younger daughter came in, and pushing her sister's feet nearer to the back of the sofa, sat down beside her.

'This is my second eldest daughter, Selina,' Turnbull said. She reached out a soft, oily hand, and Frankie guessed that she worked in a linen mill. Her face had already soaked in the oil of her calling and made her skin swarthy.

'There she is,' said the mother, 'a big lump of a girl of fifteen, and she can't settle to anything.'

'Now, now, give her a chance,' said Turnbull. 'Dammit, she's not the oldest woman in the world. And she's doing bravely in the mill, aren't you, Selina?' Twisting her hands, she looked up shyly to meet her father's eyes.

'That's it,' said her mother, 'butter her up with plenty of soft soap. This man would spoil all the children in Creation.'

'No matter, she'll make a good wee wife for some man.'

'Aye,' laughed her mother, 'the first thing her husband will

149

need to do is buy her a good loud alarm clock. She must be one of the Seven Sleepers that's mentioned in the Bible.'

It dawned on Frankie that Turnbull had perhaps brought him to the house to meet this daughter. But he could never fall in love with this girl. He looked at her — at the thin hair, untidy like her mother's, the oily hands, and the dirty finger nails. Then he looked at his own hands. They were not so clean. It was his work that made them dirty... Well, it was *her* work that made hers dirty. He imagined her with her hands clean, but it made little difference; he did not like her face, nor her drooping shoulders. Yet, she could no more help her drooping shoulders than he could his smallness. Perhaps her work, bending over the loom, was the cause of her stoop. It was not *his* work that made him small.

Tea was served; but no one took any notice of the girl on the sofa.

'Don't be a stranger now that you have broken the ice,' Turnbull said. 'Come up any time you like and see us.' Frankie eyed Selina as she sat breaking a bun and transferring bits of it to her mouth. No, she was not the sort of girl for him.

'I hope we get this big convent job, Frankie. It'll last months.'

'Do you think you'll get it?' his wife asked eagerly.

'I hope so. The nuns like a good job; they pay for a good job, and I think the architect is kindly disposed to St. Clair's.'

'It would be great if they did get it. It would mean work all through the winter,' she said.

'Aye, it sure would, and inside all the time. If they get it we shall be all right, Frankie; they'll need all the Papishes they have for it. The nuns can be sticklers for a good job. It would be better for all tradesmen if there were more like them. They don't do things by halves. You'll see what I mean if we get this job.'

The girl on the sofa cried out, a strange sound as if she

were falling down a cliff or into a fire. Frankie stopped eating. No one took the slightest notice, and Selina asked if he would like another bun.

'Don't ask him,' said her father, 'hasn't he two hands of his own and can't he reach for anything he wants. Isn't that right, Frankie?'

He mumbled a reply. He was filled with curiosity. He wanted to turn to the girl on the sofa to see what had happened to her. Again she cried out, but no notice was taken. Mrs. Turnbull asked him if his tea was sweet enough.

He recalled the conversation in the pub when he had first started to work, Toby asking Turnbull if they could not get a wheel chair for his daughter, and Turnbull replying that they would have to pay to garage it; there was no space in the house for it. He looked at the front door; there was barely enough room to let a normal human through it. He remembered, too, this was the girl Turnbull carried to the first house of the pictures every Saturday night. But could she follow what was going on at the pictures? Mrs. Turnbull filled a large mug with tea; then she broke a bun into it, and stirred until the pieces floated sodden on the top.

'Give her that, will you?' She addressed her husband.

Turnbull lifted the girl's head and pushed a cushion behind it. The girl appeared to be unconscious of what he was doing as he coaxed her to open her mouth. With half a spoonful of the sodden food he tried to part her lips, still urging her to open them. Frankie heard the spoon against her teeth. He felt that he ought not to be watching. 'I don't suppose she's very hungry,' said the mother, 'she had a good plateful of stew at tea-time.' The girl now kept her mouth open, and her father once or twice had to touch her throat gently with his finger to get her to swallow the food.

Mrs. Turnbull, sensing Frankie's embarrassment, asked: 'Do you like the painting trade?' Before he could answer Selina cut in with: 'It's no catch the painting trade. There's never no work at it during the winter.'

'You're right there,' agreed her mother.

'I haven't done that badly out of it,' Turnbull said, half apologetically.

'Aye, you have. Working five months out of the twelve, the other seven on the dole.'

'I wouldn't marry a painter if he was the last man on the earth,' Selina added.

'It's manners to wait until you're asked. You might be glad to marry a painter if you can get nobody else. There's a wee man sitting in front of you, and you could do worse than string along with him . . .' Turnbull turned to the other girl and went on coaxing her to eat. Frankie wanted to get away from the house. Like his own, there was a smell of poverty about it; a depressing house made worse by the girl stretched on the sofa being coaxed to swallow her food like a two-year-old child. If he married Selina — he could never do that — but if he did, he would have this girl for his sister-in-law . . . No, he did not like the house. Selina would never be asked by a painter and he doubted if ever by anyone else. No wonder Turnbull's thoughts went back to the woman he had met in the pub. This little woman his wife, with the mop of hair and the careless shoes with no heels on them — it was her fault that Turnbull always talked about 'Life'. At the mention of the convent job she had been all ears. So had Selina. God, no! He could never marry Selina. He liked Turnbull and would do almost anything for him, but not marry his daughter. He wanted a girl who had come from a clean home, not from a dark and dismal home like this.

Turnbull had now finished feeding the girl; he took a khaki-coloured handkerchief from his pocket and wiped her lips. She made no sound. Frankie stared at the trembling figure. Her red-rimmed eyes were closed and the flesh of her neck looked tightened and strained, with a great swollen blue vein pulsing quickly. Her stockings were ill-fitting and the heel of one curled over the back of her shoe. Her coat was fastened round her waist with a leather belt. Turnbull seemed to be the only one who took any notice of her. He was aware of her all the time. Selina and her mother went about the kitchen heedless of her presence. Before he left her, Turnbull felt her brow and gave her white cheek an affectionate little pat, then he shook his head resignedly. Perhaps she was the reason why Turnbull worried so much. She was always there, a constant reminder of nature's cruelty every time he carried her up the stairs, or down the stairs, or to the pictures, every time he fed her spoonfuls of sodden food from the mug. He could not even look forward to death, because of worrying what might happen to her. Selina would never worry about her — at least that was what Frankie judged from the way she went about the kitchen. He looked at the clock.

'She's five or ten minutes fast,' Turnbull said. His wife corrected him. 'She's right now. I put her right by the Angelus bell the night.'

Frankie stood up. He thanked Mrs. Turnbull for the tea, and said good night to Selina, for a moment he looked across at the girl on the sofa.

'No use bidding her good night or good day for that matter. She's not in this world at all,' said the mother. Selina reached out her soft oily hand. 'Good night.'

'I'll come as far as the tram with you,' Turnbull said, reaching to the chair for his cap. He turned to his wife. 'I'll be back as soon as I leave Frankie to his tram.'

'You will, I'm sure. You'll finish up by walking the shoes off your feet up the mountains. Don't let him trail you away up the mountain, son, for a walk as he calls it.'

'No danger of me dandering up the mountain tonight. I'm tired.' When they were away from the door, Turnbull said: 'She's always at me about the long walks I take. I like walking. I like looking at the mountains and the sky and the stars or a flock of birds or a tree. I could sit for hours and watch a stream running over stones. It's strange, Frankie, but I never tire of looking at the things God made. Buildings and ships and things have no interest for me; it's only the things that God makes has anything to them. I hear all the rant about these wonderful pictures they make, and as you know I take the daughter to the first house every Saturday, but it's a sore waste of time. Whether she gets any fun out of them, I don't know. When she was a child she was fond of them, so I kept up the habit. If I stopped taking her, I should have the feeling that she might be missing something. I often think it would be better for her if I could take her out into the country, but I could never carry her there; that's where one of them wheel chairs would be useful. But where could we keep it?'

After a pause, Turnbull went on: 'It's tragic you know, Frankie. If you had seen that girl when she was about fourteen or fifteen — a real picture she was; and, do you know, that came on her just like a flash. Sometimes I look at a tree in the winter and it is so bare and naked looking; and then I go back in the summer and see it in full life, and it delights me. I think too, of her; when she was, as I say, fourteen or fifteen. It may be silly of me, but I have faith. In summer, when the tree is rich and full-blooded again, I think that's what will happen to her, that she'll recover and get back her fullness of life.' Turnbull looked to the sky. 'There's the Plough up there, just between those two chimneys. You can see the Milky Way from the mountains. But there's your tram now, better hurry . . .'

Frankie ran, and from the bottom step of the tram called a loud good night to Turnbull. He looked through the window, Turnbull had not turned homewards, but was walking firmly up the road towards the mountains. He had dreaded the walk from the house to the tram. Turnbull might have asked him what he thought about Selina, and it would have been hard to refuse him anything. If Turnbull had said, 'There is Selina, she is a good little girl and I could fix it for her to be your wife; what do you say?' how hard it would have been for him to refuse. His thoughts about trees and his hope that his daughter might be cured of the sleepy sickness — there was a great sadness about Turnbull that was almost lovable. You could never imagine any different. The other men could call him 'Crying Annie', but Toby always had a kind word for him. Toby maintained that Turnbull was no 'sponger', and Frankie had discovered that that was one of the highest compliments that one workman could pay another.

What a perfect man, Frankie thought, could be made if you picked the things you liked and admired in other people. He himself would pick the height, the face, the manners of Haig; the robust and laughing manner of Toby, with his fearlessness; the gentleness and a little of the sadness of Turnbull, and his habit of looking at a naked tree or a stream laughing over the mountain stones. But he had to remain Frankie, and he recalled the rhyme from his school book about the discontented little pine tree:

> Change no more but thankful be,
> For what you are, dear little tree,
> For one, for all; what's sent is best,
> Needles for you, leaves for the rest.

He alighted from the tramcar and hurried home. His aunt was at the fire.

'Where were you?'

'I was up with Mr. Turnbull.'

'Are you sure?'

'Yes, he lives at . . .' He tried to stutter out the name of the street. She cut him short with, 'Never mind, never mind. There's a letter for you.' She flung the envelope to the table, its mouth open, its lips ragged. He read: 'Please report to the office in the morning and bring clean overalls with you.'

'Clean overalls!' she complained. 'Where am I to get clean overalls for you in the middle of the week? A nice time for them to tell you to fetch clean overalls. There's no drying of clothes this weather at all.'

He made no answer. If they wanted him to bring clean overalls, he must bring them and that was that, no matter how she talked, he would have to get them.

'What do they want clean overalls for in the middle of the week? Can you tell me that?'

'It's because I'm going to work in a convent.' He knew he had told the right lie. Anything connected with religion was always sure to silence her objections. He saw her put the smoothing iron in the heart of the fire, then she cleared the table and spread the grey cloth she used when ironing. He might be right about the convent job, for it was unusual of the firm to give such instructions.

He lay quiet in his bed, his feet touching the cold iron that pressed against the mattress. He was aware of the hardness of the tick. For a shilling a week he could have a soft bed — that was what the furniture man had told him. A shilling a week! The price of one packet of cigarettes. A shilling a week for a decent wardrobe, and a shilling a week for a sofa or a couch that you could stretch yourself on in front of a fire; your own fire. He was suddenly excited. How easy it was! Three shillings a week for all this.

The girl, that was his problem. Surely in this big city there was some girl; one perhaps like himself, lonely and wanting to get away from a jail house. He knew of servant girls shut up night after night in attics . . . One night free in the week . . . Girls from country places, lonely and afraid. Yet, there was never one of them he could have interested himself in. People seemed to despise servant girls; 'slaveys' they called them. So many of them were decent and kind. They would give you tea and want you to talk to them. He saw the books and magazines they read. Stories about Maria Martin, and other tales of girls with hidden secrets. Stories about buried babies. It was a favourite topic with Turnbull, when they worked together in some house. He would talk to the servant girl; find out all about her; if she was new to Belfast he would warn her against going down certain streets or to certain picture houses. He appeared to regard them as his own daughters. 'They're looked down on,' he said, 'but if some of those who despise them had only the wit to know it they would make better wives for them than the clarts they set up on pedestals.'

He was annoyed when a workman named Collins had brought in a bundle of letters. He had put an advertisement in the newspaper: 'Lone gentleman, tradesman, would like to meet attractive and homely girl; view matrimony.' Most of the replies were from servant girls but one was from a woman who said she was thirty-nine years of age and had eight hundred pounds as well as owning four houses. Collins maintained that if she admitted to thirty-nine years of age, you could bet your life she was on the borders of forty-five.

Frankie thought about this woman. Would she be like his aunt? Not in manner, but in appearance? She could not be good-looking if she had so much money and was not married. This surely was not a good way to meet the woman you wanted to marry. Collins had picked out one letter, saying he would answer it just for fun, that he would tell the dame he would meet her at the Albert Memorial and that he would wear a red flower in his buttonhole.

Yes, Collins could do that. But Frankie knew that he himself could not. Supposing he did put an advertisement in the paper: what would the girl think when she saw him, small as a bantam, waiting for her, and then heard him trying to talk to her? No, he could not do that. But where would he ever meet a girl to be his wife. How, when or where would it happen? It would happen. Everyone else was more confident than he was himself. Turnbull often told him, 'Wait until you are married, Frankie,' and Toby would say, 'Wait until you have a woman to look after you.' He could go to a dance hall and get a girl there, but girls

frequenting dance halls did not make good wives. Again
he thought of the woman with eight hundred pounds and
four houses. Could you be happy with a woman like that?
You would not have to worry about work, nor about a house.
Yet Collins was not interested; he tore up the letter, and that
was the end of the matter.

3   'LOOK AT THE RESPECT I have for the
     Papishes,' said Toby with a laugh. 'Turning
     up in the middle of the week with overalls as
white as a dollar on a nigger's arse.' The convent job was
to start that morning. Frankie sat in the lorry with Toby and
Collins.

'You'll finish your time on this job, Frankie,' Toby said.
'I can't wait for the night that you'll get your first pay.
We'll all be drunk that night.' He saw Toby nudge Collins
and wink. 'Is Turnbull not coming to this job?' he asked
Collins.

'I'm sure he will. The job isn't ready yet for a full squad;
we three are just going to get things ready.'

'You taking charge of it?' Toby asked. Collins nodded.

'Congratulations,' Toby said.

'This is my first charge, I'm a bit nervous.'

'You'll be all right,' Toby assured him.

The convent was about half a mile from the main road.
It stood at the top of a long avenue lined with trees, laurel
and rhododendron bushes. Turnbull will have all the trees
he wants here, thought Frankie. The trees were bare,
leafless and black, with great streaks of damp on them.
Birds' nests, long since deserted and desolate, looked like
ragged warts in their oxters.

'These places have the dough,' Toby said. 'That's the
only racket there's any money in — religion. Start up a new
religion and you're on Easy Street.'

158

'Sure thing if it catches on,' added Collins. At the back of the convent they unloaded the lorry. Already there were plasterers, plumbers and carpenters on the job. Toby stood back, looking at the windowless spaces in the walls, the bricks missing here and there. 'Jazes, this is gonna be a cold spot to work in. No windows in it yet.'

'We're all right,' said Collins. 'We are not starting the new wing just yet. We're in the old wing — in the kitchen apamments.'

'Aye, down in the soot, is that it?' Toby pretended to be angry.

'O.K. If you like I'll start you in the new wing, where you'll get all the draughts. . . .'

'No, I'll go down to the kitchen apartments. Frankie coming with me?'

Collins nodded. 'And listen, Toby,' he spoke quietly, 'put a brake on the swearing. And if you sing, let's have no "Old maid's serenade to the soldier".'

Toby eyed him with good-humoured disapproval. 'Right. I'll watch my talk and if I sing, it'll be "Oh, God our help in ages past". Will that do?'

Collins led them to the kitchen apartments. As they walked almost on tiptoe along the quiet passages, nuns passed them with bent heads and flowing black skirts almost sweeping the floor. Toby had removed his cap, and seeing him bareheaded for the first time nearly made Frankie laugh out loud. His hair was uncombed and he looked stupid; a different Toby. The loud, confident, bluff Toby had vanished. He had now a silly, gawky and almost half-witted appearance. The light caught the upper part of his fat jaws and the tails of hair that were now curving down his brow.

As soon as Collins had pointed out their particular job and they had arranged the tools, Toby said, 'Close that door, Frankie, till we get a breather.' Toby sat on an upturned bucket, and, taking his cap from his pocket, rubbed his brow with the inside of it before clapping it on his head. 'Tell me, Frankie, do you know your way about these convents? Do you have to go about all the time bareheaded? Does the religion demand that?'

'It's my first time ever in a convent,' he stammered.

'Jazes!' Suddenly Toby took in a great breath. Lowering his voice, he said: 'They can't expect us to scrape the muck off this ceiling and not cover our heads. We'll keep the thatch covered, and if anybody objects we'll show them the ceiling. Another thing, Frankie, how do you address these nuns?'

Again Frankie did not know. 'Jazes!' Another great intake of breath and lowering of the voice: 'Are you a Papist at all, Frankie?' The boy remained silent. 'During the war when I was in hospital in France we had nuns, and we called them Sister, but they were nurses. Do these ones just pray all the time?' Still Frankie did not know, and again he pleaded it was his first time in a convent.

'There's no point in worrying. They'll hardly be trucking with small fry like us. If there's any talking to be done, Collins will do it. Still, if one of them bid you time of day, you'd be happier if you could answer her properly. I'll blow out and sound Collins about it.' Toby left and Frankie looked around the apartment. It was a sort of relief kitchen. There was a range but no fire, three windows opposite and another door in the same wall as the range. The sound of laughter came from somewhere. He tiptoed over to the door and listened. He heard a voice say: 'There now, take your kettle away it's boiling.' And another voice said: 'God! There's no water left on these eggs.' Then there was laughter, louder than before, and suddenly a silence, followed by an uneven chorus of voices: 'Yes, Sister. The kettle's just ready. The eggs are finished now.'

'Well, set to about your work, and don't waste your time giggling like a lot of three year olds.'

Frankie knew this was a nun's voice. The other door

opened and Toby entered. 'Well, I've found out how to address them. If we're in contact with them we call them sister.'

Having arranged the planks and the stepladders, Toby started to scrape the ceiling, and gave Frankie the job of washing the lower parts of the walls.

'Where do we get the water?' he asked. 'Knock on that door,' said Toby, 'there seems to be some life on the other side of it.' The door was opened by a nun. She pointed across the kitchen. 'There are the taps, hot and cold water, as you like.' Her eyes looked hard and cruel. Her mouth pursed impatiently. She turned and left the kitchen. It was a huge apartment with four gas stoves and two ranges. Near the sink two girls were cutting vegetables. They turned to look at him. He went to the sink and one of the girls lifted a basin, making room for his bucket. She was a pleasant little girl, not much taller than himself. Her companion giggled, and looked at Frankie as if the other girl's removing the basin meant something more than just leaving room in the sink for his bucket. He turned the tap, glancing at the girl. She was smiling — a smile that lit up her whole face, her eyes, her lips, her teeth. It was a smile that coaxed conversation. But all he could do was smile back at her. She bent her head and went on cutting the dark green cabbage.

'Your bucket is flowing over?' she said. He liked her voice. The overflowing bucket could not take his eyes from her hair. It was soft, and rose in little waves. The edges of the waves were golden.

'Have you never those vegetables prepared yet?' The voice came from behind him. He tightened the tap and lifted the bucket from the sink. As he turned to go, he saw a nun approach the girls. She wore a blue apron over her black skirt. Her walk quiet — her shoes had rubber heels. She asked the girls if they had fallen asleep; and they answered her in confused and nervous tones. When he got to the door, he turned to look at the smaller girl. She was neat-looking, unlike her companion, whose wide shoes were so unshapely as to give the impression that she was knock-kneed.

'What's in there?' Toby asked.

'The kitchen.'

'Is it full of nuns?'

'No. There are two girls cutting vegetables.' Toby got down from the plank and lamented about the soot on the ceiling. 'This is a nice how do you do. Telling us to bring clean overalls to this kip! Look at me already — like a bloody chimney sweep.' He spat in anger, but once up on the plank again he started singing. Toby could never work without singing. This time he sang 'The shade of the old apple tree'. His version was: 'As I laid her down on the grass, and I put my hands on her arse . . .' But he stopped dead when the door opened and a nun entered. She looked up at Toby and smiled.

'I like to hear men singing,' she said. 'It shows they are happy at their work.'

'Thank you, Sister,' Toby called down. 'There's nothing beats a bit of song.'

'You've certainly got a dirty job there. We had a fire, you know, and everything's as black as tar.'

'We'll soon clean it for you, Sister,' Toby said, getting down from the plank.

'My goodness, look at your hands,' she said with concern.

'Honest work, Sister,' laughed Toby.

'It takes a dirty hand to make a clean hearth stone,' she said and left.

'She can't have heard what I was singing.' Frankie laughed. 'She looks a happy old woman that.'

Frankie had never heard nuns referred to as old women before. Now that he thought about it, Toby was right, she was an old woman.

'Would she be a forewoman or a charge hand?' he asked.

He climbed to the plank again and started singing, the 'Holy City'. Just as taking off his cap made him look different, so his singing of the 'Holy City' made him sound different. He was singing now as if he were in a church or at a service: 'I stood in old Jerusalem, beside the Temple there . . .' He broke off. 'Ach! there's neither life or love in that song.' He changed it to a parody of 'The man who broke the bank in Monte Carlo!' Now he was enjoying himself, scraping the ceiling, keeping time to his singing. Sooty flakes of plaster were flying everywhere. Frankie moved his bucket to the door that led to the kitchen. He started washing the door, which meant he had to open it. The little girl was standing by the fire stirring a pot. A man, who looked like a plasterer's labourer, entered with a four-quart can which he put on the fire. Standing close to the girl he put his arm playfully around her. She pushed his arm away.

'Don't,' she said, 'the fusilier's knocking about.' The man persisted, and the girl, withdrawing the wooden spoon from the pot threatened him with it, but Frankie noticed that when she turned to the pot again there was a smile on her face. The man went to the door, looked into the passageway, and came back to the girl, trying once more to put his arm around her.

'I don't want a second-hand man's arm about me,' she said.

'What do you mean?'

'You're a married man. If I can't get the arms of a single man around me, I'll do without any,' she said, but all the time smiling.

'A married man has more experience.' He laughed.

'What would your wife say if she knew?'

'What she doesn't know doesn't do her any harm.' Another man came in, also with a big tea can. He too tried to put his arm around the girl.

'And how's my wee love Isabel today?'

163

'Isabel's well enough and she can do without the arms of either of you two about her.'

'Any sugar, love?' he asked.

'You're always begging. If it isn't you wanting sugar, it's him wanting milk. Keep an eye to the passage and see there's no nuns about.'

She hurried to a press, and filling a cup half full of sugar emptied it into the tea can.

'Do the same for me, love,' said the other man. She complained as she walked to the press: 'Such men for begging,' but she was smiling all the time. 'I suppose the painters will be begging sugar too.' She looked towards Frankie. 'You'll be looking for sugar too. The only men who look after themselves are the plumbers. These two lads here are borrowing for the plasterers and the bricklayers.'

'What about the bricklayers?' a red-headed man asked as he entered the kitchen.

'Oh, it's you, trouble?' The red-headed man came to the fire with a kettle.

'I'm not looking for sugar the day, but have you any milk?'

'Keep a lookout in the passageway,' she said, going to the press and returning with a jug of milk.

'What did you do with yourself last night?' the ginger-haired man asked.

'She was to come out with me,' said the plasterer's labourer.

'Well, if I won't go out with Ginger here, who's a single man, I'll hardly be seen with you. You're second-hand, and I don't want a second-hand man.'

The plasterer's labourer eyed her good-naturedly. He shook his head slowly: 'Why didn't I meet you before I met my wife?' He took his can from the range and left the kitchen.

'Go on, Ginger, you've got your milk, hop it.' Ginger lifted his can and held it playfully in front of her: 'Smile in it and sweeten it.' She made to swipe at the can but he was gone through the door laughing loudly.

'You take yourself off, too,' she told the third man.

'It's very cold outside. I'd rather stay in here with you.' This man called across to Frankie, 'Don't let this girl break your heart. She has every man on the job after her.'

'Go on. On your way.' She smiled and returned to the vegetables. She was not like the usual run of servant girl, Frankie decided. He compared her ·with Turnbull's daughter. This girl was neat and tidy. Her stockings were good, so were her shoes. She was wearing a blue skirt and cream blouse. You could not apply this awful word 'skivvy' to her.

The nun in the blue apron came into the kitchen. 'Never the vegetables ready yet, Isabel?'

'I haven't four hands, Sister; I've only two and they've been doing other things as well as trying to get these vegetables ready.'

'What else have they been doing?'

'The workmen came in and I had to make the fire ready for their tea.'

'Why can't the workmen have their tea made outside? Haven't they got fires outside?'

'Mother Superior gave orders in the kitchen a long time ago that the men were to have their cans boiled on the range. I was to give them milk and sugar if they wanted it, and if they were short of bread I was to make them some sandwiches.' Without a word the nun left the kitchen. 'That'll let her know where she stands,' said the girl, with a wink to Frankie. 'She's only a lay sister but she has more airs and graces and gives more orders than Reverend Mother.'

He admired her independence. There was a great cockiness in the way she put the basin of vegetables on the range and started transferring them slowly to the boiling pot. 'Doesn't do to let Sister get away with anything,' she continued. 'She'd have you running round in circles.'

The other girl now entered the kitchen. 'What did you say to Sister, Isabel? She came upstairs as cross as two sticks, and sent me down to give you a hand with the vegetables.'

'You needn't bother helping me with the vegetables. As you can see, I'm putting them into the pot now. I just told Sister all I had to do. She thinks I've got half a dozen hands on me. I reminded her that I've only two.'

'Did you tell her that?'

'I did.'

'She'll report you.'

'I don't care whether she does or not. This isn't the only place in the world. I've two hands and a head on me and a tongue to ask for a job elsewhere, as well as eyes to look for it and feet to search for it.'

Frankie saw that the other girl was nervous. She kept turning her head in the direction of the door, and suddenly darted out of it.

'Are you eyeing the young nuns?' It was Toby's voice. Frankie closed the door. 'They're not young nuns,' he said.

'I thought they might have been apprentices,' Toby said with a laugh. 'What are they then, skivvys?'

Frankie disliked Toby referring to Isabel as a skivvy. He did not mind on the other girl's account, because she was clumsy and awkward-looking, her knees appearing to fall in to each other. She was taller than he was; much taller than Isabel, too. If she straightened up she might be better built than he was. He had no right to feel that way about her. She could easily feel the same about him: 'Look at you, two hands higher than a duck, and can't open your mouth to say three words the proper way.' He had no right to be so critical. Isabel was different. She was not afraid to give a back answer to the lay sister. And she was not telling lies when she said she could get a job elsewhere. She looked like an office girl or a schoolteacher.

When he went for the tea he would get to know her better. Toby had told him once that some girls liked to be

166

made a fuss of, while others did not like fuss at all; they liked to know a boy a while before they would even go to the pictures with him. Others just jumped at the chance, but they could cool as quickly as they had warmed.

He would ask her about making the tea, knowing well he would stutter in doing so; but he would watch and see whether she laughed at him. Some people were amused by his efforts at talking. Hudson, the van man, a little pointed man with a face like a rat, had laughed loudly at him when he tried to give him a message for the office. Was it such a dreadful thing, this stuttering or stammering, or whatever you like to call it? He had once met an apprentice plumber with a hare lip; his talk did not come from his mouth but from his nose. He had also met an apprentice carpenter with a great mark covering his cheek, like a map of Africa and the colour of bright red ink. Stammering was not so bad as these things.

He looked at the ceiling where Toby worked and sang:

> Who were you with last night,
> Under the pale moonlight?
> It wasn't your sister, it wasn't your ma;
> Ah, ha, ha, ha, ha-ha, ah-ha!

Isabel was pretty, and, unlike Sally, she was within his reach if he thought of asking her to the pictures. It was pleasant to think about her, to imagine meeting her, putting his arms around her, kissing her.

Collins entered. 'What about some tea? I see all the others gorging themselves. We might as well have some.'

'A good idea,' Toby said, getting down from the plank. 'Hop it in there, Frankie, and see if you can fix it.'

She was there alone, standing at the range with her hand on the lid of the soup pot.

'I suppose you're after tea now?' He laughed. 'I never saw such men for tea. They say that women are fond of tea, but I've discovered that men are fonder.'

He came close to the fire and looked over her shoulder. Yes, she was just about his height.

'How many are there?' She walked from the fire and he called, 'Three' after her.

He looked at her feet. Her shoes were flat-heeled. If she wore high-heeled shoes, they would make a difference to her height. He knew the change they made on his aunt when she wore them.

When they finished the tea, Collins informed them their next job was in the kitchen. Frankie, returning the cups was to tell whoever was in the kitchen, to move out of the way anything that might get stained. There were a few pictures on the walls and one or two calendars. A pile of tablecloths stood on the top of the press, and there was a clothes line with a few glass cloths drying.

'We're coming to work in the kitchen,' he said, this time stammering badly. He saw her stare wide-eyed at him. No smile on her lips or in her eyes. She helped him out, by pointing to the tablecloths and following his eyes to the pictures.

'Right,' she said, 'I'll clear all these things away for you.'

'I can help you.'

'Well, if you like, you can see to the pictures. I'll show you where to put them.' He took down two of the pictures. 'Stick them in here for the time being,' she said. He followed her along the passageway and into a room where on a long table stood a cooked chicken and a roast of meat. He eyed the food before he laid the pictures down. Reaching to the veiled roast of meat, she uncovered it and lifted a small piece, and ate it. 'Would you like a bit?' Before he answered, she had lifted a slice on a knife and held it to him. He hesitated. 'Go on, take it in your hand. Your fingers were made before knives and forks.' The meat was delicious; as he ate it she looked into the passage. 'Just making sure the coast was clear. I'm very fond of meat. It's bad for me, makes me too fat.'

'You're not fat,' he said, having a little trouble with the last word. She looked at him, still with no trace of a smile, but with an expression that told him she was curious, as if she wanted to know why he stammered.

Toby came into the kitchen with a step-ladder. 'Tell an ould heathen, and set my mind at rest, are you a young nun?' She burst out laughing. Frankie saw her white teeth.

'I'm not a young nun. What made you think that?'

'I dunno, but sometimes, daughter, I curse a wee bit you know, I let an odd switcher out of me. Like, if I caught my hand on a nail or if I bumped my head against something, I'm apt, as I say, to let the odd switcher out of me.'

'Curse away as much as you like, I don't care, though I don't suppose the nuns would like it.' Again she laughed, bending her head and slapping her knees. 'That's the best I've heard for a long time; you thinking I was a young nun.' Toby joined in the laughter and smacked her back lightly with his palm.

The thin girl entered the kitchen, and Isabel, after glancing up the passageway, told her what Toby had said. 'A young nun? You don't know her!' said the other girl to Toby.

'Curse away as much as you like,' was what she had said. That showed she was not over-religious. During the afternoon she would look at Toby and laugh. When he left the kitchen she asked Frankie, 'What's his name?'

'Toby.'

'I like him best of all the workmen I've met here.' When he came back she said boldly, 'Hello, Toby.' He bent over her and whispered loudly: 'I'd like to take you to the pictures, but I think you're a bit on the old side for me. Besides, my mother wouldn't let me; she doesn't like me talking to strange girls.' She thought this a great joke, too, and answered: 'Sure your mother wouldn't know. . . .'

'She would. Frankie here would tell her,' Toby chuckled as he climbed to the plank.

Frankie could not sleep that night. How could he ask her out? It was too soon. Better wait until he had been here a week; perhaps a fortnight or three weeks. Toby could help him. She liked Toby. Pity that Toby was so hard to talk to about girls. If Toby had only been as concerned with 'life' as Turnbull was! But then he would not have been the laughing, outspoken, fat man he was. Still, if he said: 'Look, Toby, I like this girl and I'd like her to be my girl to meet me every night, to keep me company and cure the cold, lonely feeling that is inside me,' he might go to her and say: 'Listen, Isabel, Frankie has a notion to ask you out. Would you come to the pictures with him some night?' 'Putting in a word' could mean a lot. The 'putter-in' could say so much more about you than you could yourself. . . He would wait, then, until he got Toby in a proper mood. Perhaps some day when he was praising her or when they shared a laugh together, he could say: 'Toby, I like Isabel. I would like her for my girl. Would you ask her to come out with me?'

He could dress up to meet her. His suit was not too bad, nor were his shoes, but the shirts his aunt washed looked neither clean nor dirty and the collars were limp. He liked a fresh collar, not too stiff, but firm and clean, like the collars Collins wore. His aunt was always complaining about washing his things. Why couldn't she send them to the laundry? Just another few months and he would be away from her. He saw himself in his new world, decently dressed . . . If he asked Isabel to the pictures he must have an overcoat — he could not appear in his thin canvas-like grey waterproof. A good overcoat could make such a difference — broaden your shoulders, make people say you were on the 'up and up'. He remembered what Simon had told him of the kick he was going to get out of life by buying the simple things. Maybe it was pride to think about clothes, but surely God could hardly be annoyed nor blacken his soul with sin because he longed to see himself in a heavy, grey overcoat. He could get one at so-much a week. So-much a week — in a month's time he could order a suit. Sometimes there were Sales and you could get two pairs of trousers if you ordered a suit . . . He drowsed in the vision of himself wearing his new overcoat, walking arm-in-arm with Isabel to the pictures.

Turnbull was on the job when he arrived the following morning. Frankie had never seen him looking so fresh and clean. Toby said he was like an ice cream man. 'We'll soon take the whiteness out of him,' he said as Turnbull followed them into the kitchen. But the dust and soot did not worry Turnbull. He told Toby that if there was no dust and soot there would be little call for painters. They were working now in the kitchen proper. Toby and Turnbull prepared the ceiling and the upper part of the walls; Frankie was left to prepare the doors and windows. The plasterer's labourer came in. 'Any of the dames here yet?' he asked.

'Haven't seen any of them this morning,' Toby answered.

'They mustn't be back from Mass yet,' he said, hurrying out again.

'Do they go to service in the morning?' Toby asked Turnbull.

'I suppose they do. Likely the nuns insist on that.' From somewhere in the convent a bell rang and sounds of hurrying feet came from the passage. Isabel entered the kitchen followed by the thin girl. She looked up: 'Good morning, Toby.'

'Good morning,' he answered. 'I wondered where you were this morning.'

'I was praying and I said one for you.'

'Good. I asked my mother if she'd let me go to the pictures with you, and she said it was all right as long as you didn't keep me out too late.'

Frankie watched her laughing. Would she notice him? The thin girl said: 'Gosh, Isabel, I'm starving. Get some breakfast ready as soon as you can.'

'Are you not having your breakfast above?' The thin girl shook her head.

'Don't you know I don't like it up there.' Isabel turned, she caught him staring at her. 'Good morning, I didn't see you there.' He smiled.

'Listen, daughter,' Toby was speaking, 'if you're thinking of cooking some breakfast, I think we had better get out of your way, because these dusty flakes we're scraping from this ceiling . . .'

'It's all right, I'll go to the top kitchen,' she said.

'Are you sure?'

'Certain. I'll fix my fire and then get going.' The thin girl hurried from the kitchen. Isabel took a coal bucket and emptied its contents into the range. Frankie looked at the ceiling. It would be at least another couple of hours before the two men finished. He was disappointed and slightly annoyed. She would not be near the kitchen until then. The plasterer's labourer came into the kitchen again and made for the range. 'Any tea this morning, love,' he said, as he curved his arm around her leaning figure.

'Go away,' she protested. 'Can't you see the painters are here scraping and creating a lot of dirt; I can't make any tea this morning.' The labourer tightened his arm and she tried to draw away from him. At that moment the nun with the apron appeared. Frankie dropped his head and exaggerated his movements of washing the paintwork.

'What's going on here?' he heard her ask. 'What's going on here?' she repeated.

'I'm sorry. I'm sorry . . . It was just a bit of fun . . .' the labourer kept repeating nervously as he left the kitchen.

'Look at me, Isabel,' the nun was saying. Frankie heard the coal bucket being put on the floor. 'Why was this man's arm around you? Did you give him any encouragement? Answer me.' Isabel began to cry. 'No tears. Tears won't get us near the truth. Have you been encouraging this man to put his arm around you? Come with me and we'll get to the bottom of this.' Isabel lifted her apron and rubbed her eyes. 'Please don't cry,' the nun said with anger and impatience in her voice.

In the short silence which followed, Frankie heard Isabel crying loudly.

'Aren't you going to answer me? Why must you stand there crying like a two year old. Has that man been putting his arm around you every time he comes in here? Are you on friendly terms with him? Answer me. Is this any example to be showing the other girls? Answer me and stop blubbering like a child.'

'Could I say a word, Sister?' Toby was climbing down the step-ladder. He removed his cap. 'Look, daughter,' he said to Isabel, 'go you away and dry your eyes and let me have a word with the sister.' Isabel moved quietly out of the kitchen. Frankie could see the nun's white face, caught in the light. Her glasses were rimless, giving the face a hard, cold expression; her lips had no colour, and her mouth looked like his aunt's. Her rosary beads moved and the brass Christ which weighted them disappeared into a fold beside the edge of her apron. He could just see her shoes, the black-leaded appearance of the rubber heels plainly visible.

'I'm not of your persuasion, Sister,' Toby was saying. 'But I happened to be working here. The wee girl did nothing to encourage him, absolutely nothing. I can swear to that. She was putting some coal on the fire when he came in and put his arm around her. In all fairness to him, I don't think he intended . . .'

'It isn't what he intended. It is what he was doing. We are responsible for these girls.'

'I know that, Sister, but take it from me, it wasn't the little girl's fault. She's a complete stranger to me, but it would be on my conscience if I didn't tell the truth about what I saw with my own eyes.'

'We can't have it. We can't have workmen rushing in and

173

behaving here as if they were in a cheap dance hall.' The nun slid her hand to her beads, fumbling for the crucifix.

'Don't blame the child anyway for what wasn't her fault. I know it isn't for me to butt in, but I just thought I'd say a word in defence of her.'

'I think that man is with the plasterers,' the nun said meaningly as she left the kitchen. Toby climbed to the plank. The two men worked in silence, then Toby said: 'Close that kitchen door, Frankie.' Toby sat down on the plank; for a moment he thoughtfully flicked the little flakes of dried whitening from his boot with the point of his scraper. 'I wonder did I do the right thing there?' he said as though to himself. Turnbull was fiddling with his pipe. Toby faced him. 'Did I do the right thing, Doggie?'

'You did,' said Turnbull.

'But what happens to the poor bastard of a plasterer's labourer? If she squeals to his foreman, it's a hundred to one he gets his walking papers. I don't like to be a bloody informer; no Irishman does, but Jazes, I couldn't see the poor kid taking the rap. There was no harm in what he was doing, was there now?' Turnbull did not answer.

'Was there any harm in what he was doing, Doggie?' He faced Turnbull again, demanding an answer.

'You see, Toby,' Turnbull said slowly, 'nuns are different . . .'

'I know they are different,' Toby fired back. 'I suppose that's why they join up to be nuns, because they are different.'

'Exactly,' agreed Turnbull. 'You see a man putting his arm around a girl means nothing to you or me, because we're outside in the world, but a nun looks on it as . . .' Turnbull took his pipe from his mouth as if it was stopping him from finishing what he wanted to say.

'I know what you're driving at, Doggie. There's never smoke without fire. You must light the gas to heat the kettle, I know that. . . .'

174

'These girls are orphans and the nuns are in charge of them. It's up to the nuns to see that they don't fall by the wayside. You see my point, Toby. A man puts his arm around a girl, the next thing he kisses her; then the kiss leads to something else, and something else leads to trouble at the end of nine months; you and I know about that, Toby, that's life.'

Toby looked as if he were not listening to Turnbull. 'I hope I don't get that poor bastard the sack,' he said. 'Still, it was one thing or the other; I had to tell the truth. I think I'd better go and see if I can find him. If Collins is looking for me, tell him I've a touch of diarrhoea and that I've gone places.' Toby left the kitchen. Turnbull moved the plank further along. 'He did the right thing, didn't he, Frankie?'

'Yes.' Frankie wished he had been able to do it. But the damned stammer would have prevented him even if he had thought of doing so. All he seemed able to do while the nun questioned Isabel was to stare at her hard face and her beads, and listen to the sobbing girl.

'It's all very well for Toby to say there was no harm in what that fellow was doing, but the nun just couldn't walk into the kitchen and say to him, "That's a good boy, put your other arm around her and do the right thing," could she now? She had to make some protest. You see, Frankie, it's as I say; these girls are orphans. Think of the disgrace it would be — her working for the nuns and maybe some fellow taking advantage of her.' The door opened and Toby came in.

'She's gone straight to his foreman. She's with him now. I fancy it's curtains for the poor bastard. I told him what I said, but I think it's curtains. His foreman won't stand for it, I know.' Toby looked unhappy. 'I wish to blazes I hadn't been here. Still, the nun did catch him with his arm around her. If only these nuns were not so bloody religious. I'm sorry, Doggie, but that's how I am feeling at the moment.'

'That's all right,' Turnbull replied. 'Don't have any qualms, you did the right thing.'

The men returned to their jobs and nothing more was said of the incident until the ginger-haired labourer came in with a kettle. 'I suppose,' he said, 'this place will be out of bounds for us now. Always some louser to spoil everything.'

'What do you mean?' Toby called from the plank.

'Just that we had the run of this kitchen; we could pop in and out when we liked to boil a kettle of tea. Handier than hanging around that bloody coke fire outside.' He shook his head. 'Talk about one bad apple spoiling the barrel.'

'There wasn't much harm done,' Toby said.

'Sure the man was always pestering the girl. He's married with a houseful of kids. Serve him bloody well right if he does get his walking papers. That's the second time he's been caught.'

'I didn't know that.'

'Well, you know it now, he's asked for it. He can't keep his hands to himself.' The red-headed man fixed his kettle on the fire. 'Of course the kid's a wee bit of a tease herself. She's rolling her eyes at everybody, but it doesn't do to take a friendly smile as a sign of the green light, does it?' No one answered him. 'That bloke's a bad lot. I was on a job with him before and he had to attend the hospital once a week, and take it from me, it wasn't for in-growing toe-nails.' Frankie looked over at him. He was winking his eye, a slow wink. Neither Toby nor Turnbull made any answer, and when the red-haired man left, Isabel came into the kitchen. She was quiet, and Frankie could see she had been crying.

'How goes it now?' Toby asked her quietly.

'I wish I was a thousand miles away from this place,' she said, going to one of the drawers and taking out some knives and forks.

'There won't be a word about it in a hundred years,' Toby began, but she was gone before he finished.

The kitchen was strangely silent now. Frankie worked and

thought about her. It would be impossible now to ask her out. He guessed that in future this particular nun would keep a closer eye on her. If, as the red-headed man had said, it was the second time ... And what was it about her rolling her eyes? And the sign for the green light? He might send her a note, but if by any chance the nun found it he would be reported and sacked. Toby's song broke the silence: 'There's an old fashioned house in an old fashioned town.' Frankie caught Turnbull's eye and saw that he disapproved of the singing. But the silence was gone, and the thin girl coming into the kitchen brought the atmosphere back to normal. She looked fussed and worried. She did not appear conscious of them at all, but took some more knives and forks from the drawers.

At the lunch break he asked Turnbull; 'Will they send the girl away?'

'Hardly likely, seeing she's an orphan. I suppose she knows no other home but this place.'

'I don't think you'll hear another word about it,' Toby said. 'The man has got his cards. So you'll see things will be normal again. Anyway, it's all a storm in a tea-cup. I know nuns are strict and all that, but it'll be as I say; there won't be another word about it.'

4. IT WAS AS TOBY had said. In a month's time there was not a mention of the thing, but the various foremen on the job were told to instruct their workmen to frequent the kitchens as little as possible. The relief kitchen was still free for the men to make their tea. Isabel had been sent to work upstairs. When Turnbull asked the thin girl about her, he was told that Isabel was looking after the polishing of the rooms. But Frankie learned that if he could be around the passageway about nine-thirty in the morning, he might catch a glimpse of her as she came from Mass with the other girls.

She came rushing from the little church, pushing her rosary beads into her coat pocket with one hand and playfully tickling the thin girl with the other. She wore a white knitted hat, curved and fluffy, shaped like a clover blossom. As she passed Frankie, she winked, and said: 'How's Toby? I like Toby, I like his name.'

Frankie turned into the kitchen and called Toby. 'What is it?' Toby looked up the passageway. 'Ach! is it Isabel, how are you, love? It's years since I've seen you.'

'I never thanked you, Toby, for sticking up for me that day.'

'That's all right. It's all over and done with. Are you working hard?'

'Yes, upstairs all the time. I hate it. I'd rather be back in the kitchens.'

'Why?'

'There's more life down here. Have you got a newspaper?'

'I have. Why?'

'I want to see what's on at the Palace.'

'Wait, I'll get it for you.' Toby rushed to his coat. 'When are you for the Palace?'

'Tonight. It's my night off, but I must be back for half nine.'

'I think my mother might let me go,' Toby said. But she had pushed the newspaper inside her coat and was hurrying away laughing. 'Great kid, that,' Toby said as he started to work.

Who was she going to the Palace with? She would have to be back by half nine; that meant she would be about the convent gates any time from nine onwards. He could be there, just hanging about, to knock into her accidentally; he could see whether she had a boy or not. Perhaps he could talk to her tonight, and ask her if she would come out with him on her next night off.

That afternoon Toby was singing, 'Fancy meeting you, fancy meeting you. Of all the jolly old so-and-so's, fancy meeting you.' He was dancing on the plank. He could dance up to Isabel if he met her in the street and sing, 'Fancy meeting you. Of all the jolly old so-and-so's, fancy meeting you.' Frankie knew he never could do that. Turnbull got down from the plank, muttering something to the effect that Toby would finish by breaking it. Following him, Toby slapped his back, and said: 'Cheer up, Turnbull, we never died a winter yet, and the devil himself couldn't kill us in the summer.' He left the kitchen.

'Those are terrible songs for him to be singing in a convent, Frankie,' said Turnbull. 'He doesn't understand. I'm sure the nuns, if they heard him, wouldn't allow these music hall ditties to be sung.'

Frankie liked the songs and he said so. Toby returned and Turnbull said nothing more.

A young nun entered. 'Which of you men were singing as I passed down the passage a while ago?' Frankie saw Turnbull's face flush.

'It was me you heard singing,' Toby said, with hesitance.

'I listened to you, and for a moment I thought I was back in my father's kitchen. That was a great song of his. It's remarkable that a whiff of a song can puff back the years like wind skimming the pages of a book. Thank you, thank you.' She went off muttering into her hands. Toby looked as if he was about to cry. Turnbull stood with an expression of stupidity on his face. 'Well, well, can you beat that?' Toby said slowly, his eyes glazed. 'You would never think a song like that would affect a nun.' He climbed to the plank, and after a long pause, Turnbull said: 'You know, as well as being nuns they are women.' But Frankie saw that he was defeated, as if the nun's reaction to Toby's song had upset him. Toby was silent, but he kept smiling to himself and winking at Frankie. He looked happy and told Collins at the lunch hour that one of the nuns was going to put him in the choir.

That afternoon Isabel came down the passageway and

returned Toby's paper. She was dressed ready for going out, in a black coat with large red buttons shaped like poppies. Her little round cap was almost the same colour as the buttons. She wore black flat-heeled shoes.

'Little Red Riding Hood,' Toby laughed.

'I have to watch the wolves in this place,' she said.

'You would, dear, you would,' agreed Turnbull.

Frankie wanted to be near her, to test his height against hers now that she was wearing the low-heeled shoes, but Toby standing back in mock admiration prevented this. She was excited and fidgeted with her gloves. 'Like a bird let out of a cage,' Toby remarked afterwards. The thin girl joined her, unshapely and awkward as ever even in her best clothes. They hurried away after Toby calling out a warning: 'Don't do anything you wouldn't like your friends to know about.' Turnbull shook his head disapprovingly.

She had not ignored him. He had caught her eye as he looked at her dress, and she had smiled. She was aware of him; at least if he met her again, she would certainly know him. He would be at the convent gate tonight from nine o'clock or before that. It was unlikely she would return before nine. He thought about his clothes, of the canvas grey raincoat. Sure, it was ragged and dirty looking; but he could tell her he had been doing a job after hours; that would let her see he was important, that he was able to do a job on his own . . . He must tell the lie, tell a number of lies, anything to impress her, to let her know he was keen on her, that he was in love with her. Yes, he was in love with her . . . Just to stand and stare at her, to hear her feet in the passageway; even to look at the ground she walked on; to see her hands, her movements; everything about her — it was bliss. . . .

Before they left the job that night, he hurried to the hot water tap and washed his hands thoroughly. There was lashings of hot water; not stinted as at home where a hot kettle meant more coal on the fire or an extra penny for gas.

He heard the bells as he arrived at the convent entrance.

The gates were closed but not locked, for the chain with the padlock hung over the bolt. His hands looked clean, they looked, and he thought the word silly, respectable. How could hands ever be respectable? But they could. You had only to look at the hands of other workmen to see how ignorant they were — the dirty nails, untrimmed, bulging and claw-like.

The bells had stopped. Across the road was the bus stop. She must get off the bus here and walk over the road; he could not mistake her. He hoped that the thin girl would not be with her. A bus pulled up and he moved away from the gate. He stared as the bus spluttered away; someone was coming towards the gate; it was the thin girl. She did not see him, but pushed open the gate and went to the keeper's lodge, about fifty yards up the drive. Probably she had gone there to wait for Isabel. Either Isabel was at the pictures with a boy, or the thin girl had been somewhere else; yet it was unlikely that Isabel would be at the Palace by herself. One way or the other he would see her, unless she was already in the keeper's lodge. He came to the gate again, and fixed his eyes on the lodge; there was no sign of life about the little house except the light in the small window. He withdrew from the shadows of the gate and waited opposite the bus stop. Couples passed by arm-in-arm; decent, well dressed, taller and better clad than himself.

He was here waiting to get a glimpse of a skivvy — a little skivvy no taller than himself, dressed in a black coat with red buttons. He found now that he didn't dislike the term skivvy as much as he had before. When he repeated the name to himself it gave him a feeling of superiority. Instead of being nervous, as he was now, about meeting her, he should be bold: after all he was, or soon would be, a trades-man; and not every tradesman threw himself away on a skivvy. Could he not go straight up to her and say, 'Hello, Isabel, fancy meeting you ...' Toby's song echoed in his mind, and the nun praising him for it; and Turnbull's not knowing what to say or do when he heard her . . . If only he were like Toby. . . .

A bus was coming; it stopped, and there she was, but someone was with her, though it might be only another passenger getting out at this stop. He moved out of sight until the bus slid away. Yes, there she was, her arm around the waist of a tall man, and his around her shoulders. They waited, looking up and down the road, making sure, in a carefree way, that there was no traffic; then they crossed the road, slowly, carelessly, their movements suggesting a slow waltz. Her shoe caught in a tram line and she stumbled; the man put his other arm around her to save her from falling, but she straightened herself, and now with both arms around her, he embraced her tightly. She laughed and buried her head between the lapels of his overcoat. An approaching car forced them to break and dash to the footpath. She examined the heel of her shoe, the man lighting a match and holding it close to the ground. In the momentary flame, Frankie saw the man's face. It was fresh, with a moustache that looked like a line. He wore a red bow tie. Frankie tiptoed near the gate. The light from the little window of the lodge picked them out dimly. They disappeared into the black mantle of a tree.

Frankie moved forward until his forehead touched the cold iron of the gate. He supposed this man was now putting his arms around Isabel, pressing her neat and soft little body close to his own.

The sound of laughter coming from the direction of the tree had a soothing effect for a moment. The door of the lodge opened and the thin girl came out. She whistled, and seemed to expect a reply. She whistled again. Isabel and the man emerged. Frankie stood back from the gate and crossed the road so that he might not be seen. Isabel walked up the drive to join the thin girl. He followed the man to the bus stop, watching him as he rubbed his lips roughly with a handkerchief, presumably to remove lipstick traces.

Frankie got on the bus and sat opposite to him. The man turned his head and covered his cheek with his hand as he stared through the window, like a person lost in a dream. There was nothing flashy about him; he did not look the type that was out just for a night's fun, the type that would regard Isabel as 'pick-up'.

It was remarkable the number of things in life you could not discuss with people. Here he was, in love with the girl whom the man sitting opposite had just left. He could not go to him and say, 'Look I'm in love with Isabel. If you are only going round with her for a bit of fun, please would you let someone have her who would marry her, give her a home, love her and be good to her.' You could not say things like that. But how did he know this man was not in love with her, or she in love with him? They might be planning to marry. God! how pretty, how attractive, how lovable she was, and this man had had her in his arms kissing her, crushing her sweet lips, enjoying her laughter and talk.

The bus came to a halt and the man hurried down the stairs. Frankie sat on until he came to his own stop. He walked home slowly, through the narrow streets. Here and there, at street corners and in small porches, boys stood with girls.

His own street was changing. One or two of the boys he had been to school with were getting married. He did not go out of his way to see Devlin, or inquire about him. The girls he met, some of them, no longer called him by his Christian name. They nodded and passed on with dancing-shoes under their arms or steel-ridged skating boots. Men and women now, they had all decided what they were going to do; they were what they were going to be. No one now asked him if he liked his trade. They took it for granted that he was a house-painter, that he would probably never be anything else. He had, as his aunt had said, got a trade, but somehow it meant nothing. There was so much about his trade that he did not know; Turnbull was fond of saying, 'You cannot learn everything about the trade in five years. You go on learning from the day you finish your time until the day you die.' But Turnbull had not gone on learning, nor had Toby. They both worked for St. Clair's, scraping the dirty, sooty ceilings, doing all the rough work. No, Turnbull had not learned. If he had he would not still be doing what he was. Turnbull could preach that where there's a will there's a way. . . .

To Frankie that seemed the silliest and stupidest saying of all. He himself had tried to will his hand to steadiness, his fingers to draw, his body to grow, his brain to purge itself of fear. He had, perhaps with some success, willed himself to take as little heed as he could of what his aunt might say or do. Simon had told him that when he was away from his aunt his nerves would get stronger and better, but would they? His desperate fear of heights, and his shaking hands — would these leave him? He knew he could do nothing about his height, not even if the King of England adopted him as his son; nor with his uselessness at drawing. What other job was there that he might be happy at? A storekeeper's job? Or a bin man? He was too small for the job of bin man. A storekeeper's job would be the only thing. Giving out articles and keeping count of them. Arithmetic he was no good at at all. What *was* he good at?

He was in an ugly mood. It was because he had seen Isabel with a man. Why was this bitch torturing him? This bitch with her red lips, her soft little body . . . No, he must not call her a bitch. She did not even know he loved her. The man might be her brother. Yet he could not be. Why did they disappear into the dark shadow of the trees? Yet he knew that, no matter what she might say or do, he would still love her. She was the only girl he had ever thought about since the days of Sally. He was not jealous of the other man. She was Isabel and that was enough. . . .

He could not sleep: her black hair, her eyes were everywhere in the room. Once he reached out his arms, but laughingly she darted away and disappeared into the shadows of the trees.

He awoke tired. As he approached the convent he made up his mind again to ask her to the pictures. If only she would come out with him once, give him just one memory of her!

He found Toby already on the job, sitting on a chair, examining a pair of woman's shoes. 'I'm taking up dancing,' he said, and held out a shoe. Turnbull arrived.

'What are you doing with the lady's shoe?'

'I found a dead woman in one of the bushes as I was coming up the drive this morning.'

Turnbull took the pipe from his mouth. He eyed Toby with amazement. 'A dead woman?' he said very slowly. 'Have you reported it to the police?'

'I have. They're expected to arrive any minute. Frankie here, I may tell you, is suspected.'

Turnbull looked at Toby, then at. Frankie. 'Come,' he said, 'cut out the fooling. . . .'

'I had you fooled anyway,' Toby laughed.

'You've a wonderful imagination, Toby; you should be writing for the newspapers.'

'Aye, for the Weekly Wallpaper, or the Oul' Maid's Comforter.'

'Well, set our minds at rest. What are you doing with the woman's shoe?'

'It's the kid's,' Toby replied.

'What kid's?'

'The wee girl's. Is it Isabel's her name? You know the wee dark, nice-looking kid?' Turnbull nodded, and sighed, relieved at knowing, but still not satisfied. Toby went on: 'Aye, she asked me if I'd clean these shoes up for her. I told her I'd give them a coat of aluminium paint. I've got some good stuff at home that I used on the daughter's shoes.'

Turnbull took a shoe, examined its long, thin heel. 'She couldn't do a route march in these shoes,' he said.

'She wants them for a dance. She tells me there's a big dance coming off in connection with some hospital.' Frankie reached for the shoe, just to feel its soft leather, and push his fingers where her toes rested.

'She was waiting on me here first thing this morning with them,' said Toby. 'She's a good kid that. I just knew she wasn't a skivvy.'

'Is she not?' Turnbull asked.

'No, she tells me she's only here for three months. Her mother's in hospital and there's only herself and a brother. He's a priest.'

'What is she doing here?' Frankie asked timidly.

'I suppose there's nobody at home. The mother being in hospital didn't want to leave her alone in the house. She tells me one of these nuns is her aunt, so there you have it. But she says she has to work every bit as hard as the servant girls. She doesn't seem to mind that. A good kid, full of life and laughter — the only two things I'd look for in a woman. It wouldn't matter a damn if she was the worst cook in the world; give me the love, and the laughter and Bob's your bloody uncle. What do you say, Turnbull?' But Turnbull said nothing.

That was that. She would not be bothered with him. She belonged to the class that lived beyond the tram lines, in one of the large houses with the gardens in front and garages at the side. No, it was no use. 'I'd like to take her to the pictures just the same,' he said loudly, eyeing Toby as he spoke.

'She'll be shooting higher than a housepainter, that young lassie,' Turnbull said.

'I'd think so,' Toby agreed. 'That kid has what it takes with the men. I'd put my shirt on her marrying somebody with the l.s.d. I think her old man had a public house.'

'Aye, the money is to be made in the pubs. A publican or a bookie — those are the people with the dough,' Turnbull said.

Frankie realized now that he could never marry Isabel . . .
A brother a priest, an aunt or a friend a nun: no, it was no
use. 'I'd still like to take her to the pictures.' The words
were out again, and he did not know why.

'All right. I'll see what can be done,' Toby said. He
faced him. 'I'm serious, Frankie. As soon as I see her again,
I'll tell her the wee fella has fallen for her and would like to
take her to the pictures.'

'No, Toby, don't. . . .'

'Well, why the hell do you want to take her out? I'm only
offering to try and fix it for you.'

'You're asking for a disappointment, Frankie,' said Turnbull.

'Faint heart never won a fair lady. Before I courted my
woman she said to a pal of mine, when he told her I was
interested, that she wouldn't be seen on a string of herrings
with me. But once I got talking to her, she seen the light.
Mind you, although I do say it myself, I wasn't a bad-looking
bastard in my day. I hadn't this bread basket . . .' He
patted his enormous stomach.

'You're different, Toby. You'll talk your way out of hell,'
Turnbull said.

'There's no such place.'

'There won't be as far as you're concerned,' Turnbull
agreed.

'Why?'

'Because God won't send you to hell, he'll take you into
heaven — he'll say your were ignorant and didn't know any
better.' The two men laughed and argued on about hell and
heaven. Isabel was forgotten. When Turnbull urged Toby
to lower his voice the fat man said, 'Your trouble is that
you're not ignorant, but you know nothing.'

As they walked home that night, Toby called Frankie
aside. 'I've fixed that for you.'

'Fixed what?'

'The date with the wee dame. She'll see you next Wednes-

187

day night at the Classic picture house at half seven.' He could see a twinkle in Toby's eyes.

'You're sure?'

'Dead certain.' But he did not believe it, nor could he get any more information, for Toby had now joined Collins and Turnbull. In the tram despite his manœuvring Frankie could not get near enough Toby to learn whether he had spoken the truth.

The following morning he talked to Toby again. 'Did she say she would come?'

'She sure did,' but there was still the smile lurking in his eyes. 'You'd be all right, Frankie, if you could land that wee hussy. There's money there and plenty.'

'Outside the Classic picture house?'

'Sure thing,' Toby said.

'Wednesday night at half seven?'

'Yes, it was Wednesday.' That was her free night, of course. Yet it was so hard to believe Toby. With Turnbull it would have been different. You could see a lie in Turnbull's face, but not in Toby's. Again he pestered Toby, and the big man exploded: 'Holy Jazes, do you want me to write it down for you?' So he said no more.

They had finished the kitchen apartments and were now working upstairs in the left wing of the convent, stripping the walls of old wallpaper. Close by, on the same landing were the servants' rooms. Frankie hoped to see Isabel, but he learned from the thin girl that she did not sleep in the servants' quarters but in a little attic, quite close to where the nuns slept.

On the landing was a rail for hanging coats. Once when he was passing it, he caught the old blue-aproned nun at one of the coats, taking out a letter and reading it. It was mean, he thought, to search people's pockets and read their letters. If he had written a letter to Isabel, as he had thought of doing, to make sure about Wednesday night, the nun might have found it and read it and perhaps reported him.

This incident would be something to talk to Isabel about when he met her on Wednesday. If he spoke slowly the stuttering might not be so bad. He could let her see he was a slow speaker; sometimes it helped if he counted two silently before the second word.

He would buy the new overcoat; he *must*; a nice grey overcoat, warm and heavy, with a belt. He thought of buying a hat. A hat would add to his height. Yet a hat at the moment was not so important; you could look nifty enough in a new grey coat with your hair well combed and shiny with scented hair oil. What would his aunt say if he arrived home with a new overcoat? Probably she'd start a row. He must be prepared for that. After all, in a few weeks' time he would be a journeyman, earning his first pay as a tradesman.

If he stood up to her a little more he might change her manner to him. If he went boldly and bought the overcoat, brought it home and said to her: 'There is an overcoat I've just bought. And I don't give a bloody damn whether you like it or not. I've bought the coat and you can do whatever the hell you like about it' — if he could only say that! But the accursed stammer would not let him. A speech of this kind excited him, even to think about, and trying to utter it would tie him into so many knots that he could only dance from foot to foot and babble senseless sounds.

On Saturday he went to the big tailor's shop at Corn Market. The windows were filled with overcoats. An attendant appeared, dressed in black coat and vest, with striped trousers and a snow-white collar.

'Can I interest you in some suitings or perhaps an overcoat. We have a very wide range and selection of West of England tweeds just arrived yesterday. Would you care to step this way and look at them?'

He was in the shop. He tried to get the word 'overcoat' out, but his tongue hesitated over a word of its own choosing. 'Te. te. te. top co. co. coat . . .'

'An overcoat? Yes, I think we can suit you in that direction all right,' the attendant said. But the coats he offered were all too large. 'You see, sir, you are rather small. I think we had better make you one. Or if you like, why not take one of these and I can have it altered for you. I can promise you delivery, either way, in a week's time.'

It was for Wednesday he wanted the coat. He looked up at this long-fingernailed attendant and was suddenly frightened of him. Outside, people passed the shop and two other attendants stood looking through the window, ready to pounce on anyone that stopped to look at the wax figures.

'I think we had better take your measure for one.' The attendant had flicked a tape measure seemingly from nowhere.

'No, no, I . . . ye . . . ye . . . see . . . ' He was still stuttering as he hurried through the doorway. He ran across the street, and only slackened his pace when he was sure he was lost in the crowd. He stood behind a power box and looked at the shop. The attendant was at the door again, talking to another man, his hand outstretched in invitation.

Frankie wandered along Royal Avenue, pausing now and then as he passed a tailor's shop. The coats looked the same as those in the shop he had just left. He stood for a moment inside the porch of a picture house. Opposite him was a man walking up and down. He carried his raincoat over his arm. So neatly was it folded that Frankie could not tell whether its condition was good or bad. The man doffed his hat and bowed slightly as a girl joined him. It was pleasant, Frankie thought, to wear a hat and to whip it off when you were meeting a girl. It was good-mannered and made the event important. As the man moved down the street he carried his rolled raincoat in such a way that the girl could not have been aware of it. His arm was curved behind him, and the raincoat hung down the back of his legs.

That was the way to do it. It would save him all the trouble and embarrassment of buying an overcoat; save him the ordeal of 'words' with his aunt.

He found himself against a knot of people waiting to cross the road. A tramcar was moving slowly with 'Shankill Road' on its destination plate. He would go and see Simon. He had been once or twice, but the place was deserted, with dirty window panes and crumpled papers against the door, forced there by the wind. It appeased his conscience when he made these visits; even if the old man was not at home, he knew he had done his duty by calling. Before he knocked the door, his eye caught the windows. They were clean. Even the flags in front of the door had been washed.

Simon opened the door; he was wearing strong, black glasses. They gave his large face a frightening expression.

'Who is it?' he asked, lowering his head and peering through the large glasses.

'It's me.'

'Who are you?' He stuttered out his Christian name. 'Ach! it's you, Frankie. Come in, come in. I can't see when I open the door. It's something to do with the way the light catches these glasses I am wearing. I feel like putting them in the fire, but I'm told if I persevere with them my eyes will get stronger.' Simon had difficulty finding his chair. The boy took his hand. 'No, no, I'm all right, Frankie. I've not been much in the house this last while back. I have a woman that comes in to clean for me, and I'm always frightened of her putting the right things in the wrong place, if you know what I mean. These women want to do things too well.' He sat down. 'I haven't seen you this long time.'

'I called but you were out.'

'Yes, I've been away quite a lot, both in London and other places. I might be going away for good. My brother's ones have been at me to go and live with them. They have a house out in suburbia, but I am wondering if I could stick it. It is Pearl's idea. I suppose you didn't know she was back? Well, she is. She gives out to me for living here on my own. But I've already spent a month up in their place and I don't like it. You never see a neighbour to pass time of day with. But if my eyes get any worse I'll have to go — I couldn't manage here on my own. It's either up there or else into a home. I don't get on very well with my brother, but Pearl will be there at odd times. She was always my favourite . . . You know who I'm talking about, Frankie?' Again he lowered his head as if he were having trouble with the glasses.

'Yes, yes, I know her.' He wanted to ask about Haig, but Simon went on. 'Pearl's the best of them. She's got a fine young son. They tell me he's like the father, but I can't see him well enough to pass an opinion. I'm both glad for Pearl's sake and for Haig's too. You remember Haig? You remember the fuss of the divorce and all the talk?'

'Yes, I do.'

'Did you know he had left the trade?'

'No, I er . . .'

'No, of course you wouldn't know all his doings since he left Belfast.'

'Has he started on his own?'

'I thought he might have had that in mind — business on his own account. But he's taken a job as a paint traveller. It's for a firm with good, first class material, so he should do well. Their last traveller in Belfast could earn a thousand a year with expenses. Between ourselves, Frankie, that's money — over twenty pounds a week. The job will suit him. He's a pusher. It means he can dress well and run a car and meet the sort of people he likes. With a thousand a year and expenses and only one child to keep and Pearl herself with some money, they should be on the pig's back. She tells me she's due one of these endowment policies — about a thousand pounds, so they're planning to build, at least, give half of it to a building society, and spend the other half on a motor car. You knew Haig, didn't you?'

'Yes, yes.'

'It must be years since you've seen him. You wouldn't know him at all. He has an English accent you could cut with a knife. He always was a bit of a la-di-da, but he's worse now. He's in the Freemasons and all the other orders. Says it's a good thing for business. He can have them. Outside the British Legion, I never belonged to any society in my life; secret or otherwise. I never believed in them. Pearl's her old self. Her and him's as happy as Larry, so that's everything. If you wait a wee while, Frankie, the woman that cleans up for me will soon be here and we'll have some tea.'

The glasses had changed Simon. Frankie was uneasy. He was not seeing the real Simon and he longed to ask the old man to remove them. These bulging black rings had killed the movements in the face. He could not tell whether Simon was pleased to see him or not. The old man had talked, but in such a queer way, asking him if he knew Pearl and if he knew Haig, making him feel almost a stranger. Frankie could not see where he was looking; whether it was into the fire or down at the floor, or at his knees.

Why did Simon not ask about his job? And didn't he want to know whether his aunt was still as hard on him? Why did he not mention St. Clair's and talk a little about work as he used to? Instead, he kept whistling quietly to himself. If only he would take the glasses off, just for a minute. . . .

'McCusker's dead,' he said suddenly. 'You remember McCusker, the cat?'

'Yes.'

'Well, he's dead — run over by a motor. In a way I'm very glad. You would almost think Providence had a hand in it. Here I am, thinking of uprooting, but what could I have done with the cat? If I had left him in a cats' home I would have worried in case he was fretting, and I couldn't find it in my heart to get him done in. This was the house my mother lived in; and I'll find it hard to leave it and turn it over to a stranger.'

He paused for a moment. He seemed to be crying.

'We get old, Frankie, and we ought to know what's good for us, but we don't. If we do, we don't admit it. There are few of us face up to being old. A man gets crotchety and he finds it hard to adapt himself to the ways of others. A bachelor like myself is something of a rabbit, a worn path to his hole and fixed ways inside the den. The week I spent in my brother's house made me like a stranger to myself. My very ears seemed to want to get back here, my feet wanted to touch the rough, uneven tiles in this kitchen floor; my shoulders wanted to brush along the scullery wall.'

The outside door was knocked. 'I bet that's the cleaner. I gave her a key and with the bet of a shilling she has lost it. Open the door, Frankie.'

A woman entered with a parcel. 'I've brought your blankets. I think you had better air them in front of the fire before they go on the bed.'

'They surely aren't damp?' Simon asked.

'No, but just to make sure, it would be better to do as I say.' She took two chairs and arranged them at the fire, then she spread the blankets over them.

'This is Molly, and Molly, this is Frankie, a friend of mine.'

Molly reached out a soft hand and said, 'Pleased to meet you.' She did look pleased. Her eyes, large and brown, were almost sad, as if she were not used to meeting people. She was plump rather than fat, with a kind face. Her hair was black and untidy, and her hands were rough with the veins blackened from the soda she used in her scrubbing.

'Would you be a good samaritan?' said Simon. 'Would you make a cup of tea for all hands while you're waiting on the blankets airing?'

'I will. I'll just do it now, for there's nothing to beat a cup of tea. Would you like something to eat?' Frankie shook his head. Simon told her she knew where the biscuits were, and asked:

'Did you get fixed up in your new job?'

'I did,' she called from the scullery. 'It's just the right thing for me. It's in a clothes shop, I go down every night except Sunday. I'm only there for a couple of hours every night and the work isn't hard, and the pay is good. I would rather be a cleaner; working in mill or factory would kill me. I'd rather scrub and wash. People wouldn't believe me, but I get satisfaction out of making a dirty floor clean, and I like to do a good job of making a bed; you know, a good soft feather bed that you sink into the minute you get in.'

Simon chuckled: 'Nothing to beat a good feather bed — especially if there's someone to share it with you.'

'Yes, it's all the better if you've someone to keep you company. Say what you like, it's only natural.'

She was washing her hands, her sleeves rolled up, letting the water run down her plump arms as she held them close to the tap.

'Have you lost your key?' Simon said.

'I think I've left it in my purse in my rooms.'

'I mightn't want you next week. In fact, I might be going to live for good with my brother.'

'You'd be doing the right thing. Why should you suffer on here by yourself, and your eyes not the best? You'd be better with your brother's people; they'd look after you and get you a clean change of clothes when you needed them and a bite of good food.' She returned to the scullery and made the tea.

'Frankie here will soon be a journeyman, won't you? You shouldn't have long to go now.'

'No, a few weeks.'

'Is he a tradesman?' Molly asked.

'He is. He's a housepainter.'

'I wish he'd come down to my place and put in a pane of

glass for me, I'm nearly blown out of my bed at night. I've tried to put pasteboard over it.'

'I'll do it for you,' said Frankie.

'You will?'

'Yes.'

'I don't believe you.'

'Of course he'll do it,' Simon said. She still did not believe him.

Leaning across, she put her hand on his knee. 'You'll come down and put the pane in for me?' For a moment he could not answer. Her hand warmed his knee. She kept her eyes on him, then her hand tightened a little.

'Yes, I'll come down and put the pane in for you.' He looked closely at her as he stammered the words. She showed no signs of laughing; her eyes, round and dark, held his. 'You stutter, son,' was all she said.

'It's just a form of nervousness. It'll leave him as he gets older,' Simon said.

'If you'd suck a pebble they say that's good for it. Did you ever try it?' she asked. He nodded. She withdrew her hand and his knee was cold again.

'Frankie can tell you,' she said to Simon, 'that these blankets are as white as snow. Isn't that right, son?'

'They are.'

'I washed them with these two hands. No laundry for me. The laundry ruins blankets.'

'I can well believe it,' Simon said.

'And he'll come and put the pane in for me? When?'

'What about next Saturday? You'll be in, Molly, and you have the afternoon free, Frankie. Won't that suit both of you?' said Simon coaxingly.

'God love you,' she said impulsively, bringing down her hand and gripping Frankie's knee again. He liked the warm hand and the suggestion of intimacy. 'But you don't know where I live. I'll write it down for you. It's above a shop. I've two rooms, one I sleep in and the other I used for keeping junk in; that means my bits and pieces. It doesn't take much to do me. A bed to sleep in, a chair to sit on, a wee table to ate my grub from, and it's not in my nature to crave any more.'

'You'll find me in from dinner time onwards; or, if you like, you might come and have a bite to eat with me. It's as handy cooking for two as it is for one.'

'Yes, go along and have something to ate with Molly,' Simon said. 'It'll be company for her.'

'It will,' she answered eagerly. She took the blankets and climbed the stairs.

'She's bone clean,' Simon said. 'And as industrious in her own way as an ant. Put the pane in for her like a decent lad, and listen . . .' Simon bent forward and whispered. 'Don't be too stiff in what you charge her. I'll give you something for doing the job; if I was fit I'd do it myself. Life hasn't been too good to her.'

'I won't charge her. I won't . . .'

'Thank you, Frankie. I'll regard it as a good turn done to me. Thank you. Now, I don't want to chase you, but you and I are friends enough to say to each other what's in our minds without offence being taken. I've got some friends coming. . . .'

'I know, I know.'

'Yes, you understand. Some people, if you hinted as I've just done, would take offence, but we know each other too well.'

Simon stood up. 'Frankie is leaving now, Molly, but he won't forget Saturday.'

'Right. About what time?' she asked, descending the stairs.

'About half one.'

'Half one,' she echoed. 'God love you!'

'She lives in one of the best districts in Belfast,' said Simon. 'No one bothers whether you are Catholic or Protestant, Jew or Moslem; no ghettoes down about Tomb Street.'

Simon had not exactly hurried him out, but there had not been the warm welcome he was used to. And once Simon went to his brother's he would see little of him; perhaps he would never see him again. He must be prepared for other changes. Simon knew this too; even tonight he had said something about taking it as a favour if he would put in the pane of glass for Molly. That showed that Simon was regarding him as a journeyman; not inquiring if he were able to put a pane in; but taking it for granted as one tradesman to another.

He would have liked to talk about Haig. Perhaps Simon wanted him away because Haig and Pearl were coming. Haig speaking with an English accent! Haig could carry off this sort of thing. He could wear clothes neatly as a dummy in a tailor's window. He wanted to see Haig and Pearl again. . . .

The next morning as he walked up the drive he saw Collins. When he joined him, Collins said, 'We are getting a new foreman this morning. And there he is.' Frankie could see a boy ahead of them. Collins was laughing.

'A new foreman?'

'Sure thing,' said Collins; then he called out to the boy. 'Hi! you, where are you going?'

The boy stopped. 'I'm looking for a Mister Collins,' he said.

'You're looking at him now.' The boy handed him a letter. Collins read it. 'I was right, Frankie, this is the new foreman.' The boy dropped his head. Patting his shoulder, Collins said, 'Don't blush, I'm only making fun. Frankie, meet the new apprentice.'

Frankie shook the boy's outstretched hand. 'You'll look after him today, Frankie. Show him his first job. Learn him how to make tea. Can you make tea, son?'

'I think so. I was in the Scouts.'

Frankie resented the new boy. Here he was, taking possession of the things that seemed a very part of Frankie —

lifting the tea cans and being shown where the men's coats hung, and the pockets he could get their tea packets from. He was suddenly afraid. The starting of the new apprentice meant just one thing, that he was nearing the end of his term; he would soon be a journeyman, and what would the firm do then? Pay him off? When he consulted Turnbull all he got was: 'It's only natural that the firm should start a new apprentice. You'll soon be finished.'

'Do you think they'll keep me on?' It took him a long time to get this sentence out.

'I couldn't answer that, Frankie. You know the policy of the firm; pay off the apprentices as soon as they finish. Still, I think you should be all right on this job; it's a convent and likely they'll want to keep all the Papishes they can on it. Policy should make them do that. But your guess is as good as mine.'

There had been nothing intimate in Turnbull's tone, nothing to comfort him. Frankie wanted to ask him what he thought of him as a tradesman; he wanted to ask Toby the same question, but he did not. He was soon to be told that his time was finished, that he was a tradesman, a journeyman. But was he? There was no point in shirking this question. No. He was not a good tradesman.

That he was not clever, he knew from the beginning. As the schoolmaster had said, his brain was a mass of jelly; it would hold nothing; nothing would stick there, no matter how hard he tried to learn. He could hardly sweep out a room properly; there was sure to be some spot he had failed to brush. Was there no way he could improve himself?

'Are you day dreaming?' He heard Toby's voice. 'Come, you've got to give me a hand with this ceiling. Collins has put Turnbull on another job.' He followed Toby along the passage and out to the staircase. Toby pointed to the ceiling. 'We have to wash this lady down,' he said. Frankie looked at the ladder. A plank ran from it to another ladder on the opposite wall. He counted the rungs. Twenty-two. That was twenty-two feet he had to climb and then walk across the narrow plank. The plank was at an angle because Toby was much taller than he.

He held the ladder as he climbed. His heart beat loudly. How was he to get on the plank? He looked down. Toby had gone for water. Far below him he could see a crucifix and the dark brown head of Christ.

If only he could get on to the plank before Toby returned. He pushed his body out, and with this movement the ladder scratched the wall. He lurched back suddenly, gripping the ladder again. He paused for breath. His hands trembled and he felt he was losing control of them; at any minute they would release their hold and he would fall backwards. He brought his body closer to the ladder, pressing his stomach against the rungs. This gave him a little confidence. His own head bent against the hard rung, he saw again the dark head of Christ. 'Oh Christ! why can't you help me? Why can't you? All I ask is make me able to climb. That's all I ask. It is so easy, so simple to walk across this plank, yet I can't do it, I can't do it. Oh! Christ, why can't you help me? Why can't you make me?'

Toby arrived with the water and was now climbing the other ladder. The movements of his heavy body as he got to the plank forced Frankie's ladder to sway a little. Still he held on, making no effort to get on the plank.

'What's wrong, can you not make it?' Toby was now above him. 'Come, let me give you a hand.' He felt Toby grip the neck of his overalls. Toby with a loud 'oop' lifted him to the plank.

'What's the matter? Has he got the breeze up?' Collins was below. Frankie now stood on the plank, his legs trembling, his fingers warm and stinging at the tips. 'He's not going to be much use up there, is he Toby?' Toby did not answer. He crossed the plank to the bucket and angrily wrung the sponge. Collins moved away. 'Send me some washing powder?' Toby called after him.

Frankie tried to tell Toby he was sorry. 'It's all right son, it's all right. You're a bundle of nerves. The life must have been hammered out of you when you were a child.'

The new boy came with the washing powder. He was climbing the ladder just as if he were running upstairs. Now he was on the plank handing the powder to Toby. 'I was told to deliver this.' He was off the plank and down the ladder again, all in a moment.

'Don't mope about it. You just can't climb and that's all there is to it,' Toby said after a pause. 'I think you'd better get back to terra firma. Come on, get down. If your nerves get the better of you, it's hard to say what will happen. It might be serious; maybe you'd jump off the plank. That can happen, I seen it once before. Come on.'

Frankie slid to his knees, pushed his feet over the plank and groped blindly for the rung of the ladder. Toby's hand gripping the back of his overalls again. 'Come on,' Toby coaxed, 'you needn't be afraid. I've got a good grip of you, you won't fall. Take it easy for a minute or so when you get to the ground.'

He was shaking all over. He stood breathless at the bottom of the ladder. 'Go outside into the air, it will help to steady you,' Toby called. He hurried down the stairs, glancing quickly at the crucifix, at the closed eyes of the Christ who was in too much pain, he thought, to be bothered with other people's problems. Outside it was cold and he breathed deeply to soothe his nerves. Two nuns walked up and down, telling their beads. Across the yard the plasterers worked, firm and secure on a floored scaffolding. The carpenters fitted the spouting from safely erected platforms. Painters were the only tradesmen who had to work from ready-made and insecure scaffolding.

After the lunch hour Collins sent the new apprentice to work with Toby. To Frankie it was the great humiliation that an apprentice only just started should be put to do the job that he, almost a journeyman, was unable to do. That night in the tram on the way home Collins asked Toby, 'How did the new boy shape up this afternoon?'

'Fine. One thing about him, he can skip up and down ladders and over that plank like a bloody monkey. He's shaping a good lad. He doesn't know the meaning of nerves.'

Frankie wondered what they had said about him when they were together. He had often heard other men talking about apprentices — how good they were, the things they were brilliant at, the future of so-and-so who would certainly become an employer, or of so-and-so who would finish up a botch. Yet of the botches there was always some man ready to speak out and mention some good point. Perhaps they would say about him that his smallness was useful sometimes, when there was a job that a normal-sized man could not do.

His thoughts suddenly turned to Isabel. What would she have thought of him this afternoon if she had seen him panicking on the ladder? Girls, he knew, liked men who were courageous. Christ! There was nothing courageous in climbing twenty-odd feet and walking across a thin plank. Yet he could not do it. It was a waste of time to dwell on it. There appeared no cure for his weakness. Yet if he were to get away from his aunt, from her house of fear, that might be the first step towards, if not a complete cure, at least an improvement. He was never able to relax; there was always this indescribable fear. He could not put it in words. Guilt, always guilt, as if he had committed some awful crime, was crushing down on his mind; and in a strange way the one relief he experienced was when his aunt was in her fighting mood. The awful silences of late in the kitchen were more painful to bear. When would she start again? She was waiting perhaps for the time when his journeyman's pay packet would rustle in her pocket. 'He had a trade' was her proud boast to the neighbours.

When he arrived home she said 'There's an overcoat upstairs in your room; try it on and see if it fits you.' He had

202

not expected this. The overcoat was neither black nor dark grey in colour, but looked like a mixture of both. The material was thin, and when he put it on, he saw that the arms were slightly worn. Where had she got it? Had she bought it from one of the second-hand clothes dealers in the market? She could keep it. He did not want it. He would not wear clothes that had belonged to somebody else. Besides, it was much too long for him.

'Let me see how the coat looks?' she called up. On the way down the stairs, he thrust his hands into the pockets. They were worn and bottomless.

'It's too big for me,' he almost shouted.

'Let me see,' she said. 'Stand well in the middle of the floor until I see it.'

He gathered his shoulders deliberately and let the sleeves trail down over his hands.

'Straighten yourself. Don't stand there like a sack tied in the middle,' she commanded. 'I'll put a tuck in the bottom and in the sleeves and it'll do you for Sundays. That raincoat has had its day.'

He said quickly: 'I don't want the coat. I don't want anyone else's cast-offs . . .' He tore it off and flung it to the sofa. He saw her face tighten and her mouth moving. For once she was at a loss for words.

'Is that my thanks? I tramp the feet off myself around the markets to buy something to give you a decent look, and is this my thanks? You ungrateful brute. We have got the man on us all of a sudden.'

'I want a new overcoat or none at all,' he said, stamping from one foot to the other in an effort to get the words out.

'There's no stuttering when you're flinging the angry word from you. You can talk well enough when there's evil spicing your speech.'

He stood in the hall afraid, yet at the same time determined to give her word for word.

'I want a new coat,' he repeated.

'Do you think I have a fortune to spend on a new coat for you? I suppose you'll cast up now the miserable lock of shillings you give me. Me, that tried to keep a roof over your head. . . .'

'Go on, I've heard all this before,' again rocking from foot to foot, urging the words from his mouth. He heard her move to the fire and the sound of the poker being lifted and he rushed to the yard, holding the latch of the door with both hands.

'You can run,' she shouted, 'you ungrateful pig, you can run. Me striving and starving to keep a home for you and this is the thanks I get. . .' She was crying as she returned to the kitchen. He relaxed his hold and listened. The poker was thrown back on the hob. She had won again. She was still able to cow him. Why could he not have faced her, even if it meant wrestling for the poker; he should have taken it from her and challenged her. 'Come on, you'd use the poker on me. I'm going to use it on you, just to see how you like it. Come on, let me use it just once over your arm, your head, or wherever it strikes first, come on . . .' He could say that if only he could get the words out. It would let her see he was calm about it, that he was determined; but without the words it would just be a mad rush, swinging the poker violently; without the words there would be no defiance, no challenge.

He took a deep breath and opened the yard door. He walked up the hall, slowly; if she came out, there was nothing for it but to use his boot on her. He had to be careful passing the kitchen door; she might rush out with the poker. He must be prepared to grip the poker and use it on her. She would use it on him; he must look on it all as self-defence. He glanced into the kitchen as he passed. She was looking into the fire.

The coat lay on the sofa.

He was outside now. It was cold. He wanted to cry. What with his aunt's sudden outburst and his fright on the ladder, he felt more acutely than ever that he was a failure. Was there nothing he could do?

He walked towards Simon's house. He would not tell Simon about the plank incident. He did not want sympathy, only an hour's peace by a fire. The door was opened by Molly. 'Oh, it's you,' she said. 'I suppose you're looking for Simon, but he's out. I expect him back soon. He was to be here before I left, but now that you're here I can hurry away. I clean in a tailor's shop in Royal Avenue and if I don't hurry I'll never get finished.'

He sat down at the fire.

'You haven't forgotten about putting in that pane of glass for me?'

'No. I'll do it, as I said, on Saturday.'

'God love you.' She sat opposite him. 'I've been hanging some curtains for Simon. He's going to live with his brother. It's all settled. But he's not giving up this house. He's an oddity. Wouldn't you wonder that he couldn't content himself in a posh house like his brother's where everything is of the best? I suppose everyone likes their own corner. I myself have only two rooms for the wee souvenir and myself. My wee souvenir is four years old. There's folk to say I was unfortunate, but I wouldn't give up my wee souvenir for all the tea in China; that's how much I love him.'

She laid her hand on his knee, and her big eyes searched his face. A safety pin held her blouse at the neck and her breasts, big and bulging, pushed their nipples against the brown, silky garment. 'You have a girl, have you?' she asked. 'You must have, sure it's only natural for a boy to have a girl, and a girl to have a boy, it's only natural.' He shook his head. He was quiet now within. He hoped she would not take her hand from his knee.

'I haven't a girl,' he said quietly.

'But you will have, you're a tradesman. They'll be after you like wasps round a jam pot, you'll see. It's only natural . . .' She slid her fingers further up his leg and pressed his thigh, emphasizing 'It's only natural.' He touched her hand. 'You've had it hard, son. Simon told me, the last night you were here. Your aunt must be a tyrant. I could murder anybody that would lift their hands to a child. I have a wee souvenir and will dare anyone, big or small, lift their hands to him when he grows up; I'd go out and in through them if they did.'

There was a knock at the door. 'Likely that'll be Simon now.' But when she opened it a voice said: 'I want to come in to fetch some medicine. My name is Haig, I'm a friend of Simon's. He tells me he keeps the medicine in the scullery. It's an eye lotion or something like that.'

'He's not coming home the night?' Molly asked.

'No, he's spending the night with his brother.' Haig's accent was certainly changed. He was a little stouter and was dressed in a light grey suit with a yellow waistcoat. His gloves were yellow.

'This is a friend that has come to see him,' Molly said, pointing to Frankie.

'Mr. Haig . . .' Frankie stammered. Haig bent his head inquiringly. 'Of course! I remember you . . . You started to work with me. You're a journeyman now?'

Frankie shook his head. 'A few weeks yet . . .'

'You still keep on the small side, don't you?' Molly had fetched the medicine from the scullery. 'Will I wrap it in paper for you?'

'Not at all, I'll stick it in my pocket. Oh, yes, and Simon asked me to give you this,' he handed her some money. 'He was coming over himself, but I thought I'd best pop over in the car. He says he'll get in touch with you when he needs you again.'

'Tell him to take care of himself and not worry about anything.'

'Good, I'll do that,' said Haig. He turned in the hall. 'Well, cheerio, old man, be seeing you around some time.'

'Nice chap that,' Molly said. 'He's married to a niece of Simon's, but I suppose you knew that.'

'Yes.'

'Her name's Pearl. I heard she left her first man to go with him. It's only natural, isn't it, seeing she wasn't happy.' As she spoke she took her coat from the sofa. 'I'm leaving now, and I must rush to my next job. Would you see that the back door is bolted?'

As he came back into the kitchen, she had her foot on a chair, fixing her stockings far above the knee. 'Did you bolt the back door?' she asked, looking at him, but still busy with her stockings. He was sorry she had to go; sorry, too, that Haig arrived and disturbed them. She was not married; or if she was, she wore no ring. And what was the 'wee souvenir' she had talked about?

In a little tin case she stowed soap, a scrubbing brush and some dusters. 'Now, I'm ready for the road. If you lead the way I'll see the front door is rightly closed. I'll turn off the gas.' In the darkness Frankie waited. 'Mind you don't stumble over a chair,' she said, moving slowly to the hall. 'Gimme your hand, I know my way better than you.' She pulled on her gloves. 'Well, I'll see you on Saturday. You won't forget, will you?'

'No, I won't forget.'

'And you know where I live, and you'll come for your dinner?'

'Yes, I'll do that.'

She was away, hurrying down the street. He stared after her, a dark figure, bareheaded and swinging a small, black case He thought of Isabel and suddenly felt ashamed. Why should he think of the two in the same thought? He knew he had made a friend in Molly. Simon had told her about his life at home. 'Your aunt must be a tyrant . . .' It was good to have someone who understood. He did not want sympathy from anyone, but he needed someone to talk to.

He turned the corner into his own street and his aunt was

now uppermost in his mind. Every time he entered the street it was as if her voice was recorded in the walls, in the flagstones that made the footpath, in the very air. If she had locked the door, he would knock at it, kick it until she let him in; no, there was going to be no doss house for him tonight. But the door was not closed. He looked into the kitchen. She was sewing, and on the table were several strips of paper, arranged in such a way as to suggest a pattern for a skirt. Likely she was using the coat, cutting it up to make into a skirt. There was no supper for him but tonight that did not matter. He had made friends with Molly, big, soft, kindly Molly. And there was Isabel on Wednesday night.

5   HE HAD THE KITCHEN to himself and was able to strip in front of the fire, and stand in a bath of hot water. He borrowed his aunt's scented soap, used the small scrubbing brush on his nails, put on a clean shirt, and plastered his hair with a green-coloured salve which had cost twopence for the box. With a velvet beret she wore when her headaches were bad, he polished his shoes, making them shine as they had never shone before.

He arrived at the Classic Cinema at a quarter past seven. From where he stood he could see the top and bottom of the narrow little street. The clock opposite now said twenty-five past seven. She should soon be here. He stood well away from the lighted porch and held his rolled raincoat behind his back. He looked at the posters, at the notices in neat frames, at the photograph of Cecil Chadwick at the Wurlitzer.

It was now half seven, and there was no sign of her. If she came straight from the convent she would come from the top of the street. The big hand of the clock shot forward and dragged the small hand after it. Half seven was gone.

'Tonight's the night,' Toby had said to him at the lunch hour. 'I saw her this morning and she's looking like a tulip.'

The big hand pulled itself up to the quarter. She was not coming. He looked up the street, moving from the footpath to the middle of the road. He would wait until eight o'clock: that was half an hour's grace. In the shop opposite he caught sight of himself in the mirror. God how small he was! The mirror reflected his shabbiness, the ill-fitting suit, the canvas raincoat with its shiny lining, the shoes furrowed at the toecaps.

He crossed the road to the cinema. It was eight o'clock. He would give her another ten minutes. Maybe it was eight o'clock she had said and Toby had got it wrong. Certainly it could not be any later. No girl would meet a boy at eight if they were going to the pictures. The green-uniformed attendant was looking at him. He moved further up the street out of the light of the cinema porch. The clock pointed to five past eight. Anger was rising in him, mixed with disappointment. She was a bitch letting him down like this. Why did she say she would come and then not turn up? Maybe it was Toby's idea of a joke. The terrible thing about it was Toby would ask him in the morning if he had seen her. What could he say? Be honest and admit she had not turned up, and then have the big man laugh about it all and perhaps tell her, and set her laughing too.

A quarter past eight. Something might have happened. A tram breakdown perhaps . . . Half past eight. Give her another five minutes. . . .

Nine o'clock. He turned the corner, leaving the cinema and the little narrow street. He walked slowly along Royal Avenue, pausing as each tramcar passed, searching them eagerly top and bottom. The clock at the G.P.O. said twenty past nine. She could go to hell. Serve him right to think that a girl like Isabel would show up for him. Again he was not sure whether Toby had told the truth. She might be with the other fellow, sitting arm-in-arm in some other picture house. He turned from the post office.

'Hello, Frankie.' A woman was standing over a bin outside a shop. She turned and he saw it was Molly. 'What are you doing down here?' she asked. 'Come in a minute. Push that bin out of your way. There's nothing much in it, just the sweepings of the shop and a bit of waste paper, but there'll be less in it in a minute when Turpin comes along. Turpin's an oul' fellow that goes about at night searching the bins of shops and things.' She led Frankie to a little office at the back of the shop. 'Did you not know I worked here? Of course, I told you; this is Friel's the tailors.'

She was lighting a gas ring 'You're just in time, for I make myself a mouthful of tea every night at half nine. Look, here's a bowl, go round the corner to Garfield Street — there's a chip shop there — and bring a couple of fish suppers. I had very little tea.' She took a bowl from her bag and reaching to her pocket took out half a crown which she dropped into the bowl. 'It's just round the corner; you won't be a minute, and I'll have the tea ready by the time you come back. And mind yourself going through that gate. There's a bit of iron runs along the bottom of it; you could easily trip and maybe split your skull.'

When he returned with the chips, she had spread a towel over the little table. 'I can only give you condensed milk. Do you mind?' He shook his head.

They finished the meal. 'I like this place,' she said. 'I'm not killed in it, and the manager's the heart o' corn. Him and me gets on like a house on fire. Do you see where the rain came in the other week?' She pointed to the ceiling at the brown map-shaped stain on the white surface. 'The rain came in there and got on some of the suits. He offered one to me for nothing; but I had no men that I liked well enough to present them with a free suit. Mind you, it wasn't stained that much; just what you'd know at the shoulders. I thought of giving it to Simon, but he's that independent you would never know how he would feel. So I think they sent the suits out to some pawnman. Listen, if you ever want a suit, just let me know, and I'll get you one here for half what you would pay anywhere else. Or an overcoat. Mind you, their stuff's just as good as you'll get anywhere in Belfast.'

He drew his chair closer to her, and told her why he was down town. She put her hand on his knee as she had done at Simon's. 'I know how it is. I wish I hadn't turned up to meet my scoundrel. But I did.' After a pause she pressed his knee. 'What's to be, will be. Isn't that the way of the world? I have my wee souvenir and I wouldn't change him for all the tea in China.' She stood up. 'I must finish my bit of scrubbing, no need for you to hurry away.' She poured water into a bucket, tossed a handful of washing soda and some soap powder in, and set the bucket on the gas ring. 'By the time I give the fittings a rub of polish that water will be ready,' she said. He lifted a duster and started rubbing the glass of a frame. 'God love you,' she said, 'but if you want to be helpful take this one and put a lick of polish on them for me, then I'll come after you and shine.'

She polished the patent leather shoes on the wax feet of the models. 'I have six men here every night. Six dummies who'd never ask me how I was doing. Never in a dozen years would they open their mouths to me. I have names for them all.' She laughed. 'I call that one Rudolph Vaselino.'

As he stood looking round the shop, the door was pushed, and he saw a policeman peering through the glass. Molly rose from her knees and went to the door. The policeman was looking straight at him.

'Is that yourself?' Molly asked, opening the door. The policeman came inside and lighted a cigarette. 'This is a friend of mine,' Molly said. 'He's giving me a wee hand with the polishing.'

'I'm glad to hear it,' said the policeman.

'Did you think he was somebody strange? Somebody who had broke into the shop?'

'I thought him strange, so I looked in just to check up.' He talked about the weather, giving Frankie the impression that his visit was a nightly occurrence. He put his cigarette out and slowly left the shop.

'He comes in at night for a smoke,' she said. 'He's not a bad fellow. You know the funny thing about working at night is that folks seem to be more kind. If I worked during the day, I don't suppose I'd ever see a policeman. People want to be more matey and homely at night.'

She left him to polish the few remaining frames and took the bucket from the gas ring and started scrubbing the floor.

'What time do you finish?' he stammered.

'About half past eleven. Sometimes it's near midnight — depends on how dirty the place is. But I try to finish at half eleven.'

He thought he might wait and walk home with her. Tomb Street was not far away from here, but the walk back to his own house would take an hour, and that would mean he he would not get home until after one o'clock. That was too late. It must be after ten now. He looked at her as she scrubbed, saw her breasts circle with the curling movements of her body. He put the polishing cloth back on the counter and said: 'I think it's time . . .'

'You want to leave,' she cut in. 'God bless you and thank you for looking in. I'm here every night at this time, but sure I'll see you on Saturday, won't I?'

'Yes, yes.'

'Mind that iron bar on the gate as you go out.' He expected her to rise from the floor, but with the back of her hand she swept back her hair from her brow, and said: 'Good night, and thank you a thousand times.'

In the porch, he turned and looked back into the shop. Molly was at her scrubbing again. He called out 'Good night'. She looked up and waved her scrubbing brush.

He hurried to the junction, anxious to catch the last tram. Tonight he was in no defiant mood; he wanted to go to bed and think. Think about what? About Isabel not turning up.

He was certain it had happened often before to other people. So why should he worry about it. Yet he found when he was in bed that not Isabel but Molly was in his thoughts. Was it such a bad thing that Isabel had not come? Certainly if she had he would never have met Molly in the shop. Molly he liked because he was completely at ease with her. She could be a friend to him, a friend as Simon had been. He liked her bigness, her eyes, her great full breasts. On Saturday he would see her at home. He would take no money for the little job, and if there was anything else in the line of painting that she wanted done, he would do it, do it free. He lay quiet for a while hearing his heart beats become louder as he thought of Molly's soft body.

He did not see Toby until lunch time the following day. 'How did it go last night?' Toby whispered as they sat down. 'Did she show up?' He shook his head. 'I had a feeling she wouldn't. I hear she's as good as engaged to some fellow. So the lanky dame was telling me. I thought to look at her she was a kittery wee bit; anyway, don't lose any sleep over her.'

He was pleased with Toby and felt slightly ashamed that he had doubted him.

'I ran into Haig last night,' Toby said.

'What's new with him?' Turnbull asked.

'You wouldn't know him at all. Yellow waistcoat, yellow gloves; all he was minus was the walking stick. Burlington Bertie has nothing on him, I can tell you.'

'He always had high notions, but I found him a decent chap.'

'I nearly pissed myself laughing when he started calling me "old boy", like an officer in the Navy. But as you say, Turnbull, he is a likeable bastard. He's given up the trade altogether, and I tell you his heart isn't in a drink; he brought me in and stood me a double whisky.'

'What's he going to do if he's left the trade?' Collins inquired.

'A paint traveller. That's a great racket if you've the contacts; money for old rope.'

'Is he running a car?'

'Not yet, but he's getting one. It's good to see somebody getting on in life. We can't all be failures, can we Frankie?'

Turnbull said: 'That's right, Toby, we can't all be failures.'

'Do you consider yourself a failure?' Collins asked.

The pathetic Turnbull shrugged his shoulders and said: 'Well, I . . .' He looked at the ground, furrowed his brow, and ran his finger round his collar.

'I suppose you would say *I* was a failure,' Toby said.

Collins looked thoughtful.

'You would,' Toby said with emphasis. 'From all standards you would say I was a failure. I was left a good business by my old man. I pissed it away on booze and the like; but if I did, I don't consider myself a failure. I've had a good life. I've reared as fine a family as there is in the British Isles or any other Isles. I've been contented. I married a bloody good woman; my old dutch is one of the best. There was times when life give us an odd knock; but by and large we've been bloody happy together.'

'You were different, Toby. When times were bad, your wife set to and opened a home bakery,' Turnbull said.

'All right, I'll grant you that. But there was a time when the wife didn't have the cash for the home bakery; and we were as happy as ever. No, I consider that a man who marries and is content and in love with his wife, and rears a decent family — I consider that man can't call himself a failure.'

'Supposing a man doesn't marry?' Collins said.

'Then, I've no use for him. I'd tax a bastard like that right

214

up to the eyebrows. It breaks my heart to see fine women going around single while these ould bachelors make love to their fists. Paul himself says "That it's better to marry than to burn. . . ." '

'Hear, hear,' laughed Collins. 'Let's send for the pastor.'

'If I didn't go to church, I met the people on the road home,' Toby said.

'You wouldn't measure success, then, by how much money a man had made?' Turnbull asked.

'I wouldn't. The only time I was unhappy was when I had money. The wife was out looking for me every night. She told me herself she was glad when the money was finished.'

'Would you consider a man a failure who didn't make good at his trade?' Collins asked.

'No, I wouldn't. That's our bloody trouble in this country. We serve our time to a trade and at the end of five years we're supposed to be journeymen. We have got a trade. We're tradesmen with a capital T. We would no more think of leaving the trade if we were unhappy at it than we would of flying in the air. If I didn't like the trade I'd chuck it in the morning. I'm not a first class tradesman; *that* I'm well aware of. But put me into a warehouse in charge of fifty or sixty men and I'll not disgrace myself.'

'I agree,' Collins said.

Toby went on: 'No, if I wasn't happy at the trade I'd take a job in the morning as a navvy or a bin man. That's the trouble with the bloody world, gutless people. I have a brother and his son is sweating and struggling to be a doctor. He's been at it now for ten years. With a good memory, I daresay he'll be able to learn all the data like a bloody parrot; then he'll be a doctor. He'll be as happy when he's a doctor as I would be if I was Bishop of Islandmagee; but will he give up medicine? Not on your bloody life. He'll go through life being a miserable failure and being frightened to face up to it or let the world know it.'

'Keep to the point,' Collins urged. 'That's your trouble, Toby, you cannot keep to the point.'

'Point or no point,' answered Toby loudly, 'Words like success and failure can mean sweet damn all. If people had the guts to face up to life, to look it straight in the eye, there would be less talk about success and failure. Make a man content when he's doing a job even if it's only rag-picking. Give him a good home, a woman he has a bit of love for. . . .'

'You're hot on the women,' Collins said.

'And why shouldn't I stand up for them? God love them is what I say every time. I still maintain that when a man is happy and content with the one woman and has a child or two, it doesn't matter a damn whether he's a street-sweeper. And I say that such a man has made a success of his life. . . .'

But Collins had his watch out and was getting to his feet. 'So that's the gospel according to Tobias,' he said.

'Yes,' said Toby, shaking his head and laughing. 'Thessalonians, Chapter One, Verse Two.'

'Frankie, I want you a minute,' Collins called. 'I was on the 'phone this morning to the office ordering some material. They were checking up on your time. You finish in a fortnight.' He nodded. 'I just thought I'd let you know. Likely you've been looking forward to this day for a long time. If you like I'll propose you for Union membership, and if you ask Toby, he'll second you.'

'Thank you.'

'Right. I'll fix it some night this week. You'd better see Toby yourself.'

On the way home he asked Toby. 'Sure, I'll go down and do seconder for you.'

He sat beside Turnbull in the tram. 'Did I hear you asking Toby to second you in the Union?' he asked. 'Who's proposing you?'

'Collins.'

'You'll never be poor again once you're in the trade union. I don't like them, Frankie. Some of them are sincere but there are quite a few of them members of the Orange Order and the Freemasons and behind backs they'd cut the throat of a Papist. Imagine them getting up at a union meeting and addressing you as brother, and then going off to an Orange meeting, or to listen to some of the political speakers they regard almost as Apostles of Christ, telling them to boycott Catholics, telling them they are not good Orangemen if they drink in Papist public houses. The whole business is one of hypocrisy. Look how strong the unions are in Ulster, and do the Protestants return one Labour M.P. to the Stormont Parliament? Of course they don't. I'm not saying that all the trade unionists are tarred with the Orange brush, but there's quite a few of them.'

Could Turnbull not relax? Frankie looked at him now as he clutched his pipe with his nervous hand. Poor Turnbull! Suddenly he was sorry for being irritated with him.

His aunt was bent over the table when he entered the house. She emptied the contents of a tin canister on to the table and was searching for tiny hooks to use on whatever she had been sewing.

'I come on your reference today. You should soon be a tradesman, judging by the date on it,' she said.

'Another two weeks,' he answered.

There was nothing more said. When she put his meal up she sat by the fire, staring into its red heart. She was probably planning all the things she could do, thinking how well off she would be when he was bringing home full pay. Her fingers moved against her skirt as if she were counting. He was sure she had made inquiries about how much he would get. Three pounds twelve and sixpence a week. She would want him to give it to her just as he received it from the office, the shiny, cream-coloured envelope not even opened. She would give him back the two and sixpence.

He had only another two weeks. To get away from her as soon as ever he could was important if his fear and nervousness were to be cured.

'There's a man calling here on Saturday; he'll take your measure for an overcoat and you can pay him at two shillings a week. You can get yourself a pair of shoes too, and a shirt.'

'I've to put in a pane on Saturday.'

'Who for?'

The lie came to him as he tried to stammer out the answer: 'For Simon's ffffriend. . . .'

She looked into the fire again. 'Then Saturday week.' He made no answer.

She had everything arranged — the 'tick man' calling for his half-crown, asking 'Could you not afford three and sixpence or four shillings a week and get a nice suit. I have some nice herringbone tweeds, or a good serge.' No.

6   IT WAS EASY FOR him to find where Molly lived. Even without the number of the house he could have told by the well-washed door, the clean circle in the street flags, the step scrubbed white.

He knocked and he heard her rush down the stairs. 'Come in, come in,' she said in an excited voice. 'No, not in there. That's a door leading to the shop. It's bolted in the inside. No, go right up the stairs. I have two rooms up there. Wait; better let me go first.' Pushing past him, she caught his hand and gave it an affectionate squeeze. As she climbed the stairs he could see she was wearing no stockings; her legs looked fleshy and white above the knees. 'Here we are now; in here.' She lifted a little gate, held it until they entered the room and replaced it. 'I need the gate on,' she explained. 'Them stairs are dangerous, and if Jimmy went near them at all, I'd be heart afeared of him falling down and mebbe breaking his neck. Come right to the fire. Take off your coat and make yourself at home.'

Noises came from under the table, and he saw a curly-headed child reaching for a ball.

'Come on, Jimmy, come out and see the nice man that's going to put the pane in for Mummy.' But the child had now got the ball and was beating it against the far leg of the table. 'That's Jimmy. Didn't I tell you about my wee souvenir? Well, that's him. I wouldn't part with him for all the tea in China. I called him Jimmy after my own father. I may as well tell you, I fell, as the church women told me, by the wayside. You don't know anything about these church women? They go about devoting their lives to "unfortunate women" as they call them. One of them stuck to me like a leech all the time I was carrying Jimmy, and when he was born she wanted me to turn him into one of their homes or orphanages. I told her to take a running jump over the Queen's Bridge. Says I, "Did I suffer the shame of carrying him, not to mention the pains of labour, just to let a parcel of oul' maids the like of you get him?" says I, "You ones running about, half of you couldn't get a man to sleep with you, never mind rousing him to lay hands on you?" Then she says, "Your child will get loving care and attention." Aye, loving care! What would them oul' maids know about love? They can read it in books, but books is a poor and sorrowful substitute for the real thing. So I have Jimmy and I'll sweat blood to keep him. It's a terrible thing, Frankie, for a child to be fetched up in one of these homes or orphanages. Were you ever inside one? I worked in one as a cleaner, and many's a day I pitied the poor orphans. I know there must be homes and places like that for childer, but surely they could be run better. Surely they shouldn't give weans the feeling that they have to be thanking somebody for every breath they take . . . But here, I have gabbled long enough. You must be starving. I done some spare ribs with a bit of cabbage and a couple or three spuds.'

She went to the gas stove in the far corner of the room, and little clouds of steam rushed out as she lifted the lids off the saucepans. The child crawled from under the table, and Frankie coaxed him towards his knee, but the child drew back shyly and pushed the fingers of its right hand among the curls at the back of its head.

'He's a bit shy with strangers,' said Molly. 'He doesn't see many people except a girl that comes in some nights to keep an eye on him when I'm away at work. I'll put him to bed soon for his afternoon sleep; then he won't be in your way when you put the glass in.'

The ball fell and the child searched under the table again. Molly left the room with the potatoes to drain them, and Frankie looked around him. The kitchen was clean, the floor boards scrubbed; there was a table, also scrubbed, and two chairs, a small sofa with a cushion on it and two pairs of shoes under it. A line ran across the fireplace with the child's clothes hung over it. Molly came back to the kitchen. 'I'll give Jimmy his wee bite first, then I'll get him into bed.'

She mashed a potato, skimming the cream of the milk to the plate and adding some butter. 'Nothing like the butter and the cream. The back of my hand to these foods that's advertised in the newspapers. Nothing to beat the good solid food, for putting a backbone in you.' She lifted the child to the table, reached for a spoon to sample the food:

'Maybe you would like to see the window and be doing something while I get the dinner ready?' He followed her into the room. 'This is what I call the junk room. My bed's here and all the other stuff that's cluttered up.'

But there was nothing 'cluttered' about the room. A few papers and magazines were piled within arm's reach of the top of the bed. The bed was painted white, with a quilt of red-and-white squares shaped like a draughtboard. Near the window a small table held a flowerpot, and on the green coloured walls were a few pictures.

'I got a pane of glass out of a soap picture from the shop downstairs. Will you be able to cut it?' He took a glass cutter from his pocket and said that he could do it. She left the room, and pulling the little table back he took the lower half of the sash out. He looked about him for somewhere to

220

hammer out the broken glass. When he told her, she said: 'Never mind how you mess the place up, sure ten minutes will soon clean it.' But he carried the sash to the yard, and had cleared the old glass out of it when she called him.

There was a tablecloth, a new bottle of sauce, and a great plateful of steaming, pink-coloured, fresh ribs.

'I've left you a knife and fork, but they are much better if you use your fingers, so pick them up and ate away. I was going to get you a bottle of stout, but I wasn't sure whether you touched it or not. If you like I'll run out and get you one now?' He shook his head. 'Do you not touch the drink? Maybe just an odd bottle? I like a man that can take a drink, but not one who makes a brute of himself at it. A man, I always say, that doesn't take a drink is a mean man.'

She cleared the plates and laid cups and saucers. From the oven she took an apple cake.

'I'd better get the glass in,' he said, when they had finished the meal.

'I'll put the child to bed. Will it take you long to put the pane in?' He shook his head. 'I'll put him near the wall and he'll be out of the draught,' she said.

He put the sash back in its place very quietly. The child slept with one hand under its cheek, the other cheek red as a rose. Molly was in the room looking at the sash. 'Did you manage all right?' Her eyes wandered from the window to the bed. 'God love my wee souvenir,' she whispered. She tiptoed from the room, Frankie followed her. 'I'll see to the curtains when the child wakens; no use kicking up any noise now,' she said.

'How much do I owe you for your work?'

'Nothing.'

'No, I can't have that. I must pay you for what you've done.'

'No, no, I want nothing.'

'But you must take something. If I had asked a stranger, I would have had to pay him. So come on, like a good fellow, tell me how much I owe you.'

'No, I'll take nothing.' He meant to go on but excitement was rising.

'All right, all right, if that's how you feel about it. God love you and thank you.'

She sat down. 'It was good of you. Mind you there's not much kindness left in the world today.' She was looking at him, holding him with her large eyes. Her hand was now on his knee. They heard the child murmur in its sleep. She cocked her head and smiled. She was looking away from him, listening in case the child had wakened. He looked down at her hand, at the blue vein that ran up her wrist. He touched her fingers. She did not move. He heard her heavy breathing, and his heart began to thump. She kept her head in a listening attitude. He could see her neck, tight and slightly red. Nervously he trailed his forefinger up her arm and his hand touched her breast. Suddenly she took her hand from his knee. He was about to move away, but she caught his hand and pressed it tighter.

There was a long pause. 'It's natural . . .' she said in a hoarse whisper. 'No matter what they say, it's natural.'

The child cried out. She removed his hand reluctantly. 'I'd better see to him. If you don't attend him right away he'd howl the house down,' she said. He could hear her talking to the child, telling it about the nice window Frankie had put in.

He was suddenly ashamed of what he had done and he wanted to say he was sorry. She might think his putting the pane in free was just an excuse. She might get the idea that he was a 'corner boy' or something of the blackguard, only out for that sort of low thing. He looked at her as she came from the room but there was nothing in her face to suggest that she was in any way annoyed or worried over what he had done.

She sat down with the child in her arms. 'Say "thank you" to Frankie for putting in the pane for Mummy,' she coaxed the child. 'Well, shake hands with him, if you won't say thanks . . .' Frankie reached out his hand, she took it and brought it close to the child. 'That's nice now. Say "pleased to meet you".' But the child, still sleepy and warm, shyly snuggled against her. 'He's very shy, and he isn't half slept,' she said.

As she put the shoes and the socks on the child, she played with its toes, the soles of its feet.

Was she a bad woman? A woman of the streets? He had heard often about street women, how easy they were; and he heard too that these 'street walkers' as they were called were easy to know; you had only to look at them, at their skin, their hair, the way they dressed, their talk. Molly could not be one of them. If she were, she could easily earn her living at it without going night after night to scrub out a shop. Simon would not have her cleaning his place if she was one of these women. And look at the child, clean and fat and healthy with skin like a rosy apple! He had heard the men talking about the diseases you could get from these women and how they could pass it on to children. . . .

If she did not let him come again . . . But she must. 'Now', she said, putting the child on its feet, 'Now you're ready to romp about again.' She bent to straighten one of its socks. 'What do you think of them legs, Frankie? I used to take him to a baby club when he was between two and a half and three, and they told me he was the healthiest child that came into the building.'

She fell silent as if she had suddenly remembered something. 'Aren't there some bad oul' bitches in the world too? I went to that baby club with Jimmy, and when they heard I wasn't married they used to treat me like somebody that wasn't right in the head. They thought I wasn't able, nor fit to look after him. And there were other women there, married ones, whose children had more relatives than Adam himself, and if you'd seen their weans — wee, scaldy-looking things without a pick on them! Aye, but when they heard I wasn't married, they thought I wasn't able to look after a child. Wouldn't it amuse you the attitude of some people? Well, there he is a "love child", and there's not a better looked after, nor a better fed nor clad child in the broad acres c Europe. His father done the dirty on me. Kept company with me for over two years. Come out and in here, practically lived off me; then took himself off with a tramp of a Jewess that he met in some atein' house. But I'm never tired of saying that I wouldn't give Jimmy away for all the tea in China.' The child reached under the table again for the ball. 'The world can do its damndest now; I have Jimmy to fill my life, if God spares him to me. I only hope that when he's man big he'll forgive me for his want of a name. But I've often heard that love childer are loyal to the mother. Did you ever hear that, Frankie?'

He knew nothing of matters like this, but he agreed with her. The conversation changed and she talked about his aunt. She was full of sympathy for him. 'Why don't you leave her? Far better to be in a room of your own at half a crown a week than a life like that.'

This was his chance to prolong the conversation, to twist and turn it to his own advantage. The difficulty was to utter his thoughts. A room of his own; coming down here to see Molly; having a meal with her. . . .

'Come, Jimmy, it's time we were going for a breather. I always take him out in the afternoon. If the weather's good. I go to the park.' She stood up, yawned and stretched her arms in the air, then with a quick movement drew them down again and caught his cheeks in her hands. 'God love you again for doing my wee job for me.' She draw his head forward and kissed him. He felt her soft, moist lips. 'That's a wee love for you,' she said, dropping her hands and reaching under the table for the child.

He took his tools from his pocket. 'Would you like paper to wrap them in?' He nodded, glad of any excuse to stay on. As he parcelled the tools, he stammered: 'Can I come and see you again?'

'What do you want to come and see me for?' This suddenly made her seem a stranger. He moved from one foot to the other, not knowing what answer to make.

'You don't want to come and see me. I'm years older than you. What age are you?'

'I'll soon be twenty.'

'I'm thirty-six, almost seventeen years older than you. You ought to look for a girl about your own age and marry her soon and get away from that oul' Turk of an aunt.'

He thought of Isabel, of Turnbull's daughter ... There was a long pause. The child swung itself to and fro from her body. He touched the child's curls. She caught his hand. 'Do you honestly want to come and see me?' He looked up at her and nodded. 'Why?' But he could not answer. 'Why does a young fellow like you want to come and see me?'

'I just want to....'

'Have you not got a girl?' He shook his head. 'Are you sure you haven't a girl?'

'My hand up to God,' he said.

'You were like a schoolboy when you said that.'

She released his hand, and he moved to the door. 'All right, you can come and see me again.'

'When?'

'When you like, you know the hours I work in the shop.'

'Sunday,' was all he was able to say.

'All right, Sunday, either evening or night. But listen, Frankie ...' She was beside him, lifting his head with her hand. 'Listen, son, don't run away with the idea that I'm easy prey. Because I have the child there and I live by myself, don't think I get into bed with every man I see. I don't mind a harmless bit of kissing or squeezing, but anything else, no. Remember that, don't think you're coming here to make a mug of Molly. I've had one lesson and I've paid dear for it; I don't want another ...' A long pause. 'Now do you still want to come and see me?'

'Yes.'

'Well you know when to get me in. But it's good to know where we stand, isn't that right?' He nodded. 'Now will you not let me pay you for putting the pane in, and we won't be beholding to each other?'

'No.'

'Well if you want to come and see me, as I say, you know my times.'

'Yes.'

'I'll come to the front with you,' she said. At the door she patted his head. 'God bless you for doing the job.'

'Thank you for the nice dinner.'

'It was nothing,' she said.

'Sunday,' he said again.

'Right, if you drop in about five, maybe we'll have a mouthful of tea together.' She smiled and he nodded good-bye. He was near the top of the street before he heard the door closing. She had been looking after him. If she had banged the door immediately he was away from it, he would have been slightly disappointed. He would see her tomorrow and ask her if she knew where he might get a room. She would help, he was sure, because her sympathy was with him. She had said that she didn't mind a harmless bit of kissing . . . He remembered now what he thought as she moved about the kitchen. 'Was she a bad woman?' God! if she only knew he thought of her as a street walker. He wondered if there was another man apart from the one she had the baby to. 'When you like, you know the hours I work in the shop' was what she had said. Had there been another man, she would have been more particular about the times when he, Frankie, was to call.

He turned into Royal Avenue, passing the rooms of the Painters' Trade Union, he looked up. Soon he would be climbing the stairs, Collins would tell them that here was a new man, and Toby would get up and say that everything was all right. He felt pleased with himself, not so much

226

because he was about to be made a member of the union as because he could think of Molly as a friend.

That night he lay wide awake. If she could only take him in as a lodger! He would be so good to the child; take it for walks; look after it when she was away working ... He would prove to her that he was not the blackguard type. He wanted to be her friend because she was so kind.

7 SHE WAS EXCITED and worried when he called the next day. Climbing the stairs in front of him she said, 'God! Frankie, but I'm glad to see you. Would you stay in the house until I run and get a doctor?'

'What is the matter?' He followed her into the bedroom.

'It's Jimmy,' she said. 'He took coughing fits during the night, but they got worse this morning, and he's eaten nothing all day. I must get the doctor. God! but I've been in a panic all the day. The girl that usually comes in is away, and I had nobody. I even missed the milkman; he might have 'phoned the doctor for me. But now that you're here will you keep an eye and I'll get the doctor myself. Could you use the 'phone?' He knew he would get too excited. She was going on. 'I can't use the 'phone myself. I can't even understand the books to get the number.' She was out of the room, fussing with her shoes, her coat and her hat and now she was rushing down the stairs, closing the door loudly behind her. He was alone with the sick child. It was asleep, its cheeks burning a bright red, its eyes sunken and slightly shadowed. The curls hanging down its forehead were damp and lifeless. It breathed heavily and rapidly. On the bed lay a teddy bear, one of its legs hanging by a thread, and on the floor a jotter with a pencil chewed at the end. The bed was clean, the sheets and blankets so much whiter than on his own bed.

The child moved and whimpered, then it kicked the bed-clothes. He waited until it ceased moving its legs; then he covered it. He tiptoed into the kitchen and sat by the fire. The child cried out again. Sweat glistened on its forehead, soaking the curls. It coughed violently and moved its head as if it had difficulty in breathing. Then it turned its face to the pillow, and he became frightened that it might suffocate itself. He lifted it by the shoulders, hoping the coughing would cease and that being away from the pillow and bed-clothes it might get more air. Its forehead reddened and the eyes for a moment seemed to disappear. He waited, his mind blank, staring at the coughing child. The coughing died into a violent struggling for breath. It clawed the air. If it died and him here alone with it!

Someone was tearing up the stairs. It was Molly. 'What has happened?' she asked as she fell across the bed, reaching for the child which was now crying madly. 'He has wakened and saw you and wondered where I was . . .' She sat on the bed with the child in her arms. 'The doctor will soon be here. It might be a touch of the cold he has, but I got frightened that it could be pneumonia.' She soothed the child, kissed it and talked to it, telling that the nice doctor would soon be here to cure it. She put the child back into the bed. He looked at her and saw she was crying. She turned her head away from him and he left the room. He heard her talk to the child again — strange, inaudible sounds through her crying. She came back to the kitchen, her face twisted and shiny with tears. 'I'll make a cup of tea,' she said, but another outburst of coughing from the room hurried her away. He went to the gas stove and warmed the teapot.

'Where do you keep your tea?' he called quietly.

'In the cupboard. God bless you. Will you make some for the both of us?' She had the child close to her breast, running her fingers through its hair, rubbing her eyes on its shoulder. 'The doctor wasn't in,' she said with a touch of anger, 'but the maid or wife or whoever she was said she would tell him when he got back. I hope she does. For some of these doctors are not particular.'

He made the tea and brought her a cup into the room. The child was quiet, and as gently as she could she laid him in the bed again. 'Look at him, Frankie, do you think it's something serious?' He could not answer, could say nothing to comfort her. 'Feel his cheeks and his brow?' He bent and touched the child's moist forehead. 'Do you think it's serious?' she asked, as he drew his hand away again, 'Ah, but you wouldn't know. You've had no experience of sickness. Children are queer like that; one minute they are falling over themselves with health and good spirits and the next minute you'd think they were near death's door.' She cried loudly again. 'Jimmy wouldn't die. Frankie, would he? You don't hear of four-year-old children dying just like that, do you?'

'The tea will be cold,' he stammered.

'I shouldn't worry myself until the doctor comes, but I can't help it, I just can't help it.'

'A wee bit of bread?' he stuttered.

'No, Frankie. I'll drink the tea. God love you for being here, I don't know what I would have done without you.' She kissed him, her soft lips wet and salty with tears.

'Some more tea?' She shook her head and stood up and stared at the sick child. She cried quietly now. He saw her breasts rise and fall, as if they were forcing the tears. He caught her hand, and she sat down on the bed again. Putting her arms around him she crushed her head against his chest. 'God love you, Frankie. It was a miracle you were here. There's kindness in you, son, there's kindness in you. People need friends when there is sickness about.'

She started up. 'I think that was a knock. Would you go down and see who it is?' He hurried down the stairs. It was the doctor, a fussy little man with a wrinkled face, and a habit of moving his cheeks as if his eyebrows were causing him pain.

He remained in the kitchen, hearing the doctor talk to Molly as though she were a girl of seven.

'A simple cold he has with a cough now and then. Pull yourself together and don't behave like a schoolgirl with the toothache. See that he doesn't kick the bedclothes away and keep him well covered; and take this to the chemist's. Give him a teaspoonful in water three times a day. Do you hear me now? Cease your tears and listen to me. Have you got what I said?' Her weeping voice repeated what the doctor had just prescribed. The doctor came from the room. Frankie looked at him. 'You're a friend of this woman's?' He nodded. 'Take this prescription round to the nearest chemist and wait until it's ready.' The doctor was going down the stairs.

'Will you come again?' she called after him.

'I will when there's something really wrong with the child.' The door closed.

She was both crying and laughing now. 'That's his way of going, straightforward and rough, but he's a good doctor. Just a touch of cold and a bit of a cough Jimmy has. He says I'm not to worry, that it isn't serious.'

She saw the prescription in his hand. 'Would you mind going for that for me?'

'I'll get it for you now,' he said.

He was in the street, a wild excitement in him. It would be just too bad if the chemist's shop was closed. But it was open, and he paid for the medicine, resolving that he would not take the money from her. She was his friend now. He could call again, confident that the sick child was a strong and honest excuse.

'How much was it?' she asked.

'Nothing,' he said.

'But I must pay you for it. You can't do all this for me. I'm thankful enough for all you've done already. I can't be taking your money from you like that.' She took the bottle, shook it robustly, then pulled the cork out and tasted the medicine. 'No, it isn't unpleasant in the tasting. He ought to have no trouble taking it.' She went to the room, and he heard her coax the child to take the nice medicine the doctor left to cure him.

But in spite of what the doctor had said, she was not easy in her mind. For the rest of the evening she sat with her head cocked, listening.

'What about your work?' he managed to ask.

'The girl that usually keeps an eye on him I'm sure will come tomorrow night.' He stood up, moving from foot to foot.

'If you like I'll come tomorrow night.'

'No, no, that wouldn't be the right thing. You're good-natured and kind, Frankie, and I can't impose on you.' He was excited now, and any more speech at the moment would be impossible. He would wait until his excitement died; then talk to her again. But she was winding the alarm clock, a sign indicating that bedtime was near. She yawned. 'Nerves make you tired,' she said. 'I was badly upset this afternoon until the doctor arrived. Now that I think of it, I haven't made any proper tea for the pair of us. I'm not caring about myself, but what about you?'

'I'm all right. I'll come tomorrow night,' he said.

'Would you? Just in case anything might happen. The girl mightn't turn up, and I'd need someone to keep an eye on Jimmy.'

'I'll come,' he repeated. She came towards him, took his face in her hands and crushed her lips tightly against his. 'I'll see you then tomorrow night. If you come straight from work I'll have a bite to eat ready for you.'

In the quiet street, he paused and looked up at the window as the room filled with yellow light. She was going to bed, getting in beside the sick child. He moved up the street slowly. This was a strange part of Belfast. It might be anywhere, shut off from the real city, the city that fought and argued about religion; the city that painted on its walls,

'To hell with the King', 'To hell with the Pope', 'No surrender, we love our King', 'To hell with England, we want our republic'. He liked it here for there were no reminders of what Simon had called the Ghetto; not that he knew what Ghetto meant. But here in this part of Belfast was a sense of freedom, for shops and stores were not like houses; they had no politics nor religion.

Once out of the street and the immediate district he hurried home. His aunt had tea ready. The bowl stood at the end of the table, his ration of bread resting on the mouth of it.

'That tea has been waiting for you since six o'clock. It's cold now, you can like it or lump it. This is not a lodging house, remember that.' He said nothing, but took the bowl of tea into the hall, looking at it as he moved from the light, seeing the dull brown colour of the cold tea, with a white fog streaking it. He ate the bread and gulped the cold liquid, then went straight to bed. He thought about Molly and the sick child. He was glad the child had been sick, for it had strengthened the friendship. 'What would I have done if you hadn't been here, Frankie?' was what she had said. Now, he hoped her friend would not turn up tomorrow night; that would mean one of two things; either he would go to the shop and scrub the floor for her, or else remain at home with the child. But one or the other would make the friendship stronger.

8   WHEN HE ARRIVED on the job the following morning, Toby said: 'I've fixed that for you, Frankie.'

'What, Toby?'

'Your membership of the trade union. If you come down with me tonight at half seven, I'll fix it for you. I'm getting you through in a hurry.' Toby winked. His wink suggested something of a favour, as if it were not usual to become a member so quickly.

'I'm getting you through in a hurry, Frankie, you know why? I've heard there's going to be a big start in the shipyard soon. So if you get your walking papers this Saturday, you can pop down to the shipyard and everything will be in order. You could start right away. Everything would be in order with the union, you see what I mean . . .?' Toby winked again.

For a moment he was dazed. Two things collided in his mind. One, that he was to see Molly as soon as he finished tonight; two, that Toby had fixed that he should become a member of the trade union tonight. But the thought of seeing Molly was strongest in his mind. He wanted to go to Toby and ask him if the union could not be arranged for another night. But Toby's attitude was one of conferring a great favour.

All that day the two thoughts seemed to shout each other down. While one was in favour of going to Molly's and making the excuse that he was sick to Toby, the other told him that if he were to be paid off on Saturday, it would be better if he could go to the shipyard, looking for a job and feeling confident about his membership. For, supposing he were offered a job in the shipyard, that was the first thing they would ask; was he all right with the union? He decided to rush down to Molly and explain to her. In the afternoon he asked Turnbull how long the business would take.

'There's no great ceremony. Your name is proposed, and seconded, and that's all there's to it; then you get your card. You'll have no trouble, Frankie. Toby will propose you and I'll second it. There'll be no more questions asked, for they know we wouldn't propose an impostor.'

On the way home, Collins explained that he had asked Toby to do this because he himself had another engagement. 'But Toby will see you through all right, and so will Turnbull.'

He rushed down to Molly's. As she climbed the stairs she laughed and told him that Jimmy had not coughed so much, and that the doctor's bottle had worked wonders. She had a meal ready. Crisply fried sausages with chips and mashed turnips. He tried to tell her what had happened.

'Sit down there, take your supper and tell me slowly what it is you are trying to say,' she said. She listened intently, helping him to piece together his story. 'Well, sure there's no harm done. My girl will not be here. She's threatened with an appendicitis. So what you'll do is this. Go to your trade union; it can't last any longer than ten o'clock; then come down here, and I'll leave for the shop. If I scrub the floor and run the duster over the furniture, it won't take more than an hour to do that. And I'll speak to the manager and tell him that I'm only giving the premises a lick and a promise until things are back to normal. Now go ahead and eat up your supper.'

She talked as he ate, inquiring about the trade union, and said how glad he should be to be in it. The child slept in the room; now and then she tiptoed in and returned with a smile. He thought about his aunt. What excuse could he make for not being at home for his tea? But he could not turn up at the union rooms in his working clothes. He looked at the clock. It was twenty past six. If he hurried away he could still get there and change his clothes.

Molly came from the room. 'Don't bolt your food so quickly, you'll give yourself indigestion.'

Slowly he told her that he must change his clothes. He could rush away now, but she had put before him a dish containing custard and strawberries. 'Don't rush your food; sure five minutes will make all the difference,' she said. 'It's being nervous and worried like that that affects your talking. Take things easier. I'll pour out your tea and it will be cooling for you.'

'I'll be back as soon as I can,' he said, hurrying down the stairs. He knew he would have to make some show of eating what his aunt had prepared for him, but the meal would be so slight that it would not trouble him.

'It'll soon be that you won't come home for anything to eat at all,' she said, as he entered the house. He made no answer but reached for the plate of stew. 'Are you eating in somebody's house? Are you? Answer me. Am I a dog that you must ignore what I say to you?'

'I want a clean shirt.'

'What for?' From the darkness of the hall he called out about going to be made a member of the union.

'I haven't a clean shirt ready for you. Use the shirt you wore yesterday.' He climbed the stairs, and changed quickly.

'If I thought you were eating in somebody else's house . . .' she began as he came down the stairs, but he was outside before she finished. She was evil. Always she seemed to know what he was about.

At the union rooms Toby was waiting for him.

'Turnbull hasn't turned up,' he said, 'as usual. That bloody man will be late for his own funeral. But we'll go up and wait.' They climbed the dusty stairs, passing office after office until they came to the top floor. 'Here we are,' said Toby. The room was dusty and had not seen paint nor wallpaper for years. On the walls were one or two posters with 'Unity is Strength' printed on them; above the fireplace hung a picture of a bearded man. Near the wall were a table and a number of chairs and forms. About thirty members were present. From the way they greeted Toby, it was evident that he was very popular.

Turnbull arrived and Frankie noticed that the others did not make the same fuss of him as they had of Toby. The meeting was about to start. A man with a waxed moustache opened an attaché case and took out some papers. Then Toby was on his feet, addressing this man as Worthy Chairman, telling him about Frankie, and proposing him for membership, adding that Worthy Brother Turnbull would second him. Turnbull was now standing, nodding his head and agreeing with everything the Worthy Brother had just said.

It gave him great pleasure to second the Worthy Brother's proposal. The members all agreed that Frankie should be made a member. Many of them shook hands with him, and a sandy-haired man, who turned out to be the secretary, told Frankie that he would have his card in about a week's time. Now he was a fully fledged member of the Trade Union of House and Ship Painters; he could travel any part of the British Isles he liked and be recognized by merely producing his card. The sandy-haired man shook him warmly by the hand and said: 'Let me give you one tip. No matter where you go, never let on you're a friend of Toby's.' This was meant playfully, and Toby, hearing it, put up his hands in a mock boxing attitude. Frankie moved away towards Turnbull.

'Have I any more to do?' he asked. Turnbull took the trembling pipe from his mouth, and flogged the air with the mouth-piece: 'No, you're a member now, you can stay on and hear the proceedings if you wish, but if you want to go you are quite free to. Just say thanks to Toby and tell him if you are leaving. Be good-mannered and shake the chairman by the hand if you haven't already done so.'

Frankie left the room and raced towards Molly's. It was now twenty minutes past eight. He would be there by half past, which meant that Molly could be at her scrubbing by nine o'clock.

'I didn't expect you so early,' she said. 'Did you get through all right? Are you a member of the trade union now?' He told her he was. 'Jimmy's well improved the day. But I didn't let him out of bed. It's best not to take any chances. He's asleep now, and I don't think he'll waken until I get back. I won't be long, for as I told you, I'll only give the place a lick and a promise. I can be more particular about it when Jimmy's back to normal.' She tiptoed down the stairs, and he heard the front door close quietly.

He walked to the room and looked at the sleeping child. Its breathing was much quieter, its cheeks not so flushed.

He sat down in the kitchen again by the warm fire, a strange feeling of possession within him. It was as though he owned this little place, with Molly as his wife, or the woman he lived with. He worked for her, gave her all his earnings. She in turn gave him freedom, a clean home, good food, a sense of confidence. She would not speak the angry word, nor threaten with the poker or the brush; she would give him what he had never had — kindness. . . .

He sat in the chair, letting his mind go blank, the heat of the fire bringing sleep. He heard the child murmur and he went to it, and turned the lamp flame a little higher, but the child was sound asleep again. There had been nothing exciting about it, but now he could go anywhere in the British Isles and produce his card; he was a Journeyman. It seemed sure that he was to be paid off on Saturday, and on Monday morning, he supposed, he would go down to the shipyard and look for a job. Toby would tell him how to set about it . . . Sleep was coming. He tried to fight it. He did not want Molly to come back and him asleep He drew the chair back from the fire. But the drowsiness still soaked his mind, and he closed his eyes.

When he heard her on the stairs, he rose quickly and looked at the clock. He had been asleep for well over an hour. Quickly he hurried to the room and looked in to make sure the child was covered. She opened the door, and the first thing she did when she entered the room was to take a bowl from inside her coat. 'I brought some fish and chips. I'll put them on the hob in case they get cold. We'll have them to a cup of tea as soon as we can.' She went to the room, looked at the child, and came out again. 'You had no trouble with him? He didn't waken?' Her eyes were on him, awaiting an answer. He shook his head. She bent her face close to him and kissed him. 'I knew he was safe with you. You can tell with people.'

She talked on through the meal, telling him how quickly she got through her work in the shop.

'Tomorrow night?' he asked.

'Could you come? Would your aunt object?'

'She doesn't know,' he said.

'That's the best way. What she doesn't know won't do her any harm. You're safe enough down here; no neighbours to see what goes on. The nearest I have is a night watchman in the grain store, and he's an ex-policeman. They see all but they say nothing; not that I'm ever speaking to him.'

'I'll come tomorrow night again,' he said.

'Will you come for your tea?'

'No, I'll . . .'

'Better have your tea with your aunt. The less you give her to talk about, the better.'

Her eyes followed him to the door. 'Good night,' she called after him in a loud whisper.

The door was closed when he got to his aunt's house. He knocked and he heard her coming down the hall. Her slippers were loose and flip-flapped as she walked.

The door opened. 'What hour of the night is this to be coming in at? It's nearly midnight. Do you hear me? It's nearly midnight.' There was no point in answering her. An hour meant nothing if she took it into her head to complain about late time-keeping. 'What did they say to you at the union? Did they take you into it?'

'They did.'

'And where is your card?'

'I get my card next week.'

'I hope you're telling the truth.'

In bed he lay thinking about her sudden interest in his union card. To her it probably meant, that now he was a member, he would get full wages, and she would have no further worries. He would come home like a lamb every week and put his full pay packet on the table.

9 'THE ONLY WAY you get a job in the shipyard,' said Toby, 'is to go down every morning and stand at the gate on the off-chance of being called. It's a degrading bloody thing, men standing about like sheep until a foreman wags his finger at them. It's nearly like a slave market. There's just the one difference; in the slave market a slave knew that sooner or later he'd get someone to take him on; but down in the shipyard there's no knowing that. So that's what you do; go down morning after morning until you're called.'

When Toby left them, Turnbull said: 'Listen, Frankie, don't be doing the idiot on Friday night.' He looked wide-eyed at Turnbull, not knowing what he meant.

'It's the usual thing when an apprentice completes his time for him to stand a drink all round. Well don't, as I say, be an idiot on Friday night. Don't burden yourself with the whole crew. Ask Collins and Toby in with you. . . .'

'And yourself,' he said.

'I'm not fussy. A sixpenny bottle of stout will repay anything I've done for you. But I just want to warn you. The work is anything but plentiful, and there's a good few unemployed; so take my tip and watch every shilling.'

'But Toby says they are looking for men in the shipyard.'

'Aye, it's all very well for Toby to talk like that. We all haven't Toby's influence. If they are looking for men, there's a good few on the dole they could take. But don't let me put you off going down and trying your luck, although I don't envy you having to go down to that draughty Godforsaken hole. Still, you never know, you might not be paid off here. As I said before, this is a convent job and through policy, seeing you're a Catholic, they might keep you on.'

But on Friday at half past three, when Collins brought round the wages, he said: 'I've bad news for you, Frankie, I've got your cards here.' And when Collins had gone, after giving him the broad envelope, he opened it, and there were his employment cards. He was without a job; sacked, unemployed. The thought dazed him. From now on he was a man. Yet he did not know how to go about looking for another job. He supposed he went to a contractor's office and said: 'Are you looking for men?' or 'Are you starting any hands?' or 'Any chance of a job?'

'Well, what happened?' Turnbull was behind him. He held up the cards and Turnbull nodded. 'It's the policy of the firm,' he said quietly. 'There's nothing for it, Frankie, but the shipyard on Monday morning. Go down and have a try. You'll need to put your books into the Labour Exchange anyway.'

He dropped the sponge in the bucket and went in search of Toby. Usually on Friday they did very little work after they had been paid. He was sure he would find Toby talking with some of the others. He passed the kitchen and he looked in, hoping he might see Isabel. But she was not there, nor could he find Toby. Returning to his job, he ran into Turnbull again.

'I'm looking for Toby,' he said.

Turnbull whispered, 'Toby's down in one of the boiler houses with a couple of the plumbers and some of the electricians playing pontoon. But don't say I told you.'

The whistle had gone before Toby appeared. 'Well, are you going to make us all drunk?' he asked.

'Buy him one drink and that's the limit,' Collins said. Toby winked and whispered, 'Just the three of us, Collins, Turnbull and myself. . . .'

They went to a pub not far from the convent gates. Toby had a small whisky, Collins a gin, and Turnbull a bottle of stout. They drank to his success, all wishing him luck, and hoping he would do well for himself. If there was anything they could do for him in the future, he had only to ask. He sipped his shandy. Toby had advised him against strong drink.

'Stick to the shandy and you'll come to no harm,' he said.

Turnbull offered to buy another drink, but Collins

refused, saying he had a date with an angel and he did not want to turn up smelling the wrong smell. They shook hands again as they left the pub.

'You'll come up and see us when you like, Frankie,' said Turnbull. 'The wee girl — you remember Selina? She always inquires kindly about you. So, any time, don't be afraid to give us a call. You never know, I might hear of a start going somewhere.'

As he left Turnbull, he thrust his hand into his pocket, feeling the three pound notes. He had received three pounds twelve and sixpence, his first week's pay! He thought about what he should tell his aunt. Should he tell her he had only been paid his usual wage, give her that, and keep the rest? He would want money if he was to pay the fares up and down to the shipyard, and there was the money to be paid when he went to get his Union card. It would be bad enough having to tell his aunt he was paid off. He would need the thought of the money far back in his mind to give him a little confidence as well as comfort.

He put his overalls on the stairs, letting them fall to the ground before he did so, in order to bring her attention to them.

'Take them to the yard and steep them in the bucket of water I left for them,' she said. This was more of her thrift. She had been washing early in the day, and rather than throw the water away, she saved it because of a little soap and washing powder.

'I won't need them so soon.'

'Why?' she snapped.

'I've been paid off.'

'You've what?'

'I've been paid off.' He moved into the hall, so that he could dance the words from him. 'I've finished my time, so I've been paid off.'

'You've no work then for Monday?'

God! why should she torture him, by pretending she did

not understand? She knew what he meant when he said he was 'paid off'. It was a phrase everyone in Belfast knew.

'Have you no work then for Monday?'

'No. I'm going to the shipyard to look for a job.'

'Are you getting a job there?'

'No, I'm going to look for one.'

'Will you get one?' Christ, why must she go on like this.

'That's what I am going down to see.'

'You can't be much of a tradesman if you've been paid off after your first week.' He made no answer. 'Do you hear me? You can't be much of a tradesman if they've paid you off after one week.' What could he say? Impossible to try and explain to her about the policy of the firm. There was the agony of getting the words out, and he was certain that she would pretend not to hear them and make him repeat them over again.

'Is it certain you're getting a job in the shipyard?'

'No, I'm going down to see.'

'And what happens if you don't get a job in the shipyard?'

'I dunno.'

'You needn't think you're going to lie up here and draw the dole.' No answer. 'Do you hear me? What happens if you don't get a job in the shipyard?' He walked up the hall towards the yard. 'Is there no money for me tonight?' she called. He turned and quietly put the money on the table. She picked it up. 'Did they not give you a man's wages for your first week?'

'No.'

'By God, I swear this night that if I find out you got a full man's wages and kept it from me, I'll make an example of you.'

He hurried to the yard. Would she go to the office to inquire about his wages? He did not think she would. Taking the remaining money from his pockets, he pushed it into his boot:

'Come in here. Do you hear me calling you?' She had

closed the front door. 'Turn out your pockets till I see if you have been thieving from me.'

He pulled his trouser pockets wide out, and his coat pockets until they hung like dogs' ears. It was remarkable, he thought as he stuffed the pockets back, how each knew exactly what the other would do. It almost seemed as if there were a devil in the house prompting each of them. 'Make him turn out his pockets', was the thought in her mind. 'Hide the money in your boot', was the thought in his. She put his meal on the table — two boiled potatoes, slimy with the gravy that came from the two small bits of meat. He ate the meal, changed his clothes and rushed down to Molly's.

The child was now playing about the room; Molly said it was too soon to let him out of doors.

'I'm paid off, Molly,' he said.

'You expected that, didn't you?'

'I did.'

'Will you go to the shipyard on Monday morning?'

'I will.'

'How did your aunt take it when you told her?'

'She was upset.'

'Sure it isn't your fault, you couldn't help being paid off.'

He told her about the money, and she suggested that he could leave it in her keeping, in case his aunt searched his pockets again when he was asleep.

When she returned from the tailor's shop she had the usual fish and chips in the bowl.

'I was thinking tonight, Frankie, that if you get a job in the shipyard it isn't a big distance from here; you could come up and get a bite of something to ate at dinner time.'

'I could. I'd like that very much.'

'Yes, that's what to do.'

'I er . . .'

She looked at him, her eyes wide. 'What is it?'

243

'I er . . .'

'Take it easy now. What is it you want to say?' He stood up, words would not come while he sat. 'I would like to get a room about here, about here . . . somewhere.'

'I dunno where you'd look for a room about here. But if you care, I could keep an eye open and an ear to the ground for you. There is not, I know, any living accommodation in this street except my own, and that wouldn't be here if the last owners of the shop underneath hadn't lived here themselves.'

He was silent. He looked down at her head, at the fine thread of scalp that showed grey where her hair parted. She raised her head slowly. 'You would like to get away from your aunt?' He nodded. She put her arms around his waist and pressed him close to her. He kissed her hair. For a moment it seemed silly to him that he was here kissing the hair of a charwoman. He had seen this sort of thing often at the pictures, but the woman was never a char. Then he thought about himself; what was he? A nonentity, a failure. He felt Molly crushing her breasts against him. He took her face in his hands and kissed her.

'You know, Frankie,' she said, 'the first time we met, I mean the first night you came here, I thought you were after the one thing. I was wrong. You're a kind creature. You know nothing about women,' she paused, 'do you?' He shook his head. 'I thought so.' She smiled and pressed her head against his chest. He stood, feeling uncomfortable, not knowing what to say.

'We're friends anyway, son,' she said, 'aren't we?'

'Yes.'

She turned to the fire, picked up the child's bottle and poured water into it from the kettle. He looked at the clock; time he was leaving. He stood at the door about to descend the stairs.

'Good night, Molly.' She came to him, kissed him.

'I wish you were not going home the night, Frankie.' He

looked at her. 'You'd better go, Frankie . . . go on, like a good boy, you'd better go. . . .'

'I'll come tomorrow night,' he said.

'Yes, do. Come for your tea. It is Saturday; we'll have a fry.'

10   HE LAY AWAKE most of Sunday night. He was afraid of sleeping too late, for he would have to leave the house very early to get to the shipyard at least fifteen minutes before the whistle went for starting time. His aunt had told him that he could waken himself; she was not getting up in the early hours of the morning for him. He could hear the knocker-up in the street, loudly hammering on the doors, and he knew it was about six o'clock.

He had never been to the shipyard before, but he knew if he followed the crowd over the Queen's Bridge he was all right. He saw one or two men in white overalls and he ran until he was directly behind them. They stopped at a grey building with the words 'Paint Shop' in large white letters above the door. He counted twenty other men there already, and he stood close to a little circle of them. One was saying: 'Yes, I was here on Friday. He started six. I was here on Thursday and he started five.' The breeze coming up the channel was knifelike, the men moved about to keep warm. There was a huge iron gate, and beyond it a small door. When anyone came through the small door, Frankie could see the others moving into a position from which they could be easily seen. The boss or foreman must come from the little door. One man looked at his watch.

'What time do you make it?' asked the man next to him.

'It's now dead on eight o'clock.'

'Time he was making an appearance,' said the inquisitor.

The little door opened and a tall figure wandered out casually. He was thin, with a red face, and he wore a blue suit with a white collar and a bowler hat. He looked at the crowd, and Frankie saw his jaws move as he clenched his teeth. Lifting his hand, he pointed, 'you and you and you,' he called.

Several of the men, mistaking his vague hand movements, had entered the gate. He sent them back, saying, 'Not you ... Him there ...' This time he came closer and pointed more directly to the men he was about to take on. He counted the men he had called. 'Six,' Frankie heard him say. 'That's all for the day,' he announced, and disappeared into the office.

The men left the gate reluctantly, wandering away from it in threes and fours. Frankie found himself listening to a small man wearing very thick glasses.

'Sure the bloody thing's ridiculous. Here we are, just like a parcel of dogs — whistle us and we'll come. There ought to be some arrangement with the trade union. The delegate ought to be told each night how many men are wanted; then he could send them down. That would save us from standing at that gate like a parcel of prostitutes.'

'That would only work, up to a point,' said another. 'What happens if the delegate happens to have his favourites?'

'And hasn't that string of misery got his favourites too?'

'Bejazes, it's the last time I'll go down there to make a beggar's ghost of myself,' said a third.

Frankie was hungry, but he had only his tram fare — the rest of his money was at Molly's. There would be no food from his aunt if he went home, and there would be the added terror of letting her know he had not got a job. Molly's was just a little way on the far end of the Bridge. It was early; still, there was the chance she might be up. The street was quiet and he knocked the door as silently as he could. He heard the window opening.

'Who's there?'

He looked up. 'It's me.'

'You, Frankie? Wait a second and I'll drop you down the key. I'm not out of bed yet.'

She was gone less than a minute and he heard the clink of the key on the roadway.

'What happened?' she called as he came to the kitchen. 'Did you not get started?'

'No.'

'Come in, don't be alarmed. I'm still in bed.' She pointed to the child. 'He's asleep.'

'I've come for some money, Molly. I took a hungry fit and I want to buy something to eat.'

'You can eat here; I'm getting up now. See if you can set a light to the fire; you'll find sticks in the oven. Would you like to make a cup of tea now, on the gas? You know where the things are?'

He moved about the kitchen preparing the tea. 'I'll bring you in your cup of tea,' he said, at the door. He heard her laugh and say something about doing it in style.

She sat up in bed, moving easily so as not to disturb the sleeping child. She had put on a pullover to cover her bare neck. Her face looked fresh and soft. There were no dark shadows, no sunken eyes, no traces of the moustache that he had seen on his aunt's face.

'Do you think there'll be any chance of you getting a start in the shipyard?'

'I dunno, Molly. I may just keep going down every morning.'

She looked into his eyes and let her hand rest on his thigh. He felt her fingers warm. 'If you set a light to the fire, I'll get up now.' He left the room, lit the fire, and was sweeping the hearth when she entered the kitchen. 'You could ate a fry of bacon and eggs,' she said, bending to the gas stove for the pan. She sang as she cooked the breakfast.

> Will the angels play their harps for me,
> Oh! I wonder, yes, I wonder,
> Will the angels way up yonder,
> Will the angels play their harps for me?

As they ate, she said: 'Look, Frankie, I'd like to go up to the hospital this afternoon to see my friend — the girl I was telling you about. Would you stay and keep an eye to the child for me? I don't want to take him out of doors so soon after his touch of the cold.'

'Yes, Molly, I'll come back, but I must tell my aunt first. She might think I was started to work.'

'Would she?'

'Well . . .' He tried to explain. 'You see I am afraid . . .' But he was lost again, and he had to rise from the table to move from one foot to the other to get the words out.

'That woman must have the life and soul frightened out of you. You go about like a mouse. You seem afraid to put your feet properly on the floor; you even seem scared to knock the door. God above, Frankie, you can't go on like that.'

The child's crying took her from the kitchen. He looked at the clock. It was ten minutes past ten. It would be eleven before he reached home. Better go now.

'I'll go home and tell her, Molly, but I'll come back.'

'All right. There's no hurry back if you have anything else to do. The hospital visiting hours are from two to five.'

Outside the street was now lively with traffic. He thought of what he would say to his aunt. He could only tell her that he got no job, but there was a hope for tomorrow morning. He would have to see about leaving his cards in the Labour Exchange too.

Her coat lay on the sofa. She had evidently been out.

'I didn't get s . . . ,' but the word did not come. He closed his eyes as he tried to force it out. Something made a clinking noise on his head. Little bright sparks flashed from his eyes. She had struck him with the poker. A trickle of warm blood was rushing down his nose. Dazed as he was, his immediate reaction was the old one — into the yard and hold the door tight.

'You dirty, lying thief,' she was calling after him. 'I knew you got your full week's money. And, you dirty thief, you told me a conniving lie. The liar is always found out. I found you out, my boyo. I went straight to your firm this morning, and I got the truth, word for word.' She tugged at the door, uttering sounds like some strange animal. She beat the floor with the poker, calling out: 'I'll murder you, you thieving dog. Keeping from me the money you owe me. Me that kept a roof over your head all these years! That's the thanks I get. I'll pull the lying tongue out of your head.' With two hands he held to the latch of the door. The blood trickled down his nose and ran along the outside of his upper lip; what he couldn't take into his mouth with his tongue, he tried to blow away. A few drops fell to the ground. They were black, like beads. There was no fight in him now.

He could only wait until she had cooled a little, then try to wash the blood away, get out into the street and escape from her for ever. Usually after an outburst like this she would have to sit down for nearly five minutes getting her breath back.

There was a knock and he heard her move up the hall. Now was his chance. He crossed to the entry door, man-œuvred the bolt back, closed the door quietly, and was away to Molly's.

He tore a pocket from his trousers, wet it with his tongue, and wiped the blood from his forehead.

'My God! What is the matter with you?' Molly cried. She bathed the wound with hot water and dusted it with boracic powder. When she had coaxed the story from him, she was for sending for the police. 'Go to hospital and let a doctor see what she's done. That's a case for the police. My God, did you stand back and let her do that? You, as near a man's years as makes no difference, to let anybody do that without raising a hand in your own defence.'

He tried to tell Molly how he felt about keeping the money.

'Doesn't matter. If you'd kept fifty pounds from her, she

had no right to use a poker on your head. Sit down there in front of the fire and forget about her.'

'I'm not going back,' he said quietly.

'You'd be mad if you did.'

'I'll go to the doss house in Millfield.'

'I'll make a shakedown here for you. You can stay until you get your head cured.'

A knock at the door took her downstairs. She came back with a letter. 'Who on earth could be writing to me?' She read it and was puzzled about the writer. 'It's from some connection of Simon's. The name is Haig. He wants to know if I can do some cleaning for him.' She looked again at the letter: 'Could you call about eleven-thirty tomorrow morning?' She darted from one subject to another until it was time for her to go to the hospital.

At tea-time she said there was a small mattress she could put in the middle of the kitchen floor. 'I'm not blessed with too many bedclothes, but we'll get what will cover you.' When she left for the shop, he felt tired, and lay down on the bed beside the child. The wound in his head was painful. But he was far away from his aunt, away from the house of fear. For one night he could relax. He was here in the house of a big, kindly woman. A woman whose child now lay beside him, a bastard. He wanted to be with this woman, to live with her in this quiet street. . . .

'How long have you been asleep?' She was bending over him with a lamp in her hand.

'I'm sorry,' he mumbled.

'What are you sorry about? You were tired and you stretched yourself on the bed. I'd do the same myself. How is your head?'

He followed her to the kitchen, feeling that he had slept for three days rather than three hours.

'I'm sorry . . .' he repeated.

'For God's sake don't keep lamenting that.'

'You've been kind to me, Molly.'

'Not at all. What I've done for you, I would have done for a dog — washed and put a bit of sticking plaster on your head. Nonsense, man, I was thinking in the shop tonight . . .' She touched his knee and he looked up. 'I was thinking, if I go to see this man, Haig, at half eleven in the morning, who is to look after the child? I wonder, ought you to go down to the shipyard tomorrow, your head being cut? Sure, there's always Wednesday morning and Thursday morning. You could stay, could you?' He nodded. 'Now I'll fix a bed for you.'

She looked at the fire. 'No danger of a spark flying out on you.' She assured herself that it was safe and, brought a small mattress from the room. 'This was for a cot, but I had no room for it, and I thought the child was better in bed with me.' He moved the chairs and she put the mattress on the floor. Then she got a pillow, a sheet, a blanket and a thin cover. 'I'll leave you a coat and you can put it over you. I told you, I'm not blessed with too many bedclothes.'

She left him and he undressed. 'Don't worry about turning off the light, I'll do that,' she called from the room. He got into bed.

'Can I put the light out now?' The door opened and she picked her way to the gas. The light went out, and the few flames from the fire sent their shadows dancing on the ceiling. She stood looking down at the fire. 'No, I don't think there's any danger of a spark flying out.' He lifted his head. 'It's not paining you any more?'

'No, Molly, it's fine now.' She bent down, feeling the wound lightly with her fingers. 'Good night, son.'

'Good night, Molly.' He caught her hand, and she put her arm around him and kissed him. She lay beside him. 'It's quiet here, Frankie.' His breath came out in a rush.

'Why are you nervous, Frankie?' But he made no answer.

She lay close to him for a long time. The child crying made her rise reluctantly. 'He misses me. I'd better see to him at once.' As she moved to the room, he could see that her feet were bare.

11 IT WAS TEN O'CLOCK the next morning when she woke him. The breakfast was already on the table.

'You slept well?' she said.

'I did.'

'Any pain in your head this morning?'

'No, it's all right, it's. . . . '

'You mustn't whisper so much, Frankie. There are times when I find it hard to make out what you're saying. Don't be afraid to use your voice. There's nobody here going to use a poker on you. Try and forget your nerves. Now finish your breakfast and I'll bathe your head again.' But, glancing at the clock, she said: 'Maybe I'd better rush on and see these people in case I'm late. Sure you can get some hot water yourself and bathe it.'

She dressed, powdered her face and used lipstick. 'How do I look? You don't object to lipstick do you?' He laughed. 'There now, you've got some on your own lips.'

When she left he lay on the bed and talked to the child. The child's laughter was sudden and musical like the singing of a bird. He played a game; making it stand up in the bed and pushing it down quickly. Once he turned it head over heels, and the child, for a moment, looked frightened, but when he repeated this, it regarded the tumbling as great fun.

He wondered why its father had deserted Molly. She never talked much about this. Nor did she ever talk about her friends or relatives. He did not know whether she had a mother or father, or brothers or sisters. Yet it was strange that a man should go off and not care about the child he had left with the woman. He would not do that. If he lived on with Molly and she had a baby by him, he would not leave her . . . Last night she had lain with her arms tightly around him, but nothing had happened. . . .

She returned about an hour later. 'It's Haig and his wife, Pearl, a niece of Simon's. They want to know if I'll come once a week and clean for them. I met Simon too. He was asking about you. And Mr. Haig wanted to know if you were working, and when I said "no", he asked me if you'd do a wee job for him.'

'When?'

'I dunno. I told him I'd get you to go and see him. There, he gave me that card. You'll get him there any afternoon between four and five. You could go along this afternoon and see him.'

'I could.'

'You ought to keep in with that man Haig. He looks to me to be the sort of person that might be able to do something for you. I could get two jobs if I wanted them. Pearl wants me to come to the house for her, and he — I believe, he's a traveller for paint — he's getting some sort of store in the city centre with an office; so he asked me if I'd care to come and clean for him. I told him I'd think about it, for with Jimmy here I don't want to bite off more than I can chew.'

Molly was right; Haig might be able to do something for him.

'They've just got themselves a new house out by Bloomfield way. They're moving into it next week.'

'How's Simon?'

'Simon's eyes are getting worse. But he seems to be in good form. He's talking about going to London again to see the specialist. Did you bathe your head?'

'No, Molly, it's all right. . . .'

'It's not all right. Come on, I'll bathe it now for you.' She poured hot water in the basin and washed the wound. 'If you are going to see Mr. Haig, you don't want the sticking plaster to be as big as a cabbage. I'll put it neater this time and you can comb your hair so as to hide it.'

Putting a little strip of pink plaster on the wound, she became almost angry as she talked about his aunt and her brutality. 'She might have split your skull. Jail's the place for her.' She looked at his shirt. 'The collar of that shirt is tired-looking. Take it off and I'll give it a run through. It won't take long drying in front of the fire. It's the only shirt you have, isn't it?'

'All my clothes are at my aunt's.'

'I don't suppose you feel like going for them.' She did not wait for him to answer. 'I know how you feel. Let her keep the clothes. Once you start to work you can buy yourself a shirt or two. Here, you'd better put this on you to save you from getting the cold.' She handed him a pullover. 'Off with your shirt now, and I'll give it a run through for you.'

'Thank you, Molly.'

'Why must you go on trying to say "thank you" all the time. You know, Frankie, it seems to me you are just as nervous with me as you were with your aunt. You're frightened of the wee bit of kindness. I suppose you think, any minute, I'll tell you to clear out.'

'I know you are kind, Molly, but I feel you might get tired of me. I have never been used to kindness and . . .' He could go no further. He moved excitedly, and the sounds that came in place of words died into tears.

'Don't take on like that. Don't work yourself into a panic. Have a good cry if you want to.' She left the kitchen with the shirt in the basin. When she returned she was humming to herself. 'I always like to see a clean shirt. It doesn't matter what the rest of the clothes are like, if a man is wearing a clean shirt, he's more than half way to decent looking.' She put the shirt over a chair close to the fire. 'Now, while the shirt's drying, clean your boots. You need a shave badly, but, you can call into a barber's on the way to see Mr. Haig.'

As he made his way to meet Haig, he kept to the little side streets, for there was the danger that he might meet his aunt. When he had left her house before, there had been nothing final about it. But this time, he was sure she would try to find where he was living. He was a man now, a journeyman, capable of earning over three pounds a week. She would certainly make a great effort to find him. He would never go back to her, that was certain, nor could she make him go back. He would go to jail first!

Haig was in the office when he arrived. 'Nice to see you again, Frankie. I thought you might clean up this store for me.' He led him down some stairs. 'All it needs is a lick of distemper, but I want it as bright as possible before I stock it. Could you do it tomorrow for me?'

'Yes.'

'Right, the material is here and there's a brush in the office; all you need to bring is a bucket. Here's a key to let yourself in. So start on it first thing in the morning.'

'I'll do that.'

'Listen,' Haig said, 'I might be looking for a good store-man, someone with a knowledge of paint generally, to keep check of things and do an odd delivery on a handcart. If you fancy the job there's fifty shillings a week for it. One thing, it's constant, and I am not the hardest man in the world to work for.' Haig turned from the store and up the stairs. 'Right, I'll see you some time tomorrow. Cheerio, old man.'

Why should Haig offer him the job of storeman, and tell him that the wages were fifty shillings a week and that the job was constant? Did Haig know he was a failure at the trade? Had he talked to Toby, or Collins? He remembered Toby saying that he had had a drink with Haig; perhaps they had talked about him then.

When he got back Molly was eager to know all about the job. He told her about the position of storekeeper. 'Please yourself, Frankie. It's fifty shillings a week. And that much money constant is not to be sniffed at. Ask yourself, would you be happy doing it?'

He thought about it when Molly left. He could take it for a time, because he must have something immediately, whether or not he stayed on with Molly. He could not live on here without paying her, nor could he go to a lodging house. There was the fear on him that if he got a job at his own trade there might be climbing to be done. The odd job tomorrow was not a high one, nor was the work itself of good quality — just a coat or two of distemper on rough brick work; anyone could do it; yet it was decent of Haig to have thought of him.

He lay back in his chair, took off his boots and put his feet on the hob. The front door was knocked, a quiet, uncertain knocking. He came down the stairs softly, and, as he approached the door he heard voices.

'It was here he was seen coming in. We can make inquiries. They can't kill us for asking a question or two.'

'They can't, that's right.' This was the voice of his aunt. His heart beat violently, and he was almost afraid to breathe lest she should hear him. He waited, moving closer to the door. Again a knock, this time a little louder. Quietly he felt the lock — there was a sudden fear in him now that they might push the door in. The lock was secure.

'They must all be out,' he heard his aunt say, but she knocked again, still louder. His eye caught the gap of the letter box, and he backed against the wall, away from the little rods of lamplight that filtered through.

'Mebbe they're at the pictures,' his aunt said.

'They'll hear this,' said her companion and the door was knocked so loudly that the stairs seemed to move.

'They're out at the pictures,' his aunt repeated. They moved away, one of them speaking but so low that he could not hear what was said. He heard their footsteps for a moment, and then everything was suddenly quiet.

He came back to the fire, trembling. What would Molly say when she heard they were here? He would not tell her. But if they came back? How did they find out he was here? Who could have told them? But it was useless to go on like this. His aunt knew now where he was, and that was that; it was of little account how she had found out.

He decided not to tell Molly, but she was scarcely five

minutes in the house when the door was knocked. She cocked her head, a startled expression on her face. 'Who on earth could that be at this hour of the night?' He crossed to the door as the knock was repeated. Mechanically he stretched his arms as if to bar her way.

'What is the matter, Frankie?'

'The knock, my aunt was here tonight. She, she . . .' but his words stuck.

'I suppose that's her, back again. What did she want?'

'She, she . . .'

'No, it's no use asking you questions about that. You're excited and your nerves won't let you talk. Come away from the door and sit down. Let her knock away there. Come, Frankie, don't be afraid. It's like what she *would* do. When my fellow left me, I pestered the house he stayed in for weeks after. But your case is different. Just let her knock away there. I'll not put you out, if that's your fear. So, come and sit by the fire. She'll get tired of knocking when there's no answer.' She motioned him not to speak. Going towards the stairs she listened. The knocking became stronger. 'If she knocks any louder she'll waken Jimmy. I'll go down and open the door.'

'But, Molly, Molly . . .'

'Now, don't fuss yourself. She'll never use the poker on you again. Sit down there and give over your worrying. She'll not put her foot beyond the threshold of my door.'

The old fear was coming back. He looked under the bed. He could crawl under there — he felt that Molly was no match for his aunt. She might have something with her, a poker or . . .

He heard voices. 'Yes, he's here, and what's more, he's staying here,' said Molly.

'What right have you to harbour him?' His aunt's voice was loud and angry.

'Listen, missus, I don't know your name, and what's

R APP. 257

more, I've no desire to know it. But would you take yourself away from here before I get the police to you.' Molly's tone was firm.

'How dare you threaten me with the police?' his aunt shouted.

'Now, now, keep your voice down. There's a sleeping child upstairs and I don't want him wakened. So take yourself away from here. You should be lying in Crumlin Road jail the night for lifting a poker to any human being. So now take yourself off, and don't waken my child.'

'His father might be angry,' his aunt spat this out venomously.

'No, his father won't be angry, and if you think that wee bit of dirt sticks in my gullet, you're wrong. So now, if you don't want me to send for the police, you'd better take yourself off.'

'You're decoying him. You're harbouring him. I'll send the priest on you.'

'You needn't bother sending priest, friar, minister or bible thumper, for I belong to no persuasion.'

The door was closed and Molly was climbing the stairs. When she got to the top, she stopped and listened, putting a finger over her lips — a sign for Frankie to keep silent. The door was knocked loudly again, and his aunt was crying out: 'I'll see a solicitor.' He could hear her companion coaxing her away. 'You haven't heard the end of this.' The door was given a final shake.

'Well, that's that,' Molly said, sitting down beside him. 'Didn't I take the right attitude? No fuss, just kept cool and gave her back word for word. You see, if I had lost my temper with her, it would have become a street brawl and maybe finished up with a lot of hair-pulling. But I didn't want that. So now, Frankie, we'll have a cup of cocoa and we'll forget all about her. It fairly took the wind out of her sails when I didn't rise to her taunt about the child. Isn't that the beauty of living about a place like this? You get no kick out of a row here. If that had been anywhere else the street would have been black with listening neighbours.'

'She said something about a solicitor.' It took him some time to get out the word 'solicitor'.

'And where will she get the money to hire a solicitor? Have sense, Frankie. I'll make a drink of cocoa now and we'll forget all about her. Aren't you happy now that it's all over? This had to happen some time.'

'How did she know I was here?'

'Does that matter? Do you think this is the end of the world? Aren't you only a tuppeny bus ride away from her? Belfast is a small place. But it's good to know that it's all over. If she comes back again we won't open the door to her, that's all. You must not be so afraid of her. As I told you before, you are as near a man now as ever you'll be, so you must have some guts. Get to your bed now and rise early in the morning, and see your friend Haig.'

He helped her to arrange the bed on the floor. At the door she said: 'Good night, and don't let all this keep you from sleeping. Can you turn out the gas yourself?'

'Yes.'

'Good night.'

He was glad now that his aunt knew. There was really nothing she could do about it. If a solicitor did appear, he would cost money, and she had none to spend this way. But this could not be the end of it. She was not the type to let things rest.

From the other room came the heavy breathing of Molly. She was sound asleep.

It seemed to him that she was glad all this had happened. She knew now there was nothing to hide. She could say to herself, 'He's here, lodging with me. His aunt knows, and sweet damn all she can do about it.'

In the morning Molly sang as she cooked their breakfast.

'What time will you be back at? Will you get home for any dinner?' she asked.

'I'd better take a lunch,' he said.

'Right, I'll make you some sandwiches, and you can get a cup of tea in some café.'

He was well started on the job when Haig arrived. 'I see you're going ahead. Tell me, did you think any more about the storeman's job?'

'I er . . . er . . .'

'Now, now, take it easy. Give me a "yes" or "no". I'll hold the job open until Monday next. But I should like to know soon. I'll have to advertise it. Had you anything else in mind?'

'The shipyard,' he answered.

'Well, if you get started in the shipyard, let me know in good time.'

Haig left and he did not see him again that day. When he got back to Molly's she said: 'There was someone here today again.'

'My aunt?'

'No, it wasn't your aunt. It was a clergyman. I think he's a priest. I couldn't say. For they are a race of men, priests and ministers, that I know very little about.'

'What did he say?'

'He's coming back to see you. I told him you'd be here tonight. It annoyed me.'

'Why, Molly?'

'Nothing to do with you. I suppose your aunt thinks because I've had a child to man, I'm hopping into bed with anything wearing trousers. I was very annoyed about it. I didn't show it before him. He, I suppose, is only doing his duty. It's his job. Your aunt has probably told him we are sleeping together.'

'But, er . . .'

'I know we're not. But evil minds think evil thoughts. And who are we hurting if we do sleep together? Tell me, Frankie,' she made a move towards him. 'Tell me, Frankie,' she repeated. 'You would sleep with me, wouldn't you?'

'Yes.'

'That's all I wanted to know. They'll put in between us, I know they will. I told you before, when I was carrying Jimmy a bunch of oul' maids from a church organization spied on me, night, noon and morning. They coaxed me, courted me, all the time thinking I was on the broad road to hell. Well, if I am on the broad road to hell, I can't help that. I suppose that's why hell was made, for people like me. If there must be a hell, there must be people like me, for what other reason should it be there?' There was a long pause. 'But I'm not telling you your business. If the clergyman calls back to see you, don't let anything I say colour your talk to him.'

When she left for the shop, he thought of what she had said. What would his attitude be if the priest called again? What could the priest do to him? He could not drag him back to his aunt. He knew the priest would take the stand that his soul was in danger. Well, he would not go back to his aunt to save his soul at the risk of breaking his body, for that was what had happened in the past.

The front door was knocked. He tiptoed to the stairs and listened. Was it his aunt? He heard coughing and he knew it was a man. He opened the door.

'Are you Frankie?'

'Yes, yes,' he cut in quickly and motioned the priest up the stairs. The priest sat down by the fire and took out cigarettes; 'Smoke?' Frankie shook his head. The priest lit his own cigarette, cleared his throat and said: 'Now what is all this trouble between your aunt and you?'

'I just left the house,' Frankie replied, trying to remain calm.

'Why did you leave the house? Oh, by the way, are we alone?' Frankie nodded. 'Has it ever occurred to you to give a thought to your aunt's difficulty in bringing you up? Here you had a woman with a very small income, striving to keep a home for you; and now that you have a chance of repaying her, you leave her. Is that a very honourable thing to do? . . .' Frankie was silent. 'The other aspect of the case is quite different. Tell me, are you intimate with this woman?' Frankie shook his head. 'No intimate relations at all?'

'No.'

'You are just a lodger?'

'Yes.'

'I see. You know of course there is a certain danger here? This could easily prove an occasion of sin for you. If you get yourself involved it may lead to much unhappiness. A little pleasure can easily lead to much pain. Just give that a little thought some time. "They who love the danger, very often perish therein."' The priest dropped his cigarette end into the fire. 'Are you definitely staying on here? Don't you think you would be much better back with your aunt? A good Catholic home. . . .'

'I'm not going back. I couldn't stand her cruelty,' Frankie got this out with great effort.

'Well, that, of course, is a long story. If your aunt was strict with you, it was for a very good reason. She had to chastise you. She told me of a little incident. You collected for the Missions and kept the money.' Frankie tried to speak, but the priest put his hand up. 'Let me finish,' he said. 'You were young then, I know. But even at that early age there was a tendency to steal, to take what was not your own. Your aunt was well aware of this, so she adopted the best method, according to her way of thinking, of making you drop that bad habit. She believed that if she spared the rod she might spoil the child. You see, we must look at other people's points of view. Her occasional use of the rod, shall we say, may have been responsible for your not stealing anything more.'

He was too excited now to answer the priest. The words were in his mind. 'Spare the rod!' The poker, the brush, the toe of her shoe, her long fingers twisting the tongue in his mouth! Her getting him down on the floor and jumping on him ... Yes it was easy to talk about sparing the rod and spoiling the child.

'You needn't think I'm going back, Father,' he managed to say, not very clearly.

The face of the priest reddened. He lit another cigarette. 'What time does your landlady get back?'

'About eleven.'

'I see ... well, I'll call back again.' He made for the stairs. Turning, he said 'Good night', and made his way to the street.

The priest, he knew, would come back and talk to Molly, but that did not matter. His aunt could say that he had stolen the money, but she did not tell the priest it was because he was hungry. He was finished with her for good even if she sent all the priests in the world after him. The pity was that he was no use at talking. He got excited and could say nothing, otherwise he could have put the priest right on a point or two.

He told Molly about the visit when she got home. 'He's coming again to see you.'

'Why?' she asked. He shook his head. 'What is there I can do? You want to stay here, Frankie?'

'I do, Molly.'

She prepared the supper and as they ate, she asked: 'Have you thought any more about Haig's job?'

'No. I'd still like to try the shipyard.'

'But isn't the shipyard just a chance? Doesn't it mean your going down morning after morning, waiting and waiting?'

'It does, Molly.'

'Well, couldn't you take Haig's job in the meantime? I do feel that Haig's a good man to know.'

He was worried now about the trade. It was hard to have served five years and at the end turn to a job that anyone could do. But then, was he a success at his trade? He knew he was not. Perhaps Molly had talked to Simon and that was why she was so keen on him taking Haig's job. Simon, of course, would get to know all about him. Haig and he must have been discussing him.

'I think I should take Haig's job,' he said at length.

'Yes, for a while,' agreed Molly. 'You'll have no worries at a job of that kind, Frankie. And if you stay on here, I won't take the last shilling from you. You want to stay on here, don't you?' It was the second time tonight she had asked him that.

'I do, Molly.'

When she arranged the bed, she lay down beside him; only this time she lay closer. He hoped the child would not wake. From outside came the throaty purr of a pigeon.